A FAIR TIME FOR DEATH

ADRIANA LICIO

The Home Travellers
Press

A FAIR TIME FOR DEATH

Book 2 in *An Italian Village Mystery* Series

By Adriana Licio

Edition I
Copyright 2019 © Adriana Licio
ISBN: 978-88-32249-04-0

Cover by Wicked Smart Design
Editing by Alison Jack

To Prathap,
Wherever you are

CONTENTS

1

THE TRECCHINA CHESTNUT FAIR

"I am very grateful to this splendid community for the work they're doing." The Mayor of Trecchina carried on, despite the yawns and weary expressions of the people facing him. "I do not need to remind you that over the next two weekends, many tourists will come to visit our village. We must take great care to ensure our streets and main square are clean and looking their best. Let's not wait for the street sweepers to pass by; if you see litter lying around, please be a good citizen and pick it up yourself. The reputation of the town rests with you."

He stopped, waiting for applause that didn't come. The numerous people gathered in the assembly hall of the Trecchina school were all staring at the short roundish man with salt-and-pepper hair and perpetually red cheeks, wondering if he'd ever stop talking. Oblivious, the man carried on, preaching about the duties of his fellow citizens.

One of the teachers touched Vanda on her shoulder. "I think you should take that mic. It's almost three o'clock and he hasn't gone over any organisational details, apart from the fact we should all become street sweepers."

Vanda thought for half a second, her head with its mop of red curls tilted, then raised up her hand, asking one of the assistants for a mic.

"Thank you, mayor." Vanda's mezzo-soprano voice rang out across the room. She smiled at him and gestured meaningfully towards the audience, inviting all those gathered in the hall to applaud. The mayor tried to signal he hadn't finished yet, but the applause got louder, effectively silencing him.

Vanda moved onto the stage and shook hands with him. Drowning out his protestations, she said cheerfully, "We're very grateful for your words, but I see we're running late and we still have to organise the teams. Do you want to be a team leader?"

He declined, horrified at the idea, and finally left both mic and stage to Vanda. More applause.

Both Vanda's daughter and son had left the school years earlier, but the teachers had asked her to stay on the school committee for the annual Chestnut Fair to help organise the event. She had a talent for breaking down complex problems into manageable tasks, identifying teams and singling out the right leaders. Even the generally argumentative teachers had hardly ever disagreed with her; maybe they whined and complained behind the scenes, but not to the extent that they threatened Vanda's organisational machine.

At that moment, she was asking the teachers of the youngest ones how they were packing the chestnuts by the kilo for sale. She looked at the jute bags they handed her, the red ribbons and the printed labels announcing them to be "The Trecchina Chestnut Friends", and nodded in approval.

Vanda then inspected the handiwork of the craft teams: the painted tiles and wooden spoons. As three of the boys had worked under the guidance of Giuseppe, an old farmer with a talent for making wicker baskets as well as for teaching the traditional art, their results were splendid. The work of the students trying their hands at *découpage* wasn't entirely to Vanda's taste, mostly because the art teacher's view on what was aesthetically pleasing was… let's just say questionable. But maybe there would be at least some members of the public who would appreciate it.

"Oh, Ada, these are beautiful," Vanda said, looking in admiration at the work the elderly lady had presented. Ada turned crimson.

"I'm glad you like them, dear." Despite her 80 years, Ada was as shy and modest as a little girl. She had been running small crochet classes, and her students had come up with some wonderful patterns.

"Next year, you have to run a class for quilting," Vanda told her, still looking at the slouch hat in her hands. In cream and brown colours, it had laces ending in two chestnut shapes instead of the usual pompoms.

"What's that?" Ada asked, fearful and curious at the same time.

"It's sewing together two layers of fabric, padding out the middle. And the top layer can be made from different pieces of fabric."

"A sort of patchwork?"

"That's it, exactly!"

"I'm not sure I'd be good at it, I've never done it before."

"It comes from the US, and you'd love it. As soon as we're finished, I'll show you a few videos on YouTube."

Ada turned even redder, but her eyes were shining with enthusiasm at the new challenge. She was not too good with the internet, but Vanda and her students helped. And she loved that with this *word*-wide web – or was it the *world*wide web? – you could learn all sorts of new things.

Vanda kissed Ada on the cheek and congratulated the four young girls who were with her.

The organisation of the older students, who would compete in the street food competition, was not so simple. There were to be three teams of eight students, but the school headmistress had insisted they form the teams themselves. It turned out – not surprising Vanda at all – that the more talented and organised competitors had formed two teams, while the seven boys and girls whom the two main leaders didn't want in their teams had ended up in the third team. The eighth member of the third team was Erica, daughter of the Italian teacher and the most stubborn and hard-to-deal-with student in the school.

"So, Alessandra, Daniele, Erica," Vanda called the three team leaders, "may I see your menus?"

She read and complimented the first two, nodding in approval. But when she came to the third one...

"Erica, lasagne isn't proper street food and is rather complicated to prepare. Hadn't we already agreed you'd change it for something more appropriate?"

"I think we can do it. I have given my team clear instructions, and we're sure most visitors will love a real dish instead of junk food."

Vanda raised her eyes to the Italian teacher, who was standing not too far away, clearly eavesdropping while feigning indifference. That told Vanda all she needed to know about where the idea for lasagne had come from. She shook her head as she went through the rest of the menu.

"Parmigiana? But aubergines are not in season in October and it's such a complicated dish. You need to fry the aubergines first, and you'll need heaps of them, and two lots of sauce for the parmigiana and the lasagne. How many pots will you require on your small stall? Erica dear, I think we should review this menu. I'm sorry, but I don't see a single dish based on chestnuts, and this is the Chestnut Fair."

"But the tourists will be sick and tired of the same food everywhere they go." Erica stood in front of Vanda, her pointed nose high in the air, her fists defiantly on her hips. "Chestnut bread, chestnut focaccia, pasta made of chestnut flour, chestnut jam, gelato, cakes. They will be sick of the sight of chestnuts by the time they get to our stall, so we'll serve them sensible, delicious food."

The headmistress finally intervened, but she didn't say what Vanda was expecting.

"If they are determined to try this menu, let them do it," she said with a twinkle in her eyes. "Just make sure, Erica, that all your team agrees and you give them precise instructions. Not just the recipe, but who should do what."

Erica snorted an ungracious, "Of course".

As she left, the headmistress murmured to Vanda, "The time has come for Erica to learn her lesson the hard way."

Vanda smiled. "I'm just sorry for the rest of her team."

"Then they shouldn't have chosen her as their leader in the first place, and they could have objected to the menu."

"But there isn't a single strong-willed one among them. I feel sorry…"

"Don't feel sorry. School is a safe place to learn, even when one is learning how to make mistakes."

Once she'd approved of the streamers and posters, Vanda went back onto the stage to repeat timings and tasks. The fair would be running on Saturday and Sunday for two consecutive weekends and there was plenty that could go wrong, so she answered a few questions and reminded the teams of the sequence of events.

"Remember this weekend is mainly for our community, and for people from nearby villages who prefer this part of the fair to the more touristy events next weekend. This means that by tomorrow, we must be as close to perfection as possible. Thank you all for the work you've done and see you tomorrow morning for the walk in the forest in search of chestnuts. Early afternoon, we'll gather in the main square, ready to run our stalls. The proceedings from all sales will go to buy a multimedia board to make school more fun."

Once the applause had died down, the crowd made their way out of the school hall.

"Thank you so much, Vanda, you were splendid as ever," the headmistress said.

"It's a pleasure, really. But guess what? I don't have a single chestnut and I'm supposed to bake a couple of cakes for tomorrow."

"I've got plenty if you want to call in and pick some up."

"Thank you for the offer, but going to forage gives me a good excuse for a walk in the forest. It's been a strenuous week at work, so I wouldn't mind a little fresh air."

Vanda drove her car a few hundred metres along the road just outside the town that led up to the Sanctuary of the Madonna del Soccorso. But she didn't need to drive that far; the forest of chestnut trees lay all around the town.

She parked next to two other cars – more people in search of chestnuts, surely? – and changed her office shoes for a pair of hiking boots she'd had in her car all day. She could hear voices, but needing quiet, a little time for herself, she headed for the upper part of the forest path. Most people preferred the lower areas.

The cool breeze blowing around the tree trunks carried the scents of undergrowth, decomposing leaves and fresh soil, moss and lichen. The bright yellow of the leaves was so cheerful that she couldn't understand why people looked at the autumn as a sad season. But it was a time of change for her; she was now officially an empty-nester.

Matilde had moved away years earlier to study architecture in Florence, but Mimmo had left just a week earlier. Unlike his sister, he had always been a practical child. Although he had struggled academically, he had an inborn talent for dismantling things: TVs, washing machines, mobile phones, PCs – you name it, Mimmo would take it apart, and then put it back together, often fixing any problems he found along the way.

Mimmo had got his technical diploma in June, excelling in all practical subjects and scraping his way through the others, and had received a job offer from a start-up in Brescia up in the north that specialised in automated machinery for larger companies. He had accepted with a certain amount of regret at leaving both his village and mother, but she doubted he'd be back. Yes, she felt a pang of loneliness when she came in from work to find her home empty, but she was so proud of her children and couldn't wait to see where their lives would take them.

Matilde had been back in Trecchina for the whole month of August, begging Vanda to come to join her in Florence. She'd surely find a job there; after so many years of running the biscuit company where she worked as if it was her own, Vanda certainly had a brilliant CV.

"You won't feel lonely, Mum. I mean, I'll be there, and Mimmo won't be too far away, and Florence is a splendid city. You'll have everything you'll need."

It was hard to explain to an ambitious twenty-five-year-old that all her mother needed was in her small town. It had been different when Vanda was in her twenties, but after her divorce, she had headed back home to Trecchina and all that was familiar to her.

Vanda put her jute bag down, pulled on her gloves and started to pick the prickly husks. She took the nuts out of the half-opened ones and threw in the ones that were still closed, prickles and all. As she worked, she realised she must have wandered away from the other people in the forest since she could no longer hear their voices.

Standing upright and stretching her back, a number of fat, glossy chestnuts in her gloved hands, she spotted something greyish just ahead of her. Not a common colour in the woods. She walked over, uncertain what it could mean.

As she got closer, she realised it looked like a piece of material. Wait a second, wasn't that a coat, half hidden among the leaves? It's funny how even the most brilliant brains sometimes refuse to take in what's blindingly obvious. Until her eyes ran across the hem of the coat where the leaves had piled up, until she started to remove them with her stick revealing a black shoe, Vanda simply wasn't able to process the implications of what she was looking at. Inside that shoe…

Inside that shoe was a foot. At that moment, her brain finally had to accept the unmistakable truth: the shape beneath the pile of crispy and colourful leaves was a body. Simple as that.

With a thumping heart, she frantically removed the leaves from around the figure until she could distinguish an old woman's face, framed by grey hair. The frozen grin left Vanda in no doubt that the old woman was dead.

Her hands let go of the stick and chestnuts; her dirty gloves raised up to her mouth to stifle a scream that never came out. Something heavy fell on her head and everything went black.

2

MR NASTY

"Gran, I'm going," said Agnese, knocking at Granny's flat. Granny opened the door straight away; she was already up and dressed. "I'm coming with you, Agnese. I'd better help you to choose the fruit and vegetables, or you'll come back with the most dreadful stuff."

Agnese shook her head, smiling. She might be renowned as one of the best cooks in town, but to Granny, she was still little Agnese, so easy for wily traders on the Maratea Saturday Market to trick. Granny was convinced Agnese would be fobbed off with a withered zucchini, half a kilo more lemons than she asked for, the dried up slice of a pumpkin that had been cut open the day before…

"You said you were a little tired yesterday after preparing all the chestnut biscuits for the fair, so why not take it easy this morning?"

"In fact I was exhausted, but I've had a cup of ginger and green tea, done those weird balance and flexibility exercises Giovanni taught me, and enjoyed a good sleep since then." Granny spoke nonchalantly while putting on a pumpkin-coloured coat, the brightness of which had shocked both Agnese and her sister Giò when they'd first seen it, and searching for her bag and keys.

"I'm really happy that you and Giovanni are getting along well."

"I'm telling you, he might have a peculiar temper, but he's teaching me the right things. I feel rejuvenated."

"Next we'll be looking for a boyfriend for you."

"I'd be happy to find one for Giò."

"Oh, please let her be. You know she's quite touchy on that point."

"In fact, I won't be nagging her about it, but that's what she needs," Granny said as they left.

"You know it's not her fault she broke up with Dorian after a ten-year engagement," Agnese remarked as they descended the cobbled street. "At 38, she has the right to do what she wants with her life."

"Well, that was the best thing that could have happened to her. That fop was completely unworthy of her affection. She was saved by the bell."

"Granny, please!"

"I know you feel exactly as I do," Granny replied stubbornly. "But considering it's not two months since they broke up, maybe we can give her a little while longer before we find her a suitable husband."

Agnese shrugged, hoping that the 'little while longer' would be long enough for Giò.

Granny changed the subject, dismissing the conversation as if it had never happened. "By the way, shouldn't we call for Giò? She'd enjoy giving us a hard time at the market, pointing out the most exotic and useless stuff."

Agnese laughed; Granny was right. Cooking was definitely not one of her sister's talents, but Giò was always attracted to the most weird and unusual things she spotted at the market, finding out once she got them home that she had no idea what to do with them.

"No, best leave her. She's finally working on her Scottish travel guide, and it's taken her so long to get started, I daren't interrupt her. She can be rather savage when anyone disturbs one of her writing spells."

"I can't understand that either. She says writing guides is boring: all the information is already out there, and she need only compile it in a way that makes sense. But then, when she gets into it, she looks like one of those restless artists. One day she's among the stars, the next she falls in total misery..."

"Shh, there she is," Agnese said, pointing out a skinny long-legged figure sitting at one of the bar tables in Piazza Buraglia, Maratea's main square. The table was covered in books and leaflets of all shapes and sizes, and Giò was alternating between scraping back her short dark hair with her left hand and spells of furious tapping on her laptop's keyboard. Granny and Agnese half expected the keys to fly away under her vigorous finger strokes.

"Look there." Agnese pointed to a cornetto on a dish, balanced on top of a pile of books.

"It's untouched," Granny commented. "We're lucky – it must be one of her good, productive days."

At that moment, Leonardo, the café owner, spotted the two observers. He nodded to them and gave them a discreet thumbs up. Giò was indeed having a good writing day; in fact, so good she was totally unaware of the observations going on around her. As she continued typing, her lips compressed together tightly with the effort of putting every single word in the right place.

Granny and Agnese waved at Leonardo and took a long detour around the square to keep out of Giò's eye line, although they could have passed under her nose and she probably wouldn't have taken any notice of them. They completed their loop on the other side of the square and disappeared into one of Maratea's many little alleys, surrounded by houses and narrow passageways.

The market was just as colourful and loud and cheerful as ever. Granny haggled the zucchini price fiercely and inspected every single vegetable critically as if she was looking to buy a house, shaking her head in disapproval until the seller pulled out the best stuff that he kept hidden under the stall for the most awkward customers. In the market, Granny's argumentative nature was infamous.

After the customary cup of coffee at the market – just barley coffee for Granny – she and Agnese headed back home. In the main square, the writer was still absorbed in pounding on her laptop and reading and struggling. Looking at her watch, Agnese gave a shriek of horror and left Granny to carry their shopping bags the rest of the way. It was 9.15 and she had to open her shop.

Despite it no longer being the tourist season in Maratea, which meant that most of her customers knew how to find her, Agnese disliked being late. She hurried along the cobbled streets, and when she arrived at her shop, she discovered there was in fact a customer waiting. A sturdy man wearing huge sunglasses under a flat tweed cap was shifting restlessly from one side of the alley to the other, his mouth contracting and contorting strangely.

"Good morning, I'm so sorry I'm late. You're waiting for me, aren't you?"

"No, I'm measuring how wide the street is from one side to the other."

Agnese searched for the shop keys in her bag and unlocked the heavy turquoise shutters. She then had to secure them against the wall to make sure a gust of wind didn't hurl them against an unwary customer entering or leaving the shop.

"Do you think you'll be finished by closing time?" the man asked, looking at his watch.

Agnese's mouth opened to respond with the first nasty thing that popped into her mind, then she shut it promptly as if a heavy security door had slammed closed.

Your fault, Agnese, keep your cool. After all, you're late, and the customer, no matter how nasty, is right. Bear with him.

But she was so nervous it took her some time to identify the right key for the second lock on the glass door. She was struggling and juggling with it when the customer started whistling a song, a sarcastic expression on his face.

She pushed the door open and moved between the rattan armchairs and small sofa she usually placed outside. They would have to wait until later; all she wanted right now was to get rid of this man as soon as possible.

She switched on the lights and moved an armchair aside to free up the entrance for him.

"Is this a new shop? Are you just moving in?" he asked, pointing at the rattan furniture in his way.

"No, this perfumery was opened in 1958 by my grandmother."

"Fantastic! So why does it look as though you're opening for the first time?" He smiled, but it was a grimace of a smile. He had a nervous tic, the right side of his lip twitching downwards two or three times in a row, adding to his air of contempt.

"What can I do for you?" Agnese asked, making an extra effort to smile.

"I'm looking for my cologne," and he named a brand Agnese did not stock.

"I'm very sorry, I'm afraid I don't have it."

His eyebrows climbed slowly all the way up to his forehead in disapproval. "How about this one?" He named a second fragrance.

"I don't have that either."

"Why do you keep this shop open at all, then?"

Agnese gasped as if the earth had been pulled from beneath her feet. Once more she kept her temper in check and searched for the right words, forcing herself to answer politely, unsure how long she could tolerate the man's provocation.

"Every year, hundreds of new perfumes are released into the

market," she explained, "and each shop has to select the brands it wants to stock. Even the largest stores in the cities can't stock them all, so a family-run business like mine certainly can't. Nonetheless, I'm proud to offer my clients a good choice of artisanal fragrances. I personally love to select the perfumes that have a story to tell, an emotion to share…"

"Stories? Emotions?" He was staring at her as if she were insane. "I thought this was a perfumery. You walk in, you spray a sample, you like it or you don't, you walk away with a cologne that helps make you presentable and hides your hideous smell."

"It sounds like you need a strong deodorant. Or perhaps you should shower more often," she couldn't help crying in dismay. "That's not the purpose of a perfume."

He went crimson. "So, Mrs I-know-it-all-but-I-still-don't-have-your-cologne, what should I walk away with today? An emotion? Shall I spray a story tonight before I go to visit a certain lady?"

Of all the things Agnese could have said, she picked the worst one possible. "Please, sir, come over here and I'll give you a perfume session." She regretted the words the moment they were out of her mouth, but it was too late to take them back.

Agnese moved towards a little alcove on one side of her shop where an ebony table was set with all she needed to help customers find the most appropriate perfume for them. She had so far only ever offered this service to kindred spirits, people whose company she enjoyed, or when she felt her perfumes could really help a person. This customer didn't fit any of those categories. He smirked as if he was dealing with a lunatic. But after a disturbingly long pause, he followed her. He sat down on the armchair opposite Agnese and stared at her with provocative intensity.

"So what happens now?"

Agnese looked at the door. She would normally close it. A perfume session was a sacred moment to her, so she didn't like interruptions, but she didn't dare lock herself in with this man.

She looked at the candle cupboard behind her, unable to think of the best selection to propose.

When your rational mind fails you, count on instinct, intuition and chance.

"Am I supposed to sit here for eternity?"

As he said this, Agnese's temper snapped. With the impetus of rage, her hesitating hand stopped over the clove candle.

I bet you will choose this, she thought, inviting the man to smell the eight candles she was placing in front of him and indicate his favourite. The man pulled away in disgust at most of them.

How dare you! They're all beautiful perfumes.

Then he handed her "The only bearable one". It was the clove.

On the basis of that choice, she pulled out eight bottles containing eight different perfume accords. She dipped a thin *touche* into each one and handed them to the man one by one. Again his expression was sarcastic, but he didn't say a word.

When he'd smelled the eight samples, he picked the spicy Oriental one. Agnese pulled out eight more bottles, and to her surprise, the man chose a gentle, creamy carnation.

Maybe there is something pleasant about this customer after all, but frankly, I doubt it.

She finally selected the oriental spicy perfume table. She had similar cardboard tables for each family of perfumes. On the front of each, the perfumes belonging to that family were represented.

She repeated the words she used with all her clients. "Our choices are made on the basis of our rational thoughts, but there's always an element of chance." As she placed the cardboard face down on the ebony table so the man couldn't read the perfume names, she handed him a dark purple spinning top made of wood.

The most hideous colour I've got, she thought resentfully, inviting him to twist it.

He smirked again, his lips turning downwards on the right

side to make his expression even more unpleasant. He had well-cared-for, pale hands, and with his agile fingers, he gave the top a spin.

They waited for the spinning top to stop. Then Agnese marked where it had landed with a coloured pin and turned the table.

"Outrageous Carnation by The London Dandy," she read. "I'll fetch this fragrance tester so you can make up your mind if you like it or not."

She rose up from the table, feeling infinitely grateful the ordeal was over, selected the perfume bottle from one of the cupboards and handed it to the man almost fearfully.

What did you expect from such an obnoxious man? Why did you ever offer him a perfume session? How stupid.

The man took the *touche* with his usual scornful grin, inhaled the fragrance once or twice, and his eyes widened, both eyebrows raised.

"Is this meant to be a perfume?"

"Of course."

"Aaah!"

Again there was a long, unnerving pause, him staring at her and she holding his gaze until he gave in.

"Since you've got nothing better to offer me, give me a bottle of this." He didn't ask for the price, just paid for it and left, saying, "Half an hour to choose one bottle of perfume. My goodness."

As he approached the door, Giò was coming in. With a chivalrous gesture, he bent forward, holding the door open for her.

"If you're here for a perfume, you're in the wrong place. They only do tarot readings," he said, and with that, he left.

Giò hardly had time to see the man's face, hidden beneath his glasses and hat. She looked at her sister in dismay.

"Oh my goodness, what a dreadful start to the morning," Agnese said, banging her forehead with her hand. "You won't believe what that guy was like." And she told Giò all that had happened.

Giò laughed. "Horrendous guy," she said.

"Oh, Giò, you don't understand: when I do my perfume sessions, it's such an intimate thing. I mean, I know it's just a game, but I've developed it over the years. I always feel as if I'm revealing a little part of myself. And you know how many times I've refused a session to customers because I don't feel in tune with them. I've no idea how I could have offered one to this awful man."

"You were provoked, and after all, he bought the perfume, so he acknowledged you served him well, despite what he said."

"Maybe you're right."

"Which fragrance did he choose in the end?"

"Outrageous Carnation."

"And what's that?"

"It's a weird fragrance – the London Dandy brand creates unusual perfumes. This one represents a man's – or a woman's – darker side, almost a dual personality. On one side, it reflects the refined gentleman wearing a white carnation in his buttonhole, but this carnation is not innocent. On the contrary, it is darkened with an almost animalistic trait. So who is that fine gentleman really? I confess, I'd almost forgot I stocked the fragrance, it's so rarely I suggest it to my customers."

"That sounds creepy – it reminds me of the story of Dr Jekyll and Mr Hyde," said Giò.

Agnese nodded, turning towards the shelves to pick up the tester bottle. On the back she had written a few notes. She read them now and gave a loud laugh.

Giò looked at her questioningly.

"You won't believe this!" And Agnese read out loud, "A white carnation thrown in a cauldron of violent spices, musty oud and wild civet. A perfect mix for the gentleman with a dark side."

Giò shook her head. "He didn't look a gentleman to me…"

"On the contrary, he's Mr Nasty. Anyway, I hope I'm done with unpleasant customers for the weekend."

"I almost forgot to tell you the good news I've just received. Do you have five minutes spare?" Giò's eyes were shining.

Agnese looked wistfully at the boxes of products that she still had to put away, but could she tell her enthusiastic sister to wait? Of course not.

"You won't believe it," said Giò, pulling the rattan armchair outside.

"Have you finished another chapter of your book?"

"As a matter of fact, I have, but this is more like breaking news."

"You haven't finished the whole book, have you?"

"Oh no, that will take at least another month. But it's not about my guide at all, it's something bigger than that." Giò sat on the armrest of the sofa, her long arms waving in circles around her to mean *really* big.

"Is it to do with that Travel Writers' Conference you told me about?"

"Exactly!" Giò cried. "Two inspectors are coming over tomorrow to have a look around Maratea. It will be assessed along with all the other proposed locations before they make the final choice. They said they have only shortlisted three places."

"Congratulations, Giò. I really hope you manage to convince them."

"They want me to book them two rooms at the Conference Hotel and to see as much as they can of Maratea in 24 hours."

"Isn't that short notice for such an important visit?"

"It is, but I contacted the hotel I had proposed on my application and they will be more than happy to welcome them as complimentary guests. I've already made a few phone calls to ensure everything will be ready for their visit." Giò's enthusiastic face fell all of a sudden. "But should I hire a minibus to ferry them around?"

"Can't you use my car?" suggested Agnese, fearing her sister was making her welcome plans bolder and grander with every passing minute.

"Nothing against your car, Agnese, it's small and perfect for me, but they are such important guests."

"I see," Agnese replied with a hint of sarcasm. "Should I ask Nando if he can leave you his car and use mine for a couple days?"

"Oh, that would be awesome, and save my meagre finances at the same time. Oh my goodness!" Her mobile phone rang. "Maybe it's them. Ah no, it's Vanda."

As Giò answered, Agnese listened with increasing alarm to her sister's side of the conversation.

"You're in the hospital? What happened? A falling branch? Are you OK now? I can't hear you that well, what did you see? A copse? A *corpse*? You mean someone who's... dead? Hold on, I'm coming over!"

As Giò ended the call, Agnese's face couldn't have looked more baffled.

"Someone's hurt?"

"Yes, Vanda! She is in Maratea Hospital; she was hit by a falling branch in the wood while collecting chestnuts for today's fair in Trecchina."

"And who's dead?"

"Maybe nobody, but Vanda said she's sure she saw a dead woman among the fallen leaves before she was knocked out. Only the rescuers said that when they arrived, they saw nothing of the sort." Giò thought it over. "I guess it was the shock, but I'm going to see Vanda right now. She sounded unusually distressed, and she's still in the hospital."

"Don't you have to organise things for your guests?"

"I'll have the whole afternoon for that."

Agnese looked uncertain what to do for a few seconds. She glanced at the boxes of newly arrived stock, then shook her head.

There's a right time for everything.

"I'll call Nando. It's Saturday, so he may stand in for me in the shop, especially as it looks like being a quiet morning. I'm coming with you."

3

THE MISSING CORPSE

"Giò, Agnese, I'm so happy to see you."

Vanda smiled, propped up in bed by a pile of pillows behind her back. She was a bit paler than usual, but otherwise looked fine. As the sisters approached her, Vanda took a book from her bedside table and put it in the drawer beneath.

Giò took no notice of the furtive gesture, but she recognised two words from the cover: *Love Poems*. Was Vanda trying to hide her romantic side? And was there any link between the bunch of red and white roses on her bedside table and the book?

The two sisters sat on chairs beside Vanda's bed and bombarded her with questions.

"How do you feel?" asked Agnese, her eyes flitting round the typical large white hospital room.

"Still slightly dizzy every now and then, but much better than yesterday. When I tried to walk then, I felt like I was on a sailing ship on rough seas."

Agnese's eyes stopped on the second bed in the room where an old lady lay, seemingly transfixed by the ceiling. She looked too old or too sick to be taking any notice of their conversation, but Agnese instinctively lowered her voice anyway.

"What do the doctors say?"

"I should be dismissed later on after the doctors have done their rounds. I had concussion, but a CT scan says I'm fine."

"You don't need to whisper," the old lady protested, making Agnese jump. "Can I not at least enjoy some conversation?"

Embarrassed at having made assumptions about Vanda's neighbour, Agnese asked the woman if she had everything she needed, or if they could help her in any way.

"No, I've got water, my blanket and pillows, and the nurse comes anytime I call for her. But I've switched off the TV and I'm waiting to hear your friend's story again."

Vanda winked at the two sisters and pointed towards her temple. "She's nuts."

Amused, Giò asked Vanda how she'd got hurt.

"I'm possibly not the best person to answer that. After the school meeting, I went straight to the forest, realising I hadn't got a single chestnut for my cakes. I was searching for them when a branch fell from a tree and hit my head."

"And you passed out? You could have been lying there for hours!"

"Yes, but I was lucky. Matilde tried to call me, and when I didn't answer the phone, she called my neighbour, Carmela. She knew the school meeting had finished a while earlier and I was supposed to meet her to cook chestnut pies together. She spoke to Giuseppe, and he told her he had spotted my car along the road…"

Agnese smiled. "In small places like Maratea and Trecchina, everyone knows your every move."

"And I was glad of it on this occasion. Giuseppe came out to look for me, and when he found me – mainly thanks to Kia, his dog – I was still unconscious. I could have spent the whole night in the forest if it hadn't been for them. And it was cold. I was shivering all night and didn't warm up till the early hours of this morning, despite the hospital staff providing me with plenty of blankets and even a hot water bottle."

"So what's the weird story about the body?" Giò asked, uncertain whether she really wanted to bring the subject up.

"Well, that's the tricky part." Vanda pushed herself into a more upright position, as if to prove she was perfectly coherent now. "The nurse told me that I was murmuring about the old woman when I got to the hospital, but I didn't really seem aware of what I was blabbering about. All through the night, I've had this vague memory of an old woman's face: a bluish face; one that's known suffering. The doctor said it was the shock."

"Certainly," said Agnese. "After concussion, we can have all sorts of nightmares."

"But it wasn't a nightmare at all. This morning I had it all clear. The fog was gone from my head and I remembered exactly what happened." And she told them about how she'd found the body among the fallen leaves.

"Oh my goodness, and has someone gone to search for the body?"

"Oh yes. I phoned the carabinieri, and they said they would come over to take my witness statement. I guessed it would take some time for them to do anything, so I also called Giuseppe. After all, he and Kia knew exactly where they'd found me, so I asked them to go and have a look."

"And?"

"Giuseppe called me an hour ago, saying he found nothing. Apparently the carabinieri are there too, but it seems the body's gone."

"Don't take her seriously," the old lady lying in the next bed said. "She's been talking about the dead woman all night. She sent an army of carabinieri to search for her, and that poor gentleman too, but nobody's found nothing. Her brain's no longer working; concussion is a much trickier thing than many doctors believe."

Vanda shot her a dirty look. "Agnese, Giò, yesterday I thought my mind was playing tricks on me, but this morning I know that what I saw was real. There was a dead body in the forest, and she hadn't met with a natural death."

Giò and Agnese looked at each other uncertainly.

"Oh she's mad, I'm telling you. Out of her head," the old woman cried, rotating her finger on her temple, ironically using the same gesture Vanda had used about her earlier.

"I'm sure they will continue their searches, let's wait and see what happens," said Giò pensively.

"If I found her, I'm sure they can find her too."

"Give them time," said Agnese. "There will be other people foraging for chestnuts in the forest this morning, quite a number of them. They will find her."

"At best," squawked the old woman, "they will find a pile of rags she's mistaken for a person."

"Shut your mouth or I will tell the nurse I saw a stack of chocolates on your bedside table. Or was that another result of my concussion?"

"Those are to offer to my visitors."

"I saw you munching them."

The woman turned her back on the three of them resentfully. Satisfied, Vanda switched on the TV and kept talking in a soft voice so as not to be overheard by her belligerent room companion.

"I wonder who she was, because I'm sure she wasn't anyone from Trecchina."

"Well, there are already quite a few tourists coming for the fair."

"But she was all alone in the woods... that's weird."

"She wasn't that alone if you suspect she might have been killed," Giò threw in.

Vanda nodded. "That's exactly what I fear. She had a pained expression on her face." She shook her head as if she didn't want to remember. "The bluish colour, the open mouth, the tongue... oh my goodness!" She glanced at Giò. "Do you think she might have been strangled?"

After having been involved in murder cases on a couple of occasions now, Giò was starting to be regarded locally as an amateur sleuth, but she hadn't expected the same from her friend.

"I wouldn't really know, but what you've described matches what I've read in mystery stories. Let's wait and see what the carabinieri find."

Vanda sighed. "You're right, I have to be patient and wait."

"Granny has prepared some light food for you, my cool box is full of all sorts of goodies. You won't have to cook…"

"…for a couple of months!" Giò chuckled.

At that moment the door opened and a short, thin woman with tanned skin and an expressive face came in.

"Giò!" she cried.

"Carmela, how are you?" said Giò in delight. She had met Carmela during a murder mystery weekend on an island retreat owned by a mutual friend not too far from Trecchina and Maratea. The game had turned into a nightmare when guests started dying for real, but Carmela had saved a group of the survivors from an awful death with her very own secret weapon. "What are you doing here and not on the Isola di Pino?"

"The season is over, and Mrs Belardi didn't even want to entertain the idea of having guests for the Halloween weekend. But we worked quite a lot during the summer. She's over in Marseille right now, but we will have guests again for the Christmas season."

"But what are you doing *here*?"

"When she's not on the island, she's my neighbour," said Vanda, as pleased as punch to see two of her friends already knew and liked each other.

"The nurse said the doctors are going to discharge Vanda today," Carmela told Giò and Agnese, "and I want to accompany her home."

"Do you think you could stay with her tonight?" asked Agnese.

"Yes, I plan to do just that."

"Come on, I really don't need all this fuss. Mrs Brando has cooked me some delicious food. All I need is a lift."

"No, the doctors say that if you are going to go home tonight, you need someone with you, just in case. If you'll be alone, then you'll have to stay in the hospital for an extra 24 hours."

"Oh my goodness, I will of course be glad of the company. I just don't want to put you out, Carmela."

"It's fine with me, really."

"How about the fair? It's a pity I won't be there. Maybe I will try to sneak in for a while tomorrow. How about you two?" Vanda asked, looking at Agnese and Giò.

Agnese replied, "I need to return to the shop this afternoon. I left Nando covering for me this morning, but I doubt he can cope with my clients all day. But Lilia and Luca are curious so we are going over tomorrow."

"As for me, I will have guests," said Giò. "If they are interested, I'll take them to the fair tomorrow. They're looking for a suitable place to host a writers' conference and are part of a panel of judges who will make the final decision on the location."

"Judges can always be corrupted. Be ready to bribe them properly if you want to get something out of them." The old woman couldn't resist jumping into the conversation again, despite the changed subject.

"Not all people are the same," admonished Vanda.

"Of course they are, but you won't listen to those who have more experience."

Vanda rolled her eyes; the others smiled.

"I wish you good luck, Giò."

"I'll need it, thank you. We have to go now. Carmela, such a pleasure to see you again and know you'll be keeping Vanda company. I'll phone this evening to find out how she's doing."

"I'll drop by for a short visit tomorrow, if you're not too tired," said Agnese. "Carmela, if you come with me, I'll be able to give you the cool box I left in the car. You won't have to cook anything for dinner then."

As she and Giò were heading back to Maratea in the car, Agnese glanced at her watch.

"It's almost half-past one. The carabinieri haven't called for Vanda yet, so it looks like they haven't found the body of the woman. Do you believe she imagined it all?"

"If it was someone else, I would suspect just that, but you know how sharp Vanda is. I frankly doubt she would imagine something like that even if she had the most severe concussion…"

"But they haven't found the body. It shouldn't have been difficult for Giuseppe and Kia to locate… if it was really there."

"Hmm," said Giò. "Strange indeed."

That afternoon, Agnese knocked at the door of Giò's attic flat before going to her shop. As she went in, she saw maps, a phonebook, brochures and lists of local attractions spread messily all over the table, which was par for the course for Giò. Her panicked 'I'm lost' expression wasn't so typical.

"Giò, what's happening? I thought you'd be going to the fair."

"Maybe tomorrow if the judges want to come along."

"That's a good idea, I'm sure they will appreciate the village atmosphere. But what's happening?"

"I… I don't know. I had booked them into the Conference Hotel, so they could have a look at what the guests would get. But one of the judges, Mrs Advantage, just called me. She's discovered the Buon Giove Hotel and wants to go there."

"But there won't be room for a whole conference at the Buon Giove Hotel. And it would be outrageously expensive. I don't think the attendees would appreciate paying so much for the accommodation on top of their conference fee."

Giò shook her head vigorously. "No, the judges will go to the Buon Giove for this visit only, but the hotel for the conference itself would stay the same."

Agnese thought it over. "That's kind of weird, isn't it? I thought they'd be checking the Conference Hotel's standards, the food, the rooms, the service and overall location."

"We'll be heading up there to check it out," replied Giò without her usual enthusiasm. "But I had to cancel their reservation."

"Well, if it ends up being the location for the conference for three nights in low season with how many guests?"

"The last conference had almost 400 attendees," murmured Giò.

"Then I'm sure it can put up with a cancelled reservation. You also mentioned the manager was allowing the judges to stay for free anyway, so the hotel isn't really losing anything."

Again Giò nodded, but she didn't look that convinced.

"Don't you worry, Giò, it will turn out fine," said Agnese, opening the door to go. "They will be enchanted by Maratea and you will win, I'm positive. Let me know if I can do anything for you; I need to rush to the shop now. By the way, Nando said you can have his car, and I've brought you his keys. Take care."

"Thanks."

What Giò had not confessed to her sister was that due to a misunderstanding with Mrs Advantage, she would have to pay for the judges' night at the Buon Giove. While the Conference Hotel was happy to allow them to stay free of charge in return for a chance to host the writers' conference, the Buon Giove had no such incentive. Giò had learned that elsewhere, the judges had always been offered their accommodation free, so she had promptly said the hotels in Maratea would do the same. And now she didn't dare renege on that offer, even though the judges had chosen a different hotel. She had bargained as ferociously as she could with the Buon Giove reception staff, something they were evidently not used to, but it would still deplete her finances rather alarmingly.

She shook her head and went back to her local brochures – where would she take them? She went over the whole itinerary for the tenth time, phoning her chosen restaurant to book the judges in for dinner and planning an informal lunch at the Trecchina fair. Then she called the Palazzo De Lieto that housed the only museum in Maratea. It was normally closed at this time of year, but would open especially for her guests.

Her mobile rang.

It was Mrs Advantage.

Panic.

"Good afternoon," Giò said shyly.

"Hello, Giò dear, we're so happy we're coming to visit you and your beautiful Maratea. We've looked at the photos you sent us – it's a gorgeous place."

"Oh, I'm so pleased you think so." Giò immediately felt much more at ease.

"And as for your blog – you've got a real knack for writing. And believe me, I've read an incredible amount of stuff in the travel writing world."

Giò was mute, but a feeling of joy was beginning to replace her anxiety. Her mouth went dry, her heart was thumping.

"But we'll talk during our visit. And that's exactly why I called. I've checked the trains and we would waste an awful lot of time travelling from the airport to the train station, then to Sapri and finally to Maratea. Why don't you come over to pick us up at the airport? Then we'll get time to chat."

"That would be a pleasure, and on the way back we could stop in Trecchina for the Chestnut Fair. The road passes right through the town."

"Certainly, dear, we'll do as you please and discuss all details on the road. We need to focus on the conference and the places the attendees can visit during their stay, but I won't fill your head with all these details before time. Just meet us at 8.30am at the airport. Wear something yellow so that I can spot you right away. And again, congratulations on your blog. I'll expect you to tell me all about it, and whether you plan to write a book. Because you're thinking about it, aren't you?"

Giò couldn't believe her ears! After years of struggling, both practically and inside herself, could she really consider herself as an author?

"But I'm talking too much, as usual. I'll see you tomorrow, and remember – wear something yellow."

4

CHESTNUTS AND THERMOMETERS

"Ouch!" cried Nando, letting go of the prickly chestnut husk and shaking his hand vigorously up and down.

"Dad! Mum told you to wear the gloves," Lilia reproached him, her red pigtails jumping around as her head jerked up and down to emphasise each syllable. Agnese pointed her finger in the air, wearing her best 'I told you so' expression. Luca laughed, and poor Nando had to explain himself to his whole family.

"I forgot chestnuts were this thorny."

At 12, Luca was grown-up enough to know his father's weaknesses. Looking his tall, well-built dad in the eyes, he added his two penn'orth.

"Dad, you said exactly the same thing last year." He paused meaningfully. "And the year before... and the year before."

"In fact, we should write it on a Post-It note and pin it to his forehead for next year," Agnese suggested.

Nando rolled his eyes, used to being the butt of the family jokes. He was a former rugby player, but not even his size was enough to earn him any respect from them, maybe because of the belly that was starting to make itself obvious over the top of his trousers.

As the others teased him mercilessly, he said, "I'd better stay here and look at this chestnut tree all day to make amends," and he did just that, "while you go to the fair and have some fun."

"Oh, Dad, never!" Lilia felt a rush of pity. After all, he was her favourite dad, as she used to say. A split second later, she was in his arms, kissing him all over his face.

The forest was gorgeous this morning, the yellow and red of the leaves standing out against an intensely blue sky with fluffy white clouds skidding over the tops of the chestnut trees. The air was slightly chilly; despite being only 12 kilometres from Maratea, Trecchina was much higher up in the mountains. Maratea was a seaside town, Trecchina most definitely a mountain one.

"Hey, our bag isn't even half full," Luca complained.

"You're right, captain, let's get back to business," Nando said, putting Lilia down.

"And let's hurry up," Agnese said. "I'm starting to feel hungry."

They kept searching the forest floor, moving the deep piles of leaves with their sticks. It was a long, laborious process, probably because they were latecomers. Most of the husks they found were empty due to the flocks of greedy chestnut seekers who had preceded them.

"Can't we just buy a bag at the fair?"

"Dad! That's cheating!" Lilia felt she had a moral duty to educate her father.

Luca laughed. "Auntie Giò would do just that."

"A pity she's not here, then."

"She'll be free next weekend," Agnese said. "Today is a very important day for her. My poor sister was up at five o'clock this morning to drive to the airport."

"Hey, what's that?" Luca cried, his stick pointing at something among the leaves. Horrified, Agnese ran over to him, stopping him from removing the leaves around the shape.

"Stop it! Stop it!"

"Hey, Agnese, it's just an old boot," Nando soothed her. "It must have been here for ages."

"But it could be Vanda's body. I mean, the body she saw."

"This part of the forest has been searched thoroughly, there was nothing here."

Ushering her children away from whatever it was that Luca had found, Agnese calmed herself by renewing her efforts to fill their jute bag with chestnuts. To her relief, Lilia and Luca spotted a less trodden path, and within minutes the jute bag was bulging at the seams.

"Let's go to the fair," she said, suddenly impatient to leave the forest.

PIAZZA DEL POPOLO, TRECCHINA'S MAIN SQUARE, HAD BEEN planted with so many trees that it looked more like a part of the forest than a proper piazza. In actual fact, it was only separated by a string of houses from the wild woods that surrounded the little town. Evergreens were scattered among yellow lindens and a few red-leaved shrubs. Agnese loved that the stalls had been laid along the piazza, which was closed to the traffic. A paved clearing hosted a band that was playing live music, alternating the ever popular ballroom dances with tarantella tunes, and a few people were already on the dance floor.

Their stomachs growling ferociously, Agnese and her family decided it was time for some serious food.

"Shall we go to check out the school's street food stalls?" Agnese suggested.

"Sounds good to me." Nando nodded, remembering that the previous year the students had cooked extremely well.

The queues at two of the three food stalls were already seemingly endless Strangely, the third one looked deserted – a bad omen, but they were so hungry, they started there rather than joining one of the two long queues. It wasn't long before they found out there was nobody in the queue at that particular stall because no food was being served.

A blonde pony-tailed girl was shouting at her team.

"You stupid idiots, you're too slow! Can't you do anything but stand there staring? Do something!"

The others were, in fact, doing something, but they all seemed flustered by their leader and aware that they wouldn't be serving any food for quite a while. A couple of them were stirring huge pots containing far too much liquid – it could hardly be called sauce – another was frying an incredible amount of aubergines, which to Agnese's expert eye were either too burnt or too raw.

"Is that water boiling?" The pony-tailed girl was shouting at a little boy, who looked down at his feet.

"No, it's not," he mumbled. "The flame isn't high enough... actually, it's dying." Looking horrified, he shook the gas cylinder and cried, "It's empty." And the flame flickered out, leaving everyone at a loss. That is, apart from the blonde girl, who screamed and shouted at each of her companions.

"Why did I have to end up with the seven most stupid people ever? I can't believe this. The headmistress will pay for this. You're just a bunch of..."

"Mum, that girl is the meanest I've ever seen," murmured Lilia in dismay. "If I were one of her team, I'd answer back and throw her off the stall."

"I'd throw her in the sauce pot." As Agnese gave him a reproachful look, Luca amended his statement. "I mean, once the sauce has cooled down."

"Let's split into two teams. Dad and Lilia, you go to first stall; Luca and I will go to the other one. And, you two, fetch some sensible food," Agnese added, catching the mischievous look that passed between father and daughter.

"OH MY GOODNESS, THAT WAS A MEAL AND A HALF." AGNESE looked with some concern at her waistline. She was always struggling with the extra kilos that tend to rack up over the years.

The whole family sat on one of the benches around the square, their trays empty. Not a crumb of chestnut bread or biscuit or focaccia was left.

"I'm happy we don't have to judge the street food competition," said Luca, his dark eyes, so similar to his mother's, gleaming with satisfaction. "I couldn't say which team did the best job."

"I could say who did the worst." Lilia eyed the third stall, where the team hadn't made much progress. There was still no food on display, but at least the bossy girl seemed to have stopped shouting.

"I'll fetch some coffee," Nando said.

When he reappeared holding two cups, Agnese's nostrils twitched as she caught a familiar scent.

"Smells like cinnamon – cinnamon and chestnuts. Delicious."

Nando looked at her quizzically. "I don't think the coffee smells of anything but coffee."

"It's coming from the third stall, and a few people are queuing up there… finally!" Luca said. "Mum, can we go and have a look while you and Dad drink your coffee?"

"I'll tell you what, I'll come too. I'm just too curious." For Agnese, the world of scents wasn't limited to her perfumery. She loved good smells of any kind.

At the stall an Indian girl, looking distraught, was frying fritters. Another girl was putting them into absorbent paper and then scooping them into a dish, and a third was selling them to the customers. Their faces were dark with shame, their young eyes dulled by the failure of their team.

"Hey, they smell delicious, you've done a great job," Agnese encouraged them. "And you didn't give up, even when things went wrong. It happens. You're doing great."

The good folk of Trecchina who were queuing behind her burst into wild applause, and the Indian girl gave Agnese a look so full of gratitude that she was moved. She bit into a fritter from the dish she'd just been handed.

"They are so delicious and show all the effort you put into preparing them."

The blonde pony-tailed girl threw a tray of empty dishes she was holding onto the ground and ran off, leaving her team once more humiliated and speechless. But the Trecchina folk, although good-hearted, were intolerant of bad behaviour.

"You guys will do better without her."

"Hey, get your claws out!"

"Yes, show your grit and get on with your work."

The Indian girl pursed her lips and told her friends more fritters were on their way. Then the seamless workflow between the three of them found its rhythm again.

"Weird," commented Agnese to Nando, biting into another fritter and thinking that her diet would start on Monday, as is traditional.

"I can't stop eating them," he replied.

"I love the combination of chestnut flour, rosemary and raisins. The dough is perfect, and that's not easy with chestnut flour. That girl has done an excellent job."

Nando knew that his wife's judgement on food was as precise as her decisions on the perfumes she stocked in her shop.

"I think it's time for me to visit Vanda," Agnese said.

"We're going to look at the other stalls. Dad, will you join us to play the games?"

"Of course, but if I win anything, I won't split it with you two. You cheated me last time."

"Oh, Dad!" Lilia said as Agnese left them to walk along the main street, flanked by single- or two-storey houses. The buildings were packed in, one right beside the next as they would be in a city centre, but Agnese knew that behind each door, a courtyard opened directly onto the forest with a beautiful view of the mountains behind, the inner door to the house being to one side of the courtyard.

She stopped at a red wooden door with an ancient rustic portal made with uneven blocks of local stone, a rose bush climbing all around it, and rang the bell.

"Yes?" A man in suit and tie opened the door. Agnese thought she must have rung at the wrong door.

"I'm Agnese, Vanda's friend. I've come to visit her."

"Oh, Agnese, it's such a pleasure to meet you. I'm Edoardo, another friend of Vanda's, and I'm here for a visit too."

They shook hands cordially, as good friends of friends do.

"How is she?" Agnese asked as Edoardo showed her in.

"Like a lion in a cage. She's awfully put out at not being allowed to go to the fair."

"Oh, the poor love!"

The 'poor love' was sitting on the sofa with an icepack on her head, a thermometer on a little table beside her, and a blanket over her legs that she quickly moved away as she got up to greet her friend.

"Wait, Vanda, wait, don't strain yourself!" Agnese cried.

"No strain whatsoever, I can assure you I'm fine." Following Agnese's stare at the sickroom objects that suggested otherwise, she added, "Ah, that's to discourage gossips from lingering for too long. When they start to bore me, I suddenly get an awful headache and I can barely speak, let alone listen to them."

Agnese laughed.

"By the way," Vanda said, "Edoardo is the new owner of the bookshop in Trecchina. Edoardo, Agnese runs a beautiful and unusual perfumery in Maratea. She's a wonderful consultant."

"I'd love to pay your shop a visit. I'm fond of colognes in the English style."

"I stock quite a few of them, and you're welcome anytime. How are things in your bookshop?"

"Not thriving as they should, but I'm positive people will rediscover the joy of good reading."

They chatted about the difficulties of running a small business, and the amount of rules and regulations they had to comply with as if they were multinational companies, creating common ground between them. In fact, it was a few minutes before Agnese remembered the reason for her visit.

She turned towards Vanda. "By the way, how are you for real?"

"I'm fine. I could have gone to the fair, but the doctor made me promise I would stay home. And here I am, missing all the fun. Have you been there at all?"

"I've just come from there…"

"Ahem, ladies," Edoardo interrupted. "I know perfectly well how keen you are to chat freely and speak your mind about the villagers. This is when a man can be nothing but a nuisance."

The two burst into guilty laughter.

"You can stay, Edoardo, really," Vanda said. "We can share all our gossip with you."

Edoardo shook his head, unconvinced. "That I will never believe." Vanda carried on laughing, but she flushed slightly. "Enjoy your chat, and later on, if you feel up to it, have a look at them." He gestured towards three books lying behind the blood pressure cuff.

"I certainly will, thank you so much."

"Please stay where you are, I know my way out. Agnese, it's been such a pleasure to meet you, and if you don't mind, I'd love to visit your shop."

"I'll be waiting for you." Agnese smiled, shaking hands with him.

When they heard the door shut behind Edoardo, Agnese teased Vanda.

"That's what I call a perfect gentleman, and a good-looking one, too!"

This time, Vanda turned crimson: an unusual reaction for this independent woman, who had divorced her husband when her kids were very young and brought them up by herself, turning them in two healthy, positive young people.

"You're right, he's a good man."

"I don't think I have ever seen him before, though."

"He moved to Trecchina a year ago, taking over the bookshop from the previous owner who was going to close it for good. But against all the odds, Edoardo has managed to give it a new lease of life. As he said, it's not easy, as you know yourself, but he's trying hard, organising monthly book clubs for teens, romance lovers, DIY enthusiasts…"

"But he's not from Trecchina, is he?"

"That's the interesting bit: he moves from place to place, taking over bookshops on the brink of failure in small towns around the country. He stays with each one for two to three years, then sells them to a new owner. He says that's the best way of travelling he knows."

"How interesting, Giò will love that idea. But how about the carabinieri and the body? Anything new on that front?"

"That's the incredible thing. They searched all day yesterday, but they couldn't find it. Giuseppe took them to exactly where he found me, but nothing. They are sure I made it all up."

"Well, maybe they're right. After all, concussion may…"

"No they aren't!" cried Vanda vehemently. "I'm telling you, I saw her. I can see her face in front of me. It was not a bad dream."

Agnese stared at her. Vanda calmed down.

"You know, I've got blurred memories of when Giuseppe found me. I remember his voice sounding like it was coming from afar, and I hardly remember the paramedics and the ambulance ride at all. Just the hospital bed; the cold; the hot water bottle finally giving me some relief. Everything immediately after I was hit on the head is blurred and confused, but all that happened before has come back, slowly but clearly. I'm sure I saw that woman."

"But you didn't recognise her? I mean, she wasn't someone you knew by sight?"

Vanda shook her head. "No, not at all."

"Do the carabinieri know of any missing person corresponding to your description?"

"I asked the maresciallo, but so far no one of that description has been reported missing from the area."

"Well, I think people have to wait 24 hours before reporting someone's disappearance, unless it's a child, and if the old woman wasn't from the area, it may take a while before they connect her with what's happened here." Agnese trusted her friend, but the idea of an old lady coming all the way to the small town of Trecchina just to be killed didn't seem to make any sense.

"How about the fair?" asked Vanda, abruptly changing the subject.

"I'm so sorry you couldn't come and join us, but you'll be able to go next week and see for yourself. The number of stands seems to increase each year; the students have done a splendid job." And she told Vanda about the performance of the two successful street food teams and the troubles encountered by team number three.

"That Erica will never learn, because after all, it's not her fault. It's her mother, feeding her with the idea that she doesn't need to take any responsibility whatsoever for her failures in life, while taking all the praise for victories. The headmistress is determined to teach her the hard way."

"So far, the hard way has been pretty hard for her team. Erica blamed them for the stall's failure."

Vanda shrugged her shoulders in resignation. "Some things never change."

Agnese looked at her watch. "It's time to go, before Lilia and Luca get too tired. I asked them to finish their homework yesterday, but there's no way they've done so."

"Don't spoil their Saturdays. It's the best day of the week for schoolkids."

Agnese laughed. "I really thought you would recommend that things be done well in advance."

"As with everything else, so it is with organisation... it should be done in moderation. Let them enjoy their lives. You're not like Erica's parents."

"Parenthood is a pretty hard job, though," Agnese said, more to herself than to her friend. "You're never sure you're doing the right thing: you're either too severe or too laid back, never in the sweet spot."

"Well at least I'm done with my self-doubt. My little birds have left the nest, and I'm proud of them."

As they got up from the sofa, Agnese asked, "Do you have enough food left for tonight?"

"You're kidding me? With all the food Rosa sent, there'll be enough for Carmela and me for a whole week. Tell her I'm so grateful, and I'll come for a visit as soon as I'm fit."

"Where's Carmela? I was half expecting to find her here."

"She's coming over tonight; she's gone home for a little break this afternoon."

"I'm happy she's with you. And I'll get Giò to come over, as soon as she's done with the Travel Writers' Conference judges. I must say, she's got quite a flair for solving mysteries, so maybe she can help you understand what you saw in the forest."

"Yes, before the carabinieri commit me to an asylum. They're angry with me because I won't retract what I told them. But I saw that woman! I'm sure someone strangled her, and the killer is still out there somewhere, maybe even enjoying the fair."

"We'll find out what happened. After all, the woman must have disappeared from somewhere, so surely someone will be missing her. But now, please take a break from those thoughts. Are you going back to work tomorrow?"

"No, the doctor said if I don't experience any vertigo or

nausea or further signs of concussion, I can go back to work later in the week."

Someone rang the bell. Vanda peered out of the window, hidden by the handmade curtains, recognising her neighbour, Teresa.

"My goodness, not her, not now."

Agnese decided what to do. "You sit on your armchair and pretend to be asleep. I will answer the door."

As Vanda sank under her blanket, her head leaning against the pillows, Agnese opened the door and held a finger to her lips.

"Teresa, so kind of you to call. Vanda's sleeping; she's had a tough day and her head is aching awfully."

The woman peered inside, not happy until she'd spotted Vanda, the icepack on her head, shivering and muttering as if she were delirious.

"Oh, the poor thing! I didn't realise it was this bad."

"Yes, she's only just fallen asleep. Let's leave her to rest for a while. Carmela is coming over later to take care of her."

As she picked up her bag, making sure Teresa left the house with her, Agnese saw Vanda's hand sliding out from beneath the blanket to give her a surreptitious thumbs up.

5

ETHOLOGY OF THE TRAVEL WRITER

The next morning, before heading to her shop, Agnese knocked on Giò's door. They lived in the centre of Maratea, Granny on the ground floor, Agnese and her family on the first floor, and Giò in the two-room attic. One main door connected all three flats to the steep cobbled alley outside. But despite living so close to Giò, Agnese hadn't heard from her sister since Saturday.

"Hope it's not too early for you," Agnese said when Giò opened the door, already up and dressed.

"No, I needed to get up early. We've got things to do this morning, then after a light brunch, Kate and Mike are heading back to Naples."

"Are you driving them to the airport?"

"No, the hotel offers a shuttle service."

Agnese nodded in approval, then asked, "What are they like? Do you think they've enjoyed Maratea so far?"

"Kate seems delirious about it." Then Giò added, with a little embarrassment, "And both she and Mike have taken a liking to my writing."

"Really?"

"Really. They asked me to write a few pieces for the blog of the Travel Writers' Association. But most importantly, during the conference, they are going to introduce me to a couple of publishing houses. These are the guys who publish people like Bill Pryson and Paul Terroux."

"Oh my goodness, Giò, that's terrific news!" Agnese hugged her sister, who despite all her efforts, couldn't help letting out a couple of sniffs as her eyes went strangely watery. Giò could get so emotional about her own hopes and dreams.

Controlling herself, the aspiring author said in a husky voice, "Imagine if I were to pitch an idea for a travel book – not a guide, but a travel memoir, or a trek taking me way up north." Her green eyes were shining. "But I'd better not count my chickens before they're hatched."

"Agreed!" said Agnese who knew the pain of disillusionment, but she squeezed her sister's hand nonetheless. Giò was so full of vigour and positivity. "I didn't see you at the fair yesterday; I was sure you'd pop by."

"No, the judges preferred to stay in Maratea. They had such a short time here."

In fact, she had only managed to take them to see the statue of Christ the Redeemer that dominated Maratea and the gulf from one of the highest mountains in the region, and then on to the harbour for an aperitivo. Kate had insisted on spending the rest of the day chattering with Giò and sunbathing beside the Buon Giove's heated swimming pool, while Mike appreciated the delights of the hotel's golf course with olive trees on one side, and the ocean and private beach on the other. But Giò thought better than to go into detail with Agnese; for some reason, the whole visit was making her slightly uncomfortable.

"I see," Agnese said, imagining her sister taking the judges all over the place until she'd exhausted them completely with sightseeing.

"Did you visit Vanda?" Giò changed the subject.

"Yes, she looks fine and fully recovered, I'd say. She hopes to be back at work later in the week."

"And the old woman?"

"That's the strange part. The carabinieri found nothing in the forest, but Vanda is more convinced than ever that she saw her."

"Concussion?"

"If I didn't know Vanda, I would have thought that. But as you pointed out on Saturday, she's such a pragmatic person, I hardly think she's the type to indulge in daydreams."

"Maybe the woman wasn't actually dead. Maybe she was just lying there unconscious for some reason, and she left as soon as she'd recovered."

"Leaving Vanda all alone in the forest with a head injury?"

"Maybe the poor woman was homeless and scared. If the carabinieri have searched everywhere and found nothing, I can't think of any other solution."

"I didn't think you would be so quick to trust the carabinieri after the mess the maresciallo made investigating the death of poor Elena."

"I don't, but I trust their dogs." Giò winked and Agnese chuckled.

"By the way, I haven't told you the big news. There was a man at Vanda's."

"Really?" cried Giò in surprise. Vanda was a charming woman, but not exactly a romantic soul. After her divorce, she had taken up with a couple of men, but as both relationships ended in betrayal and lies, Vanda had sworn to herself and her family she was done with men. With her usual determination, she had brought the curtain down on her love life, and since then nobody had known her to so much as flirt. She had cared for her kids, provided them with a good education, gained her boss's trust, worked for her community, but falling in love had become a complete no-no.

"Who is he?"

"The local bookshop keeper, a charming man with an almost British air... you know, the sort of gentleman you read about in books."

Giò was not quite so enamoured with Englishmen after her 10-year relationship with Londoner Dorian Gravy had ended poorly just a month before they were due to get married. But she conceded that a charming bookshop owner could be an altogether different species to her arrogant and faithless ex.

"She didn't mention anything to me..."

"I'm not sure anything has started between them yet, nor that she's even aware of the possibility. But I can tell you, he's very much taken with her."

The sisters recalled the book Giò had seen at Vanda's bedside in the hospital and how Vanda had blushed and hidden it, and the incredibly beautiful bunch of flowers. Agnese had noticed similar flowers in Vanda's home.

"So maybe he visited her at the hospital, and the next day at her home. You're right, he sounds like he's falling for her."

"But don't mention any of this to Vanda. Pretend I've told you nothing. I wouldn't want her to raise her defences. Now the kids have grown up, I'd love her to find a companion for life."

"Is this the way you talk about me with Granny?"

"Maybe, but there's not a charming bookshop owner in Maratea... yet!"

"I hate you!" Giò laughed, then added more seriously, "When the judges have gone, I'm going to visit Vanda. This story about the old woman isn't adding up. As you said, it's unlike Vanda to imagine things. It may be worth having a look around and speaking to people in Trecchina, just in case."

"I was hoping you'd suggest that. Now I'd better get to the perfumery, double quick. If Mr Nasty catches me coming in late again, I'll never hear the end of it."

THE MAN AT THE BUON GIOVE RECEPTION DESK LOOKED DOWN HIS nose at Giò. With his well-trained eye, he could distinguish between Donna Baran ripped jeans selling at 900 euros a pair and ordinary high-street clothes. She was definitely below average when it came to expensively branded items of clothing.

With a derisive sniff, the receptionist allowed her to pass him and go into the garden, where Kate and Mike, to Giò's horror, were still having their breakfast. They were sitting comfortably under a white gazebo at a wrought iron table where fine porcelain cups, a Sheffield silver teapot and silver cutlery had been arranged on a white Flanders linen tablecloth. When the waitress arrived, bringing the most delicious, colourful food, Giò regretted having had her breakfast at home.

"Oh, dearest Giò, you're already here. I love your work ethic."

Mike was more of an introvert than Kate, but he pulled out a chair and invited Giò to sit with them. "This salmon is delicious, we couldn't resist a full breakfast."

Giò smiled but her heart sank, anticipating that the breakfast would inflate her bill for their rooms.

"Shall I ask the waitress to lay the table for you too?" Kate asked.

"Thanks for asking, but I've already had my breakfast, I'm fine." But her mouth was watering.

"We really want you to know how much we appreciate all of this." Kate stretched out her arms to take in the perfect lawns running between lemon and orange trees with their glossy dark leaves, the huge infinity pool overflowing into the sea, and the elegant mansion house's façade made from local stone, roses climbing up its walls. "Maratea is an incredible place, I'm so glad you brought us here. It's quite a trek, but well worth the effort."

Giò was befuddled. Maratea wasn't exactly summed up by the Buon Giove Hotel, any more than The Savoy epitomised London or the Hôtel Ritz Paris.

"I really hope you're going to like the Conference Hotel. The staff are very kind, and they are waiting for us."

"Do you have some brochures?"

"Yes, of course," said Giò.

"I knew we could rely on you. Let's finish breakfast and get down to work."

It actually took 45 minutes for the judges to finish their breakfast. Giò couldn't believe how much food two stomachs could contain. Then Mike said he was going for a round of golf.

"After all," he said, "it's always women who decide on the accommodation."

"But we should visit the hotel, and I wanted to show you Maratea town centre. They're going to open Palazzo De Lieto just for you…"

"Kate can sort out all that stuff, the golf course is calling me."

Kate laughed at Giò's disconcerted expression as Mike left. "Dear Giò, you should know what men are like. You're 40-something, aren't you?"

"I'm 38!" Giò, prickly as a chestnut husk, corrected her. She was used to people thinking her younger rather than older.

"Sure, 38. Still old enough to know that most work gets done by women at the end of the day, and women only! Let's move to that gazebo closer to the edge of the cliff. It will be a pleasure to work there."

When they had moved, Giò couldn't help but relax and feel less put out by the strange behaviour of the two judges. It was a glorious October day: the sky was a deep blue with no mist on the horizon, the whole gulf saturated in soft light. The sea was a sight to behold with different degrees of colours, from deep green to deep blue. As she gazed at it, Giò planned to go out for a paddle in her kayak the very next day. She had plenty of time to make the most of what the heavenly place had to offer, but the two judges had a mere day.

They sat down at the table and Kate asked her for the brochures. She checked them, turned them over, put on her glasses and examined all the room details.

"You know, Giò, I'm not really sure this is up to our standards. The rooms don't look that large and the decor is not as nice as here."

"But Kate, they only have 40 rooms at the Buon Giove. There's no way they could accommodate hundreds of guests."

"That's such a shame!"

"And even if they could, one day at the Buon Giove costs as much as a week at the Conference Hotel. And one of your requirements was a reasonable hotel price."

"Giò, I know, I was the one who sent you our specifications. What I'm saying is that I fear this hotel isn't really what our attendees are looking for."

"But the rooms are spacious, they all have balconies, and most of them have a view over the sea," Giò said, gesturing towards the beautiful bay before them, the green mountains embracing the whole gulf. "Why don't we go and have a look? I'm sure the pictures don't do it justice."

"I don't think it would be a good idea to rub it in their faces that their hotel isn't up to our standards."

"But your guests are world travellers, used to spending nights in the most unlikely places. They will simply love the hotel and its surrounding area. There's a nice park all around the hotel and a lift to take them down to a beautiful private beach. The hotel also has two swimming pools and serves good food."

"I see you really care about this conference, Giò. You're such a dear, I'll see what I can do. I promise you, I'll do my very best…"

"So you don't want to come along and see the hotel with your own eyes? Or at least have a look at the town centre and see what kind of activities your guests could enjoy?"

"Oh no, dear, it's been an awful week, and yesterday you took us all over the place. I think we deserve a couple of hours to relax before plunging into another week of hard work. We've seen a lot, thanks to you."

Giò was too befuddled to smile.

Kate squeezed her arm. "Hey, dear, you don't really need your hometown to host a Travel Writers' Conference to get your books published. You only need to meet the right people, and they happen to be the folks I normally deal with. Your writing is great; we just need to bring the two things together, which could happen at a conference anywhere. It doesn't have to be in Maratea."

The meaning behind Kate's words finally dawned on Giò and a smile spread across her face.

"And I'm not saying the conference won't be in Maratea, but I'd hate to see you disappointed, so I don't want to pull the wool over your eyes. The other possible venues are closer to airports and provide more comfortable accommodation, which are both important criteria because all those travel writers who claim to be able to sleep in third-class carriages, crowded coaches, yurts and hostels are in fact very picky when it comes to conference accommodation, I can assure you. And I've been in this industry for over 30 years."

And Kate went on, shattering Giò's illusions about the renowned travel writers she so admired, who as it turned out were nothing but pains in the neck when it came to pillows, mattresses and fresh orange juice for breakfast.

"I feel so naïve," concluded Giò when the woman had finished her masterclass on travel writer ethology.

"Don't you worry, there's good old Kate to take care of you."

"What should we do now?"

"Giò, I think we're done. You were brilliant, splendid organisation. Take back all the brochures and maps, then run home to do some more writing. I will spend the rest of the morning relaxing and thinking about how to sell Maratea to the judging panel. And I want you to know that both Mike and I would be delighted if you were to invite us here again."

Before Giò could suggest they could make themselves comfortable at her parents' old house any time, Kate added, "We love this hotel, it has all the luxuries we like, but we'd prefer to enjoy a longer stay next time."

Giò nodded, not trusting herself to speak. After being hugged by Kate and waved at by Mike from the adjacent golf course, she wandered back to the hotel building. She glanced back at the huge park surrounding the hotel, the spa, the gazebo restaurant serving delicious food all day long – the heavenly place had definitely enchanted the two judges. Giò only hoped that the missed visit to the Conference Hotel and Maratea town centre wouldn't be an impediment when they came to deciding whether to host the conference there.

Turning her back on the Buon Giove paradise, Giò made her way past the snooty receptionist and returned to her attic flat, overcome with emotion. She was unsure whether she wanted to yell out loud for joy or burst into tears. No matter how strong and independent they are, human beings have an innate need for validation and recognition, especially if it comes from someone with influence. And Kate Advantage had just given her that validation.

Giò fell onto her armchair, yelling, "Hooray!" and throwing her arms in the air. Then she sobbed like a child, indulging in a certain amount of self-pity, thinking of the years of struggles and self-doubt she'd finally leave behind. Her new life as an author, a real travel writer, was about to start.

6

THE ROAD TO TRUTH PASSES THROUGH LIES

When Giò rang the bell at Vanda's house, she found her friend unusually flustered. As she stepped in, a strange man was waiting for them inside, and from his brooding expression it didn't take Giò long to realise her visit had interrupted something. A sturdy man, he glowered at her, his eyebrows moving up and down strangely and an unpleasant lopsided grin stretching into his right cheek. Was this the good-looking gentleman Agnese had talked about? Giò had trusted her sister to have taste.

"I'll make a coffee for the two of you," Vanda said, disappearing into the kitchen.

"So are you another one of those people who likes to turn up unannounced?" the man demanded of Giò without even pausing to shake her hand.

Giò wasn't often wrong-footed by someone else's arrogance and would have been only too glad to respond just as bluntly, but believing Vanda to have a soft spot for this man, she bit her tongue.

"I was going to come over early this afternoon, but I messaged Vanda to tell her I could make it earlier."

"And who are you?"

"I'm Giovanna Brando, Giò to most people…"

"Why are you not working on a Monday morning?"

"I was supposed to be working, but it was cancelled, and… but why should I justify myself to you?"

"No need to get defensive, I was simply wondering what you actually do for a living."

"I'm a travel writer."

"No, not your hobby, I mean for a living."

Giò couldn't believe her ears, but the arrogant visitor hadn't finished with her yet.

"You know, when you do something productive, something useful to society, and then you're paid for it."

Before Giò could reply, Vanda joined them with a tray of coffee cups and a few brioches made with chestnut flour. Her cheeks were on fire. A tense silence filled the air and Giò wished she had come round later as she'd planned to, but she had been encouraged by Vanda's positive reply to her message.

"The sooner, the better."

"You're useless at making coffee," the man snapped at Vanda, the strange grin back on his face. "I can't drink it. And anyway, why would I want to waste my time talking to two women? I'd better leave. And the flowers? Put them in water soon. No need to accompany me – you don't live in a castle. I can find my way out."

He banged the door loudly behind him, and only then did Vanda sink onto her sofa, holding her head between her hands.

"Thank goodness you came!"

"What was that? A man or a troll? I've never experienced such rudeness."

"He's a new customer for our company in import/export, and he is interested in taking our products to the US. They haven't sealed the deal yet, and I don't want to ruin things, but it was hard not to answer back."

"Is he always like that?" Giò said, relieved that he wasn't the charming Trecchina bookshop owner after all.

"Even worse. But he is good at business deals. I don't want to know about his private life."

"Talking about private life, what was he doing here?"

"That was most unexpected. At the office, he's been anything but appreciative of my work. He's even scathing about the company and our products, to tell you the truth. But he had a meeting with my boss, and when Pompeo told him what had happened to me, he came for a courtesy visit…"

"Well, that's a misnomer if ever I heard one!" chuckled Giò. "I don't want to be present if he ever pays a discourtesy visit."

"Me neither," said Vanda, caressing the flowers. "But the bouquet is really beautiful. I just have to forget who it came from."

"There's something familiar about him, but I can't place him. But enough about that man. How about the old woman, have the carabinieri found anything?"

"Nope. They've not only found nothing, but they insist I imagined it."

"But you're still positive that you saw that woman…"

"As surely as I'm seeing you right now."

"And you're sure she wasn't just feeling sick?"

"I didn't have time to touch her, but her tongue sticking out, her expression of intense pain, the blue colour of her face… she was dead. And I mean dead, dead." A shiver went down Vanda's spine and she had to pause. "The carabinieri have checked with the hospitals in the area, but no old woman has been admitted. Her description doesn't match anybody who's been reported missing in Basilicata, or even in Italy. I was asked to examine a photo line-up of women in the right age range who have gone missing from places all over the country, but none reminded me of her."

"Do you know if anybody noticed her in town?"

"I've asked all the people who've visited, but none of them noticed her. But then, it was the day before the fair and there were quite a few tourists around."

"It's incredible that you found a corpse here, it's not the kind of thing that happens in a place like Trecchina. And it's even stranger that you were hit on the head by a branch at that very moment…"

"What do you mean?"

"When too many coincidences happen together, they are not coincidences at all."

"And?"

"I'm wondering if it wasn't a branch that hit you on the head after all. Perhaps you found something that you weren't supposed to find, and whoever killed the woman decided to put you out of action for a while. How simple to hit you on the head, remove the corpse, and leave a branch next to you so that the rescuers would assume it had fallen from a tree."

"I didn't dare voice it before, but that's exactly what I think too."

"The point is, where's the body? Because the killer had to dispose of it somewhere."

"The killer?"

"Well, you said the woman looked like she'd been strangled, which indicates a murderer of some kind."

"You're right! Of course, you're right, but isn't it strange that the carabinieri found nothing?"

"It'd be highly unlikely for someone who's not really looking properly to find anything. I'm sure they believe she was just some vagrant, perhaps a drunk who woke up and decided to leave on her own two feet."

"But she wasn't dressed like a vagrant. Maybe she wasn't wealthy, but her shoes were in good condition – I noticed those first – and the coat seemed to be a fine one."

"Was there a bag nearby?"

"I didn't see one, but it could have been hidden by the leaves."

"Let's use our brains. The woman is certainly not from Trecchina, otherwise we would have heard about her disappearance. I can't think of any elderly person here who's so alone that nobody would notice her disappearance for three days. And the same goes for the villages around here. So shall we assume she came from somewhere further away?"

"That's a good hypothesis."

"In which case, how did she reach Trecchina?"

"By coach?"

"And which coach is the most likely to bring in people from a distance?"

"The Naples coach to Lauria, then the local service to Trecchina."

"Exactly!" Giò cried triumphantly. "Let's check the timetables."

On Vanda's laptop, they searched for the times of the coaches.

"The first Lauria-Trecchina service is early in the morning." Giò started off mumbling, but got more excited as she went on. "That's mainly for the locals, but the second one looks a more likely choice for someone coming in from Naples. The third one would arrive too late and wouldn't tie in with when you found her. That was pretty easy, wasn't it?"

"I'm impressed, but what now?" asked Vanda, seeing Giò putting her jacket on.

"How are you feeling today?"

"Like a lion in a cage."

"Do you feel like having a walk in the village?"

"I'd love to, but it's not yet time for the bus to arrive…"

"Bus drivers love coffee and fags. Let's go and find out who was driving on Friday."

"HELLO, I'M WONDERING IF YOU CAN HELP ME," SAID GIÒ, entering the tobacconist's shop behind the bus stop. "My auntie left her make-up bag on the bus from Lauria last Friday afternoon. Have you any idea how to get in touch with the driver?"

"Did you phone the coach company?" replied the tobacconist harshly. Standing on the other side of the counter, she had long, greasy hair hanging lankly over her creased blouse.

"I did, but they found nothing. It could still be sitting in the bus's overhead compartment."

"It wouldn't be the first time. A bag can travel the country for weeks before it's recognised as left luggage – that is if it doesn't get stolen in the meantime," said the woman, shrugging in disapproval. "Anyway, it's usually Enzo doing the driving on Fridays."

"And could you give me his phone number?" Giò asked.

"Of course I can't! But we can phone him from my mobile and you can speak to him." She scrolled down to the correct number, told Enzo briefly why she was calling, then passed the phone to Giò. The red lacquer on her nails was chipped away.

"Hello, I'm Giò Brando. My auntie came from Naples to stay with me on Friday, she was travelling alone…"

"I see so many passengers each day…"

"I know, but please bear with me. I'm sure you'd remember her. She's in her seventies and was wearing a long grey coat. She loves that coat, even though it is too warm for our climate…"

"The lady is from the north?"

"Yes."

"Would she have asked for the town hall? Loudly?"

"That sounds like her, and I met her there. Did she leave a small red bag on your coach?"

"No, unless someone else has picked it up. There was nothing on the coach when I reached the depot."

"Did she have a suitcase?"

"Yes, I helped her with it. She's lost that too?"

"No, I just wanted to make sure we're talking about the same person."

"With that funny voice, there's no chance of mistaking her for someone else. No offence," the man added.

"None taken. What days do you drive to Trecchina?"

"What do you want to know that for?"

"Ahem… my auntie said she forgot to tip you for your help."

"Oh thanks, but it's not the custom here…"

"You know how stubborn old people can be. She won't leave me in peace till I give you her tip."

"In that case, I'll be driving the 3pm coach for the whole week. Today included."

"Great, Enzo, I'll be there!" Giò handed the phone back to the tobacconist, who had of course been listening to the whole conversation.

"Had you told me you wanted to give him a tip, I'd have given you his phone number. I was afraid you wanted to cause him trouble."

Giò smiled. "And did you notice my aunt at all?"

"Nope, but maybe she didn't come in here. You should try the bar – they have toilets, you know, and old ladies are always hunting for toilets."

When they left, Vanda looked at her friend in dismay.

"I don't know if I should congratulate you or not for telling so many fibs one after the other in less than five minutes."

"You know I'm a creative!"

"But how did you know about the lost red bag?"

"I don't, but it's easier to get people to speak if you ask them specific questions. It lowers their defences."

Vanda shrugged and gestured towards the outside tables in front of them. "Are we heading for the bar?"

"Yes, I think the tobacconist may be right. If you're desperate for the toilet, you go into the first place you're likely to find one. And your coffee was so bad," Giò mimicked Vanda's unpleasant visitor's grin and voice, "we'd better drink something decent."

"Hey, stop teasing me!" Vanda laughed.

In the bar, they ordered an orange juice each. When the

waitress came back with the drinks and Giò had tipped her generously, it was the right moment to question her.

"Can I ask you if you were working on Friday afternoon around three?"

"I work here every day except Sundays."

"That's great! My auntie arrived on the Lauria coach and she's lost a red make-up bag. We just phoned Enzo, the coach driver, but he says nothing was left on the coach."

"Maybe one of the passengers to Maratea took it. People are no longer as honest as they used to be."

"Auntie said she stopped here, you know... she badly needed to use the toilets. For an old person, it's quite a long journey from Naples to here."

"No, she didn't leave anything. I found nothing." The woman narrowed her eyes, looking at Giò suspiciously.

"Oh no, there was nothing important in the bag, just her make-up..."

The other woman relaxed instantly. "Oh, you know, people forget things all the time, and then they decide they left it here and I end up getting accused of taking all sorts of things. But as I say, if something's really valuable to you, you won't leave it behind in the first place."

"You're absolutely right. But the poor love has got herself so worked up about losing her bag that she can't remember where she went after leaving the coach. So I was wondering if you had seen her at all. An old lady, grey hair and a long grey coat. She had a suitcase with her."

The other woman shook her head.

"And she has an unmistakable voice and a northern accent," Giò added.

"Ah, *that* old woman. I didn't even realise it was Friday I saw her. But she didn't seem the type of person who forgets things. I was imagining someone fragile."

"Oh no, on the contrary, she's quite a character!" Giò smiled encouragingly.

"I wouldn't want to be around if she's in a bad mood. But no, she didn't leave anything here."

"And did you see where she was heading?"

"Well, she asked me for directions to the town hall."

"Did she say anything at all about her reasons for visiting?"

"No, she didn't say anything, and she wasn't the kind of person I wanted to chat to."

"I know, she can be a little pugnacious every now and then. So she didn't say anything other than asking for directions to the town hall?"

"No, nothing at all."

"But she left in the direction of the town hall?"

The woman took a second before replying, going back to that moment in her mind. "Yes, she did."

"What are we to do now?" asked Vanda as they left the bar. "We're not even sure it's the same woman I saw dead."

"Let's go to the town hall and consider all the options she had there. But I'll tell you what, I can't imagine too many elderly people were travelling to Trecchina by themselves last Friday. I say she's our lady."

The town hall was on the other side of Piazza del Popolo. As they walked its full length, passing by a bookshop, Giò noticed Vanda peering through the window, but as there were a few customers inside, she marched on without stopping.

When they reached the town hall, Giò checked the opening times on the noticeboard. On Fridays, the offices closed at 1pm. She asked the man on reception if anybody had shown up on Friday afternoon, maybe the mayor had held a special council, but all she learned was that the offices had closed at their regular time, as had the whole building.

"So," Giò said doubtfully to Vanda, guiding her away from the town hall reception desk, "our woman made her way from Naples to the town hall to find out it was closed, and it wouldn't open again until Monday."

"What if she was a tourist planning to visit the Chestnut Fair?"

"That would explain why she was in the woods," Giò said. "But where did she leave her suitcase? Did she stop off at her accommodation before going out again? If so, why is nobody in town admitting to having seen her?"

"Well, maybe she asked for the town hall because she was to meet someone here? We could ask around," Vanda looked at the few shops along the road, "but all the shops would have been closed around that time. What do you think?"

The town hall receptionist leaned forward. He was a slimy looking man and Giò was sure he wanted to eavesdrop on their conversation. She signalled to Vanda that they'd better leave the building, cross the road and not look back so as not to arouse the man's suspicions.

Once they were at a safe distance, Giò replied.

"Unfortunately, 3pm is the worst time she could have arrived. The town centre is deserted, the shops are closed and nobody is around. But we know the rest of the story, we only have to fill in the gap."

Vanda looked at Giò dubiously. "The gap? It's an abyss."

"I wouldn't say that. Everything that happened, happened very quickly. At around three o'clock, our woman was here in the town centre. You found her around five, lying under a shroud of leaves. That only means one thing to me: whoever killed her didn't waste time. He, or she, acted fast, as soon as he saw her. What we still don't know is whether they had arranged to meet or encountered each other by chance. Was it a robbery that went wrong?"

"We don't have robberies here."

"Nope, that's true, but imagine a drunk or a drug addict trying to mug her then losing control."

"But if this woman came all the way down here from the north, I assume someone was expecting her. Why didn't they raise the alarm when she didn't show up?"

"That takes us directly to our other hypothesis: she came to meet her killer, who of course wouldn't have raised the alarm, just made sure nobody saw her. He hid her in the woods, maybe temporarily, but then you showed up and he hit you on the head and took the body away."

"Shouldn't we tell the carabinieri?"

"Tell them what? That we know a lady from the north was on the bus and she stopped in a bar and asked directions to the town hall? They will say that her family or friends have picked her up and she's with them right now. No, we'd be better off finding the body first. Just to grab their attention."

"But they were in the forest with dogs and found nothing. We can't do any better…"

"I don't agree. In less than one hour, we have found traces of our lady in town. Don't you see? We now know she's… I mean, she *was* a real person. We've given her a face – well, a voice at least – and we know she comes from the north. And possibly she had a date with her killer. I say we go back to where you found her and use our brains to try and work out what the killer's next move would have been."

Vanda looked reluctant to go back into the forest.

"That is," Giò added provocatively, "unless you imagined it all."

"You're so unfair! Let's go."

7

NO GLORY FOR HEROES

"Here, on the right," Vanda said, indicating a parking space. "I left my car here. Do you really want to go into the forest?"

"Yes please, if it isn't too hard on you, I mean."

"I'm not exactly looking forward to it, but I want to know what happened. Let's go."

Vanda showed her the way. "I can't really remember exactly where it was. You know what it's like walking in the forest – one tree looks exactly like another. But I'm positive I was in this part of the forest; I wanted to keep away from the other chestnut pickers."

"Why did the killer leave the body in a place that was going to be thoroughly searched in the next few days?"

"As you suggested, maybe it was only temporary. He hadn't planned to kill her and left her here while he decided on the best place to hide the body."

"That's an interesting hypothesis."

They looked around some more, Vanda indicating a couple of places as possibly being where she'd seen the old lady. As they searched, they heard a vehicle passing by.

"The road is close," said Giò. "Let's see where it is exactly."

They came out onto the road a little further up from where Vanda had parked her car on Friday.

"This makes sense. See this parking space? It's hidden from the road and close to where you found the body. The killer could have brought the body here without much effort. But then you turned up and he needed a new plan."

"But why did he kill her? Was it really a drug-related crime or a robbery that went badly wrong?"

"They're not the right questions to ask at the moment."

"So what is the right question?"

"We should be asking ourselves, 'What next?' The killer had thought to bury the body in the wood, but your appearance reminded him what a risk he was taking. He could be discovered digging her grave by multitudes of chestnut seekers at any moment, so he took the body back to his car." And Giò turned back to the parking space. "What now? Let's put ourselves in the killer's mind. We've got a dead body on our hands and we certainly don't want to take her home."

"There's the rubbish dump and loads of places along the road to Maratea."

"Oh no, there might be carabinieri along the road. If you've got a corpse in the car and you're already up here, you'd be better off sticking to this road."

"But it goes to the Sanctuary."

"Not too many people there. Let's get my car and drive that way."

As Vanda settled in the passenger seat, Giò started the car. "Now, Vanda," she said, "let's carry on imagining we're the killer. We've still got the body in the back of our car, we need to find a solution soon. Let's keep our eyes open and be ready to find the right place to offload it."

"My goodness, Giò, I never suspected you could get this passionate about a murder."

Giò flashed a grin in reply. There was something true in what Vanda said.

Arriving at the Sanctuary of the Madonna del Soccorso, Giò parked the car and walked along the path leading to the church. She hadn't been there for a long time and it gave her a real thrill, seeing the small church perched on the ridge of the mountains, overlooking the sea. The church itself was closed, so they stood on tiptoes to peer through a tall window. Everything seemed fine inside.

They moved beyond the church over to the cliffs, the landscape opening out onto breathtaking views. On one side, the Maratea coastline stretched away into the distance; on the other, the two women gazed down to Calabria and the Isola di Pino where Giò had first met Carmela. Unfortunately, the fun weekend to celebrate the opening of their mutual friend's guesthouse had given way to terror when a ruthless killer had turned a murder mystery game into a very real fight for survival. And now, here Giò was, on the hunt for a murderer yet again.

Turning away from the spectacular views and the not so lovely memories, Giò nodded encouragingly at Vanda and they explored the grounds thoroughly. But they could find no traces of recent digging. Giò sighed, disappointed but at the same time happy that the sacred place hadn't been violated by human madness and violence.

"What are we looking for?" she asked herself aloud.

"Signs of digging, somewhere suitable to bury a body," Vanda answered simply.

"The ground here is too rocky, the grass carpet too thin. I don't think our killer would have found a suitable place in here…"

Vanda looked around, nodding. "Think you're right."

"Correct me if I'm wrong, but didn't we pass an adventure park along the road? Do you know anything about it?"

"It's new, due to be opened next weekend. It's a joint venture between the local council and private investors. There's not a lot there, just a tubing track, giant slides, tree-top climbing routes, maybe a couple more rides and a restaurant."

"Maybe that's the kind of place we're looking for, especially if they haven't quite finished all the work. Let's go back."

When they reached the gate of the new park, it was closed and bolted. With the exception of a curious goat, there was nobody around.

"Nicola, the watchman, should be here somewhere," Vanda said. "Maybe he's running a few errands. Shall we come back later?"

"To tell you the truth, if nobody is around, it's all the better for us. We can do what we please and search to our heart's content." Giò was already checking along the fence to see if there were any gaps.

"But, Giò, he might come back any moment…"

"We'll tell him we were too curious to wait till the grand opening next weekend. To get in, we'd be better off climbing over the gate. It looks easy enough." As she spoke, she vaulted over the low gate, her actions validating her words, and she was standing within the boundaries of the park. "Come on, it's easy."

"Giò, that goat doesn't seem very happy to see you."

As Giò turned around, she saw the goat staring at her, his yellow eyes fixed on her body, his right leg scratching the ground.

"You're not going to charge, are you?" she asked. The goat inclined his head as if taking aim. He wasn't a big animal, but he wasn't small either, and he seemed well aware of the threat his horns posed.

"Giò, I think you'd be better off on this side," cried Vanda. Giò jumped back to where she'd come from just in time as the goat hit the gate.

"My goodness! They don't need a guard dog."

The goat looked at Giò and let out a satisfied, "Naaa!"

A voice came from the dense woodland to the right. "Who's there, Guglielmo?"

"Nicola, is that you?" Vanda cried.

"Yes, who's there?" A man was making his way through the

vegetation. "Ah, it's you, Vanda. How are you?" The man unlocked the gate and Vanda followed him in, giving Giò a smug look.

"Will we be safe in there?" asked Giò, still watching the goat whose yellow eyes never seemed to leave her.

The man laughed. "Guglielmo, they're friends, just friends. You'd better not show him you're scared, he takes satisfaction from seeing humans afraid of him. He's a braggart, I fear."

"I've never seen the like of him."

"His mother passed away when he was young and a sheepdog took care of him. He half believes he's a dog himself."

The man gave Guglielmo's head a good scratch, and the goat seemed to love that.

"My friend Giò and I were having a walk around the sanctuary, then on the way back we wondered what the adventure park looks like. By the way, how come they're opening this time of year?"

"It's one of those bureaucratic things. We were too late for the summer season, but if we don't open within the year, we'll lose some of the EU funds we applied for…"

"And now, are you all set for the grand opening on Sunday?"

"Yes, we're ready, we're just finishing a few things here and there. But the safety test team has already visited and given the OK. If you start on this path, you'll see it all: the tubing track, the slides, the pendulum."

"What was the last area to be completed?"

"The restaurant. They're still busy with some of the interior decoration, and the pavement outside has not been properly laid yet. They'll have to redo the part closest to the building, so it's been cordoned off so that nobody walks on it for a couple of days."

The man took an apple from his pocket and with his strong hands broke it into two halves, giving one each to the women. "You'd better give something to Guglielmo so he accepts you as friends. His head butts are not pleasant, I can assure you."

Guglielmo munched the apple from Vanda, but kept looking with some suspicion at Giò.

"Off you go, Guglielmo," Nicola encouraged him, and only then did the goat take his treat. Feeling serious admiration for the animal's strength of character, Giò stroked his flank and then his head as she'd seen Nicola doing. The goat nodded and rubbed his head against her.

"Now you're friends and he won't forget you," said Nicola.

Still stroking Guglielmo, Giò asked, "Do you think we can have a look around?"

"Of course you can. I'm cutting some wood for the winter, so do you mind if I leave you alone?"

"Not at all, Nicola," Vanda said. "We don't want to take up any more of your time, so we'll give you a shout when we're done. It looks like a beautiful walk," she added, pointing to the rocky mountains beyond the restaurant.

"You'll have quite a view from there."

Guglielmo was determined to do the honours, and he either followed or preceded them. Giò enjoyed calling him and seeing him coming as if he really were a dog.

"What are we looking for, Giò?"

"Freshly dug ground," Giò answered, looking towards the tubing track. Their eyes followed its meanders, but they couldn't spot anything suspicious. It was the same over by the giant slides.

They moved towards the panoramic restaurant. The doors were shut, but through their large windows the women could make out the beautiful rustic interior. The patio outside had a spectacular view onto the mountains and the sea below. Part of it had been cordoned off as the watchman had told them.

"I don't think I would hide a body beneath a pavement such as this. Too much foot traffic, too close to people, and the bad smell could easily give the game away."

"Oh, Giò, please don't go into details. I don't think the killer could dig deep enough, anyway, it's so rocky here."

"You're right, but if it's not here either, it will be more difficult than I thought to find our body." Giò had been enjoying how easy it had been so far to find clues, imagine the old woman's movements. She had felt almost triumphant…

They moved towards the powerful iron arms of the pendulum, glittering in the sun. And the view from there was breathtaking, the rocks falling directly down to the sea below from a great height. The coastline was sparkling, and Giò thought that if she was getting a touch of vertigo just by standing close to the ridge, the brave people being swung around 360° by the pendulum would feel far worse.

"My head is spinning," she said, looking down. "I wouldn't dare go on the ride."

"I love rides, the scarier the better," said Vanda. "I love the precarious feeling when in actual fact I'm perfectly safe."

Guglielmo, who had been nibbling the thorny leaves of a bush which clearly tasted really good to him, disappeared behind a group of rocks.

"There's a passageway," said Giò. "I thought it was just one big boulder." With her usual eagerness, she followed him, only to find herself facing a concrete mixer. In front of it, a concrete platform had been laid, on top of which a cabin hid all the park's electric cables. Here, like the pavement by the restaurant, a few square metres of the platform had been cordoned off. It looked like an add-on rather than part of the area occupied by the electric cabin.

Giò and Vanda locked eyes meaningfully as if to say, 'This might be the right place.'

"But what can we tell them, Giò? That the body of the woman whose disappearance nobody has reported, who the carabinieri don't believe ever existed, is here under this concrete platform?"

"I know, I know, but let's address one problem at a time or I'll go mad."

At that moment Giò's mobile rang and she remembered she'd wanted to say goodbye to her Travel Writers' Conference guests.

"Hello, Kate, I'm so sorry, it's been a hectic morning."

"Giò, don't you worry. We've had a splendid day, just finished our brunch since we realised you weren't coming over, and now we're on the hotel shuttle to the airport. We wanted to thank you so much, it's been wonderful. And remember, I'm going to find you a real publisher. We'll get that book out."

Giò didn't even know exactly what 'that' book was, but gosh, Kate knew how to make her heart go pitter-pat!

She had only just ended the call when her phone rang again.

"You're rather popular," Vanda said, but her laughter died on her lips as she saw Giò's face getting paler and paler.

"No, I didn't forget," Giò was saying. "I was called away for the morning, but I'll certainly drop in this afternoon." Ending this call, Giò explained, "Good and bad news always go hand in hand. I put my two guests up at the Buon Giove Hotel, and the manager wants to make sure I don't run away without paying their bill."

"The Buon Giove? They must have been very special guests!"

"They were." Giò had to shake her head energetically to dispel the visions of fame and a prosperous career as a travel writer and concentrate on what was in front of them.

"Should we search around? Maybe she dropped something we'll recognise," Vanda suggested.

Around they went, but they found nothing.

"What if we're getting carried away by our speculations?" Giò wondered. "Imagine if we convinced the carabinieri to break open the concrete and they found nothing."

"They already think I'm mad, and I can see that asylum coming closer than ever," moaned Vanda. "But what's that goat pulling at?"

Guglielmo, who had been munching by the corner of the platform, was now engaged in a tug of war. Giò gave him a look, then walked over to see what he'd found.

"Guglielmo, you're munching away our evidence!" she cried, trying to pull the goat away and convince him that grass was better food. Half hidden by the soil was a piece of grey cloth, emerging from one side of the concrete.

Finally they had enough evidence to call the carabinieri.

IF IT HAD BEEN HARD TO CONVINCE THE GOAT TO LEAVE THE CLOTH alone, it was even harder to convince the local carabinieri to come and investigate. Only when they arrived with the German shepherd who had found Vanda, and the dog started howling and digging with his paws where the piece of half-munched grey coat was sticking out, did the carabinieri finally decide it might be something worthy of their attention. Although still rather sceptical of Vanda and Giò's declarations, they got the official papers signed, gathered all the authorisation they needed, and broke the concrete platform apart.

Inside was the body of a woman in a grey coat.

The interrogations at the carabinieri station in Trecchina were every bit as bad as Giò had experienced during a previous case in Maratea. She found herself saying, "Maresciallo, if I'd had anything to do with killing that woman, why would I have insisted you come over and dig her up?"

"Maybe so, but then how could you know the body was exactly there?" Maresciallo Bevilacqua asked.

"But we've told you already, Vanda had seen her! You wouldn't believe her, but I was certain she hadn't imagined it. By the way, do you have any idea who she is, how she died?"

"Ms Brando, I'm the one asking the questions!"

"Thank you for your help, Ms Brando," Giò replied sarcastically. "Without us, that woman would have stayed there forever."

The maresciallo didn't reply to that, just icily requested that she not leave the area because he might have to call her and Vanda in for further questioning.

Now she was finally driving back into Trecchina in the dark, starving hungry since both Vanda and she had skipped lunch, and freezing cold as the park was in a rather exposed area.

Her phone rang. "Gran, I'm coming."

"Such a pity you weren't here for the news. The carabinieri have found a body in the adventure park in Trecchina. I thought it might be your friend's body. I mean, the body she found."

"It is," Giò said, wondering not for the first time if her gran wouldn't make a better cop than the cops.

"They have no idea who she is, but the carabinieri gave a description and asked anyone who has met her or knows of an old woman who's missing to go to them with information."

"If they are as welcoming as they've been with Vanda and me, anyone would be mad to call them," Giò thought aloud.

"So you *were* there, I knew it! Was it you who found the body?"

"I'll give you all the details in a while, I promise, if you prepare dinner. I'm starving."

"You're lucky, I've just cooked a pumpkin and onion soup, and baked a focaccia."

"I'm on my way. Just listen out for any snippets of news."

"Don't you worry." And Giò knew she could rely on Granny, whose investigative skills could rival those of Scotland Yard.

Giò dropped Vanda off at her home and was negotiating the U-turns carved into the rocks along the road descending from Trecchina to Maratea when her phone rang again.

"Good evening, Ms Brando, this is Deborah from the Buon Giove Hotel. It seems you've had two guests staying here for a night, but you haven't paid yet. Do you want us to charge their credit card?"

"In fact I'm on the way to your (damn) hotel." She whispered the D word; she'd forgotten all about paying for Kate and Mike's rooms. Passing through Maratea, she carried on towards

Fiumicello and the seaside. She was tired, hungry, dirty, her hair was wild after a whole day exposed to the Trecchina wind, and she knew her appearance wouldn't go unremarked upon in the five-star hotel. And nor did her cry of dismay when she looked at the invoice.

"How's that possible? We had agreed a third of that sum."

"But that was for the rooms only. There's the extra of two cooked breakfasts, the golf course, the spa treatments, the dinner, the lunch, and two bottles of champagne as room service."

"But I was their guest at dinner…"

"They said you'd take offence as you were the host. But if you want, I can give them a call…"

"That dinner alone won't save me from bankruptcy." Giò stopped the woman, handing over her credit card gloomily. There would be barely any credit left after this – assuming the transaction went through.

"We're done," Deborah said, giving her the invoice. "I hope your guests had a good time with us, and that you'll consider us again if other friends are visiting."

"Not even if I win the lottery," Giò said, turning her back and heading for her car. If she were a proper heroine, she'd be celebrating having found the body. The carabinieri would have thanked her, the local journalists would be inviting her for interviews. In real life, she was tired, so hungry she was fit to collapse, lonely as Wordsworth's cloud, and hopelessly broke.

It had been quite a day.

8

OLD FRIENDS

When Giò woke up, the sun was shining on her small terrace. Even now, almost at the end of October, she could have her breakfast on the little table outside, the whole gulf in front of her, the mountains, the vegetation and the sea glistening in the far distance.

After 15 years in the UK, Giò was still savouring being back home as a novelty. She would miss the UK every now and then, not only Scotland where she had lived for five years between Dufftown and Glasgow, but also (and she could hardly believe it!) frenetic London. The big, chaotic city, with its hidden secrets and world-famous places, had touched her heart.

But she didn't like to indulge in memories of London for too long, because they mostly included Dorian Gravy. She had moved there because of him, and after a weird relationship that had lasted for too long – 10 years, in fact – she had discovered he'd betrayed her. Just in time: one month before their wedding.

While she had come to appreciate the coincidence that had opened her eyes to her fiancé's true character, she still felt she had wasted 10 years of her life with a person who was very different from what she'd believed. She had become aware of the tweaks she had made to her personality and life values in order to accommodate his ego, but even with the benefit of hindsight, the whole thing still hurt… a bit!

She was reading about Scotland's history, finishing off the historical section of her own Scottish guide, and she wanted to make sure she had got all the facts and dates right. But while reading of wars, battles and murders, she wondered if the carabinieri in Trecchina had discovered anything about the identity of the old woman. Who was she? Where did she come from? Why was she in Trecchina, and most importantly, who did she meet who wanted her dead?

Giò had a rule: no internet or mobile phone till 10am, to give her a head start with her work. But it wasn't set in stone. A murder took precedence over any rules, however sensible and virtuous they might be.

She grabbed her mobile and texted Vanda. *"Any news?"*

"Nothing. They still don't know who she is."

"Didn't she have any ID on her?"

"Not sure. If she did, the carabinieri have kept it quiet."

There was a big flaw in the people-carabinieri relationship, at least in Giò's eyes. Facing the same problem – an injured woman claiming she had seen a dead body – the carabinieri had deliberately ignored her, Giò hadn't. In fact, she had been stubborn enough to carry out her own investigations and had found the body. And now, the carabinieri would treat her as a nuisance. Even worse, they seemed incapable of moving the investigations forward.

Didn't she have a moral obligation to do something? Of course she did. She dropped her book and notes and got back onto her mobile.

"Hello?"

"Hello, Paolo. It's Giò here."

"Hi, Giò, it's been a long time…"

She cut him short. "Are you investigating a dangerous group of gangsters today, or can you spare ten minutes to meet me at Leonardo's?"

He laughed. "I'm buried in a pile of paperwork, but yes, I can meet you at Leonardo's in about 30 minutes. What are you up to? Nothing too dangerous, I hope."

She ignored the unconscious irony of his words. "See you soon."

~

WHEN GIÒ ARRIVED IN PIAZZA BURAGLIA, MARATEA'S MAIN square, a slightly chubby man with light brown hair was already sitting at one of Leonardo's tables. He was wearing a carabiniere uniform and was chatting with the bar owner.

"Hello, Giò," said Leo cheerfully.

"You two weren't talking about me, were you?" She looked at them suspiciously; they had cut the conversation short as soon as she joined them.

"As a matter of fact, Leo was asking me if I'd heard about the lady who was killed in Trecchina…"

"And we wondered if you had anything to do with it."

"I don't go around killing people, despite what the carabinieri like to think," snapped Giò, resenting the fact they'd already guessed the truth.

"Come on, Giò," Paolo smiled appeasingly, "we'd never think of you as a killer. Just nosey."

"A strong cappuccino for me, please, Leo," she said to the short, fat man, ignoring Paolo's words.

"No cornetto today?"

"Nope!" Was she really that predictable? She wouldn't give them the satisfaction of hearing her agree… even though Leo's cornetti were among the best in town. "OK, and a cornetto too. An empty one!" she barked as Leo went inside.

"By the way," said Paolo, extending a hand, "hello, Giò, how are you?"

She shook hands with him, uncertain how much to tell him. Should she let the guy know he was right, that she was looking into the murder of the old lady? She wasn't keen on the idea, but on the other hand, if she wanted to get some confidential information out of him, maybe it was a necessary evil.

"Doing fine."

"I've not seen you around since you solved the Rivello case," Paolo said, his hazel eyes smiling at her.

"Correct. I've been doing as much work as possible."

"Is that for your Scottish guide?"

"Exactly." How many more things did he remember about her? Of course, he was a cop.

The waitress put a cappuccino and cornetto for Giò on the table and a gassosa for Paolo.

"Are you still going out on your kayak?"

Relaxing in his company, Giò launched into a description of all the places she had discovered during days out on her kayak.

"And Romolo told me that there will be days good enough to go out right up to December."

Paolo stayed quiet. He knew she had called for him for a reason, and he would just wait for her to spill the beans. Carabinieri could be smart, at times.

"Well, I called you because I wondered if you knew anything about the old lady found dead in Trecchina."

"Why? Is she going to feature in your next mystery book?"

"Nope, I just write travel guides," she muttered, embarrassed. "And maybe a travel book."

"So may I ask what your interest is in the matter?"

"My friend Vanda was hit on the head when she found the body on Friday, and the carabinieri wouldn't believe her. So we had to find the body ourselves." And she gave him a detailed explanation of what had happened.

"I can't believe it! So you've somehow managed to get involved in this case too." Paolo had a strange expression on his face, but unlike the maresciallo in Trecchina, he didn't look annoyed. Surprised yes, maybe a tiny bit worried, but not angry.

"I just wanted to know if they've found out who she was, how she was killed."

"Wouldn't it be better to let the carabinieri do their job this time?"

"Without me and Vanda, they wouldn't even have known that a woman had been killed at all!" Giò couldn't explain even to herself what was screaming inside her, why she wanted to know more. Why, just like when she had found the body of a young woman crushed under a rock, couldn't she simply walk away and move on with her life? She suspected it was a little like when you rescue a dog or a cat, and then you want to find out if the poor creature is OK, whether a family has adopted him, if he is having a good life. True, a corpse means someone is gone and, unlike a rescued pet, cannot come back, but there is the same emotional involvement: an inner voice howling to reveal the truth and bring the culprit to justice. So difficult to explain, but something in the way Paolo was looking at her reassured her that he understood, and maybe even shared those feelings.

"We have actually become involved in the case," he admitted. "The woman came from Lauria to Trecchina with a suitcase, so she must have intended to sleep somewhere, but nobody has responded yet to the carabinieri's call to come forward if they knew her. Maybe she was planning to spend the night in booked accommodation. There are so few hotels in Trecchina that it was easy to check them out. None had a booking for a single woman. So the Trecchina carabinieri asked us to check with the hotels in Maratea."

"But there are hundreds here…"

"Thanks to the Tourist Board, we were able to send an email to them all. An old woman travelling on her own is not a typical booking in this part of the world, so we should get some results by lunchtime. We've asked them to come forward whether or not the guest turned up, just in case."

Giò was impressed.

"Of course, if she was meant to stay with friends or family, it's a totally different kettle of fish. The carabinieri in Trecchina are also going to interrogate the man who drove the coach from Naples to Lauria, but as three days have passed, it may be hard for him to remember unless he's very observant..."

"Her voice," Giò interrupted him, "seems to be what everyone we spoke to remembered. It was loud and rather nasal."

"I'll make a note of that, it might help."

"And do you know how she was killed?"

"She was strangled. She had died somewhere else, then was taken to where she was buried under the cement."

"Do you think the adventure park owners have anything to do with it? Or maybe some of the workers?"

"I still wonder why you don't apply to become a policewoman." He smiled. "The Trecchina carabinieri are asking questions, but the workers weren't there on Friday or over the weekend. But the watchman and the owners were – they're checking their alibis and movements. But that may just be a formality; the site is accessible to anyone who wants to get in through the secondary gate: there's a walkers' right of way as it's part of a mountain path. What's strange is that a woman has been missing since Friday and no one's raised the alarm."

"Maybe she's from another region..."

"There are shared databases. No recent missing person's profile matches our woman, unless she's been missing for a long while and happened to reappear to be killed in Trecchina. Nevertheless, we're checking older profiles, but I don't think we'll find anything, unless there's an unusual story behind this case."

Giò had no idea what the brigadiere meant. He read the question in her eyes and continued.

"Old people who have been missing for a long while have generally become homeless. But this woman was wearing good quality clothes. Her body doesn't seem to have undergone any trauma – except for her violent death. It looks as if she lived a comfortable life before she came here."

"It seems you're doing everything possible, this time…"

"I'm glad you think so. Maybe this time, *you* won't expose yourself to any risk. I promise I will share as much information as possible with you, but I simply cannot disclose everything. There's a killer on the loose somewhere, he knows we know about him, and when they're backed into a corner, killers become even more dangerous. Please don't go searching for trouble."

"I don't want any more adventures," Giò said, but as she spoke, she realised she wasn't being entirely truthful.

9

NEWS FROM SWITZERLAND

"I'd love to find a good mascara, but they never seem to do the job," a pale and rather unhappy looking young lady said to Agnese.

"We've just received this new one. It has an excellent thick brush that's ideal for coating the lashes individually. From a natural look with a few strokes to a very sophisticated one, you can coat them as many times you want."

"And do you think it works?"

"My other customers are enthusiastic about it. Shall I try it on you?"

"Maybe later," the customer said, skipping to another counter opposite the one at which Agnese was standing. "I was looking for a foundation. I can never seem to find one which works well on me."

"What sort of problems do you have with your current foundation?"

"It doesn't last. It turns patchy, and my face ends up yellow."

Agnese left the mascara she was holding on the main counter beside a blusher, a couple of eyeshadow palettes and some eye cream. Each was there to solve a problem the customer had detailed before leaving the issue suspended at the moment of decision and moving on to something else. Waiting patiently, Agnese scrutinised her customer's skin, which showed a number of impurities indicative of the fact she wasn't in the habit of using a good cleansing product to remove her make-up each day. But no, she wouldn't lead her customer down yet another path.

She sighed inwardly and showed the woman a number of different foundations, detailing the characteristics of each.

"This one give a light to medium coverage, but once applied it's undetectable and looks like a second skin." So saying, Agnese invited the woman to sit on a chair in front of a mirror and started to apply the foundation to her face with the help of a brush.

The door opened and a gentleman came in, smiling and wishing them both a good morning.

"Hello, Edoardo," said Agnese, recognising the bookshop keeper. "It's such a pleasure to see you. Can you wait for a short while? I'm just serving this lady." As he nodded, she turned back to her customer. "Don't you think that this almond shade looks perfect on your skin?"

"I don't know," the woman said, looking critically at her face in the mirror. "I have so many doubts. Maybe we should look for something different."

"Why? What's wrong with this one?"

"I don't know, really. It's just I'm not sure. Maybe we should look for a good perfume for me." She smiled as she left the chair to cross the aisle and reach for one of the turquoise Provencal cabinets full of essences. "What's the best perfume?"

"Madam, if I may intrude, I'd go for that foundation if I were you. It makes your skin glow," Edoardo said.

The woman flushed with pleasure. "Do you really think so?"

"Absolutely," he replied, nodding.

Quick as a flash, Agnese seized the opportunity. Forgetting the perfume, she invited the woman to take a seat again, and in a few minutes she'd applied all the products the customer had selected and then rejected in the last 45 minutes.

"What a transformation!" Edoardo declared. "You have delightful features without make-up, but with it, you shine. It brings out the best in you. My congratulations, madam, on having such refined taste."

"Oh, thank you. I think I will go away and see how it all goes. After all, I didn't really come in here with the intention of buying anything."

Agnese could have banged her head against the wall – she had guessed correctly. The woman had taken up nearly an hour of her time for nothing. Of course, she didn't mind; customers liked to browse and satisfy their curiosity, but there were times, like this one, when she felt cheated.

Only today, she had an accomplice.

"I simply adore you determined women," Edoardo declared. "You know what you want and you never waste your time. You've selected some gorgeous products, maybe with a little help from Agnese…"

"Indeed! Umm, I think I might buy the mascara. Can you tell me its price?"

With Edoardo dropping in another couple of well-timed remarks, within five minutes the woman was walking out of the shop with a bag full of foundation, blusher, mascara, lipstick, an eyeshadow palette, and an impulse buy of a perfume that Edoardo had sprayed in the air and said he would fall in love with any woman wearing it.

"Edoardo, I should pay you to talk to every customer who walks in." Agnese laughed, going over to greet him.

"The funny thing is that it doesn't work in my bookshop."

"Maybe we should swap shops every now and then."

"I love my books, but I'd be happy to take a dip into the world of perfumes. Shall we sign an agreement right now?"

"Not before I've found your perfect scent."

"I was hoping you'd tell me. I've heard you're some sort of magician…"

"That's an exaggeration, but I do have a game I like to play with my customers, and I'd be pleased to give you a perfume session." She went to put a 'Back Soon' sign on the perfumery door. "How's Vanda, by the way?"

"Much better, and now the carabinieri have found the body, she feels she's done all she had to do."

"I wish my sister was like that," Agnese replied, inviting him to take a seat next to the ebony table in the alcove.

"Huh?" He looked at her in surprise.

"You haven't met Giò, have you?"

"Unfortunately not."

"But you know it was she and Vanda who found the body?"

"Oh, Giò is Vanda's sleuth friend, I see. I hadn't realised she was your sister. She's done quite a lot to help the carabinieri, from what I've heard."

"And I'm afraid she will carry on until the villain is sent to prison."

"Wow, she's a brave one."

"We just call her stubborn as a mule. I only hope she won't get herself into trouble."

"I'd like to meet her. But what are those?" he asked, looking at the ceramic vases Agnese was putting onto the table, selecting them one by one from a drawer behind her.

"Just candles. Without giving it too much thought, tell me which one you prefer."

The man made his choices as the game progressed.

"Carnations seem to be your favourite." Agnese smiled, imagining the white carnations that British gentlemen wore on their smart jackets. When Edoardo had chosen the *touches* with his preferred accords, Agnese picked up the oriental spicy cardboard table and handed him the spinning top. When she turned the table over, she laughed in surprise.

"Outrageous Carnation, again!"

"Should I be concerned?"

"Not at all. It's a carnation-based scent, but isn't typical of its genre, and it's come up twice in the last few days after years of silence. I find that a strange coincidence."

"Who was the other person?"

"You really don't want to know. I'm afraid he was as unlike you as it's possible to get. But I am distracting you with my chatter." She left the alcove to cross to the cabinet which contained the perfume testers, sprayed some Outrageous Carnation on a *touche* and handed it to him.

He smelled it, closed his eyes and said after a pause, "It's not really what I had in mind. Rather different from the fragrances I generally use."

Agnese forced herself to smile rather than show her disappointment. She was proud of her ability to guess what her clients would like.

"Would you spray a little on my pulse?" he asked, pulling up his sleeve. Agnese did, staying silent. She had learned that words could spoil the way her customers perceived a perfume.

He smelled it again. "It's so unusual. There's something powerful behind the delicate petals of this carnation. I think I'd better buy a bottle before I become obsessed with it."

"I'm glad you found it interesting," Agnese said, relieved that her talents hadn't disappeared overnight after all.

"Now, I need you to help me further. I'd really love to buy Vanda a bottle of perfume, but I don't have a clue what she would like."

"I do, but I won't take the pleasure of doing a little guesswork away from you. When you give perfume as a gift, you always put a little of yourself into the choice."

More bottles, more *touches*, more words followed. *I really love my work,* thought Agnese as she smoothed the white ribbon with which she had bound the wrapped packet. She slid it into one of her Tiffany bags and shook hands warmly with Edoardo.

I think this man is totally in love with Vanda. And a frisson of pleasure unexpectedly went down her spine. *Ah, love, love, love!*

~

AFTER A LONG AFTERNOON OF WAITING, IT WAS AROUND FIVE o'clock when Giò's phone finally rang. It was Paolo.

"We've found out who the old woman was. Early this afternoon, one of our officers recognised the picture of a woman who'd lived in Chandolin and had only been reported as missing yesterday. But it seems she's actually been missing since Friday."

"Chandolin? Where's that? The French Alps?"

"Nope, Switzerland, canton of Valais, not far from Sion."

"And she came from Switzerland to Trecchina to be murdered?"

"We printed out her photograph and showed it to our witnesses, the ones you met…"

"The waitress and the bus driver, you mean?"

"Exactly. They both recognised her without any hesitation. Also, in the description of the missing person there was a reference to her peculiar nasal voice. There's not much doubt it's her. Now, how's your French?"

"My what?"

"We need to get in touch with the Swiss police. We've exchanged a few documents, but I need to phone the *police cantonale* – I've got the contact details of the officer who's been interviewing the family and is following the case – and I told the maresciallo in Trecchina I have a friend who speaks fluent French."

"Should I come to the carabinieri station?"

"I'd appreciate that. Let's say in 30 minutes?"

"I'm coming right now."

It took Giò under two minutes to change her sweatpants, which she only wore around the home, for her jeans and the first cardigan that came to hand. It was no harder to change her overall demeanour: her expression went from dejected and frustrated to fulfilled and cheerful in a matter of seconds.

Driving the car her sister hardly used, Giò was soon at the

carabinieri station in Fiumicello. This hamlet was one of the seven villages that made up the Municipality of Maratea.

The gardens surrounding the building had a shady car park under the trees that was almost empty at this time of day. Entering the station, Giò was dismayed to find herself face to face with Maresciallo Mangiaboschi. The man not only had a real dislike for her, but he had wished so badly for Giò to be the murderer of a young woman earlier in the year that he'd never forgiven her for being innocent, even though she'd solved the puzzle that had led to the arrest of the real murderer. She greeted him politely nonetheless.

The man stopped short, snorted a "You again!" and left. Giò wondered how she would ever get on with the local authorities. Even the maresciallo in Trecchina seemed to have taken a dislike to her. On the surface, Giò didn't care; for the most part, she wasn't even aware of her convoluted thoughts and inner feelings herself.

The carabiniere at reception informed her that Paolo was waiting for her on the first floor. He normally shared his office with another brigadiere, but the other man had already left. Both desks were covered with piles of paperwork.

"I thought you were a carabiniere, not a clerk."

"Don't rub salt in the wound. We're understaffed, we have too large a territory to cover, and our paperwork and bureaucratic procedures have multiplied."

"Criminals know that and enjoy pulling your leg."

"That's exactly what I suspect." Paolo smirked, looking at a piece of paper on which he had jotted down a few questions. "What we need to ask the *police cantonale* is why they only raised the alarm yesterday if the woman disappeared on Friday, what they know about the victim's background and what her connection was with Trecchina. I'm hoping they either know why she came here or can find out."

"I only hope he doesn't deliberately speak French too fast to be understood," said Giò.

"In that case, threaten to switch to English. I'm sure that will snap him out of it." Paolo grinned, picking up the phone and dialling the number for Giò.

The Swiss policeman was actually a policewoman and was quite helpful. She confirmed that the victim's name was Tina Melly, formerly Tina Mica, although she couldn't clarify why the elderly woman had travelled to Trecchina on her own. Mrs Melly had married a Swiss man 20 years earlier and moved to Chandolin. Her husband had passed away three years ago. Although he and Tina hadn't had any children since they had married at a mature age, Mr Melly had a daughter from a previous marriage, Martine, who kept in touch with her stepmother and knew Tina was meant to take a short trip to Naples. She'd said it was just a holiday to see the places she had worked in as a young woman.

Tina Melly had called her stepdaughter on the day of her arrival in Naples to let her know that her journey had gone well. But on Sunday, when Martine had tried to call her stepmother to say hello, the woman hadn't replied nor called her back. Martine had kept calling her at regular intervals without any luck, so on Monday – yesterday – she had gone to the police.

This morning, Martine had been called back by the *police cantonale* to look at the photos from Trecchina carabinieri to see if she recognised pieces of the coat, its label, the shoes. And since she did recognise them, she'd be arriving in Naples tomorrow with her husband; they'd rent a car, and by lunchtime they'd be at the carabinieri station for an official identification of the body. No, Martine had no idea why her stepmother had decided to go to Trecchina.

"This is really mysterious," concluded Giò, taking notes among the piles of papers on Paolo's desk. "A woman comes all the way from Switzerland to Trecchina and meets her death in a small town where nothing ever happens."

"But in a sense, the strangeness of it all might help us to confirm it was premeditated murder."

"What do you mean?"

"Our first hypothesis was that the woman was the victim of a robbery that ended badly. But if she came all the way from Switzerland to Trecchina, she must have had a good reason to do so, and possibly her death is connected to that reason."

"You mean she came over specifically to meet her murderer?"

"That's the working hypothesis with the scant evidence we have at the moment. But we'll see what Martine Melly says tomorrow."

"Do you need me to act as an interpreter?"

"I will need to ask the maresciallo in Trecchina. It's an official interrogation so we should use a certified interpreter, but if no one is available, he might accept your services."

"He? You won't be there?"

"Nope. The carabinieri in Trecchina will do the questioning. I was only allowed to make the phone call today because they didn't have anyone handy who could speak French."

"I see, so it was our lucky day. But how are we going to know what Martine Melly says?"

"I've got a colleague and good friend in Trecchina who thinks that sharing information will help the investigation."

An idea flashed into Giò's brain and she couldn't hide the twinkle of excitement in her eyes. Paolo caught it.

"What?"

"Nothing really, I was just thinking how useful this call was, and I'm pleased to know that at least one colleague of yours is a decent person." Giò lied without remorse, then, feeling Paolo's eyes still on her, she tried to distract him. "Anything new from the local hotels?"

"Oh, I forgot to update you on that. Tina Melly had booked an agriturismo on the outskirts of Trecchina. She was supposed to call them by four o'clock on Friday afternoon and agree on a place so they could pick her up. The landlady is accustomed to her customers turning up late, but when it got to the evening, she called Mrs Melly repeatedly between 6 and 8pm. The woman's mobile phone was switched off, which she took as a sign Mrs Melly wanted to cancel the booking without bothering to explain."

"Why didn't the agriturismo respond to the Trecchina carabinieri?"

"This agriturismo is close to Trecchina, but in the Municipality of Maratea, so they weren't questioned by the carabinieri in Trecchina. They came forward as soon as they received our email."

Leaving the carabinieri station, before getting into Agnese's car, Giò sent a text to Vanda.

"Can we do lunch tomorrow in Trecchina?"

"Certainly. I'm not yet used to my empty nest, so I'll appreciate the company."

Giò grinned mischievously.

10

MARTINE AND GASPARD

No calls came for Giò during the morning, so she assumed the carabinieri in Trecchina had found an official interpreter. She was pleased that she had thought of a plan B; by midday, she had struggled enough with her Scottish guidebook and was ready to go.

She drove to Trecchina and parked her car in front of the local school. From there she could see anyone going into or out of the carabinieri station, and she didn't mind waiting. The view of the mountains stretching all around was simply beautiful. In a couple of months' time, their peaks would be dressed in the winter snow. And all this 15 minutes from Maratea, which was a Mediterranean seaside town with plenty of hot weather and sunshine. Despite the pleasant climate, though, the local people could still enjoy the changes of the seasons.

And from there, Giò's thoughts turned to Christmas. *This will be my first Christmas at home after such a long time away. I wish I'd never left Maratea, except for my trips.* The moment the thought appeared, she knew she was back home for good. It's strange the way we make decisions: we spend long nights without sleeping, mulling things over and over, paralysed by indecision and the inability to evaluate the pros and cons, then all of a sudden the solution appears by itself, as if it's popped out of thin air.

One year. I will spend one more year in Maratea and see if I can make a living here.

She was in the middle of her thinking and planning when she saw a blue Ford coming towards her. A couple got out of the car and, from the uncertainty on their faces, Giò guessed it was Martine and her husband. They disappeared into the low apricot-coloured building that would have looked more like a modern condominium than a military establishment, were it not for the stop signs.

At 1pm, Vanda rang Giò to discuss where they should meet, and Giò told her to come to the school.

"What are we doing here?" Vanda asked as she joined her friend in Agnese's car. "There are no restaurants in this area that I know of."

"We're waiting. Tina Melly's stepdaughter is in there to identify her stepmother's body and answer some questions," Giò replied and, gesturing towards the carabinieri station, she updated Vanda with what Paolo had told her.

"So, what's your plan now?"

"Nothing much. We'll try to have lunch with Martine and her husband. Even if Paolo's colleague is going to share info with him, there's nothing like hearing it first-hand. And I'm sure we'll get more out of them than the carabinieri."

"Giovanna Brando, that is pure bragging!"

Giò laughed. "Guilty as charged," she admitted. "There they are! Let's see if they take their car."

Martine had a tissue in her hand and was pressing it against her eyes. Her husband had an arm protectively around her shoulders. They looked around and clearly decided to leave the car where it was and walk.

"They are likely to be looking for a restaurant," Giò said. "Let's get out of the car and follow them, and as soon as we're far enough from the carabinieri station, we will introduce ourselves. How's your French?"

"It's been better, but I believe some of it is still there."

The couple moved towards the main square. Once they were on the road surrounded by trees and vegetation, Giò signalled to Vanda it was the right time.

"Good morning," Giò said in French, approaching the couple, "I'm Giovanna Brando and this is my friend, Vanda Riccardi. You must be Martine, the stepdaughter of Mrs Tina Melly."

The woman looked startled. "Did you know her?"

"Not really, but it was Vanda who first found her in the woods and raised the alarm."

"The woman who was hit by a branch?"

"Let's say the woman who was hit *with* a branch."

"Yes, the carabinieri told us that too. I'm so grateful, though." Martine's eyes, already red, started to water again.

"Shall we take a seat somewhere?" Vanda suggested. "If we're not intruding too much, perhaps we could have lunch together?"

"That'd be great," the man said. "I'm sure my wife will appreciate having a few more details, we really can't understand what happened. What a piece of luck to bump into you. My name is Gaspard Savioz, by the way."

After they'd all shaken hands, Vanda led the way.

"I know a small family-run trattoria on the opposite site of the square," she said. "It's a cosy place, the fire will be on, and you look like you need a little comfort."

Martine nodded at her in gratitude.

They chose a table next to the redbrick fireplace, dried red peppers hanging from the wall as was the regional tradition, and the environment made Martine smile for the first time since they'd met. She was tall and sturdily built, with brown hair, fair skin and slightly red cheeks.

As they gave their order and a white focaccia with olive oil and oregano appeared on the table, they tacitly agreed they wouldn't talk about the murder until the meal was over. Martine said that Tina had married her father when she'd already left home, and they had been very happy together. He had met Tina at a client's home in Brescia where she'd worked as a nanny and fallen in love with her. Martine had never called Tina 'Mum', but they had always got on well, even though Tina was a forceful character who liked things to be done her way. Martine smiled again, possibly at the memory of some long-ago quarrel, but it was clear she had loved and cared for her stepmother. Every other week, Martine and Gaspard would go to visit her in Chandolin, or she'd come to them in Berne. She suffered from heart problems, and even though the doctors said she was doing well, Martine liked to see her as often as possible.

"Had she ever thought of going to live in Berne or returning to Italy?"

"Oh no, she'd never have left Chandolin. She simply adored the place, had some good friends there, and she loved walking, so it was ideal for her to be able to get everywhere she needed to be on foot."

By now, they had finished the simple but tasty meal of homemade ravioli and porcini mushrooms, but their glasses of red wine were still full. It was time to talk more seriously.

"Was it really a holiday that brought Tina to Trecchina?" asked Giò softly.

"It was a holiday, yes. She wasn't a great traveller, but she said that she wanted to explore more of Europe; she didn't fancy exotic places at all. Italy in particular was one of her favourite destinations. But anticipating your next question, I never knew she was planning to come to Trecchina. I didn't even know the place existed."

"Oh, really? I thought you would be able to explain to us why she came here," said Vanda in dismay.

"As far as I knew, she was going to spend a week in Naples. She said she had worked there a long time ago, and she wanted to rediscover the city as a tourist."

"Did she book a hotel there?"

"She was quite independent. She did all her bookings online, and she told me she'd stay in Naples. That's all I can say."

"Maybe she mentioned Trecchina to you in the past? Could it be that she had connections here? Did she work as a nanny here?"

"She certainly worked in a few places in Italy, and I do know some of the names of the families who employed her. You know what old people are like – they love to tell stories from their younger lives about the work they did and the children they brought up. But I can't remember her naming any places down south except Naples."

"Maybe she was only here for a short time."

"I can't be a hundred per cent sure, but you see, when Tina was young, people would stick with the same family until the children were grown up. Most people stayed in one place for years, so it's strange that I can name quite a few families that Tina worked for, but as I said Trecchina doesn't ring a bell…"

Giò couldn't hide her disappointment. She had felt sure that the Savioz husband and wife would be able to explain the mystery of Tina's visit to Trecchina.

"And what did the carabinieri say?"

Gaspard replied for his wife. "We were asked to bring them a few pictures of Tina. The ones from the autopsy couldn't be published to see if people recognised her. I could hardly recognise her myself."

"Nonetheless, you're sure it's her?" Giò asked.

"Yes, the clothes, shoes and watch are definitely hers. And though her face has been disfigured by the cement, I could tell it's her. A beauty spot on her left cheek and an old fracture on her left arm, pointed out to us by the forensic team, prove it beyond doubt."

Martine shook her head, not wanting to hear the gory details about the disfigured corpse.

"And you said the carabinieri asked you for some photos?"

"Yes, they asked for both recent and older ones. They want to see if local people can recognise her from having seen her on Friday, or in the past when she worked as a nanny."

"I see. I'm sure we will find out that yes, she did once work here."

"But why would she decide to come back here *now*?" said Martine, shaking her head vigorously. "Why would somebody wait 20 years to kill her? And if she knew it might be dangerous, why didn't she tell me anything?"

"This is the problem," commented Giò. "I thought that once we'd found out who the victim was, we'd be able to solve the mystery. But actually, we know less than before. Though there's no apparent reason for Tina to have come to Trecchina, the next step is to discover why she was here, then we should be able to solve the puzzle. By the way, did your stepmother keep a diary?"

Martine shook her head. "No, she wasn't really the type of woman to do that."

"Maybe some old personal organisers?"

"She used one every year, but she was in the habit of throwing them away when she'd finished with them."

"Well," Giò said, sipping her last drop of wine, "when you return home, maybe you should try to put together her working life. For example, when she worked for each family and for how long."

"That will be a hard job. I do have some photos, but they don't have more than the first names and locations on the back. She often spoke of Mrs Alfonsina Aldobrandini in Fiesole and Elda Caracciolo Sciarramanna in Naples, but there are no work records. You know, back then nannies weren't necessarily given a contract, so there are no official documents."

"Elda Caracciolo Sciarramanna in Naples, you said?" asked Giò.

"Yes, why?"

"Well Naples isn't too far from here compared to Fiesole and

Brescia. Did she have a friend, someone she kept in touch with who may not have thrown away the letters?"

"She often mentioned a distant cousin, Antonietta, but she passed away a few years ago, and she had no kids. They both worked as nannies and they kept in touch, reminiscing about their experiences and all…"

The waiter came over with two bottles and small glasses to ask them if they wanted to try the restaurant's homemade specialities, a limoncello or a nocino – two sweet liqueurs made from lemons and walnuts respectively. They inhaled the fragrant liquid silently before tasting it.

"The nocino is delicious," Vanda finally said before asking, "What are your plans now?"

Gaspard replied, "We're leaving tomorrow morning. If the carabinieri have other questions, they can call us."

Martine added, "I want to go back and search Tina's home for clues, though I doubt I will find much. But how about you? The carabinieri said you found her in the forest near here – would you mind accompanying me there?"

"Are you sure you really want to go there?" asked Vanda.

Martine nodded vigorously. "The carabinieri also mentioned a bar where she had a cup of tea as soon as she arrived."

Giò pointed to the bar, which was not far from them. "That's the one."

THE SAME WAITRESS AS GIÒ HAD SPOKEN TO SERVED THEM A COFFEE, and when Martine showed her the pictures of her stepmother, she recognised the woman instantly.

"I've been expecting you. The carabinieri came here with the same photos and asked me the same questions. I told them what I'm telling you: it's her, beyond any doubt."

Giò translated Gaspard's questions. Had Tina mentioned where she was going? No, she hadn't. Had the waitress noticed the direction she'd taken? Yes, towards the town hall. Had she seen anybody approaching or looking at Tina? Nope, there aren't many people around at 3pm in Trecchina, as they could see for themselves.

They all looked around. Apart from a few older people playing bowls in the park, they could hardly see anybody. Gaspard insisted they go and speak to the bowls players, who confirmed they had also been there on Friday afternoon, but none of them had noticed Tina. Giò and her companions then went to the last place Tina had been seen, heading towards the town hall. Maybe she had been heading there because it would be a recognisable landmark to describe to the agriturismo owner so she could pick her up.

On the way back towards the car park, they spotted a pharmacy. On its left was a bookshop, and stooping to look under its half closed roller shutter, Vanda recognised Edoardo.

"Why are you still in your shop instead of having your lunch?"

The man came out, ducking under the shutter. "There's so much to do in a bookshop, you'd hardly believe it." He smiled and looked at the other three. Vanda made all the introductions, not surprised to discover Edoardo spoke French well. He offered his condolences to Martine, turning pale and quieter than usual, clearly sensitive to the fact it wasn't the right time for chitchat.

But he smiled at Giò. "The famous sleuth, I finally get to meet you. Both your sister and Vanda have told me so many good things about you, I hope I'll get the chance to talk to you in happier circumstances," he said, and he looked up at Vanda.

"Certainly, we'll make sure of that," she said.

"I simply love bookshops," said Giò, looking at the section of shop window visible under the roller shutter, which was displaying travel books.

"You're welcome anytime. Maybe you could give me a few recommendations."

"I'd be happy to do that." Giò's excitement showed for a

second, but on seeing the expression on Martine's face, she composed herself. "Can I ask whether you stayed on in the shop on Friday afternoon, as you have done today?"

"Friday?" he replied. "Let me give it some thought. It was the day before the fair. No, I'm afraid I closed at 1.15pm and reopened at 5pm. Why?"

Vanda explained what they had found out about the disappearance of the woman and showed him Tina's picture. Edoardo scrutinised the photo.

"No, I've never seen her before. I wonder who could have done such a thing. Trecchina is such a small place, you can hardly believe someone here is guilty of murder."

"Nonetheless, it happened," murmured Giò.

"I'm afraid someone wanted to rob her and it went wrong. I can't see any other reason for what's happened."

"I'm not so sure. You see, even Martine and Gaspard don't know why Tina Melly came all the way to Trecchina. I suspect she had a strong reason to do that, and if we discover that reason, we have the key to solving the whole mystery."

Edoardo couldn't hide his concern. Looking at both Giò and Vanda, but mainly at Vanda, he said, "Leave that to the carabinieri. It might be dangerous to play the sleuths."

"We will only be keeping our eyes and ears open." Vanda smiled. "You've no reason to worry."

"I've got a feeling I'd better keep an eye on you," he replied, winking at her. "How about the three of us have dinner together this evening? If you're free, I mean."

"If that's your way of keeping an eye on us, it's fine with me," said Giò, smiling. Looking at the Swiss couple, who'd wandered a few metres ahead, she added, "But now, we'd better take care of our friends."

"I won't keep you any longer, then." Edoardo shook hands with Giò, and when he turned to go back into his shop, she noticed his concerned expression.

Agnese is right, he really does care for Vanda. It's time for her to put an end to her no-romance rule. She grinned to herself as they left for the cars to take Martine and Gaspard to the forest to show them where Vanda had found Tina.

Vanda showed them the spot where the branch had come down on her head and Giò pointed out how close the road was, but the visit didn't turn up anything new. Martine then asked to visit the amusement park, where they were welcomed by Nicola and Guglielmo. The watchman told them that the area where Tina Melly had been found was still cordoned off with carabinieri tape and not accessible, but by Friday it would be cleared and the organisers had been reassured they could still have their opening on Sunday.

By now Martine looked exhausted, and it was Gaspard who reminded her it was time for them to drive to their hotel to check in and rest before their return journey the following day. They agreed to keep in touch with the two friends, and that the first thing Martine would do when they got home would be to search her stepmother's house for old photographs and letters. They could all only hope that she'd find a lead to link Tina to Trecchina.

11

IN A STEW

"It was great to have the opportunity to meet Martine and Gaspard," Vanda said as she and Giò walked back to the main square. "I'm sure the fact that they now know someone locally other than the carabinieri has brought them a little comfort. But on the other hand, the mystery looks more complicated than ever."

"At least we have two leads…"

"Have we?" Vanda looked at her in surprise.

"First of all, if Tina Melly ever worked in Trecchina, it would only have been in one of a few houses. There aren't many people here who could have afforded a nanny."

"Well, that's true, and we're looking for families that would have had young children 20 to 30 years ago or more. I can only think of two people who would have been rich enough."

"Who are they?"

"Miss Maria Antonietta De Fino and Mrs Rachele Roselli."

"The first one sounds like a spinster."

Vanda laughed. "Indeed, she is the epitome of spinsterhood."

"She sounds like a candidate for my collection of weird characters, but we're more interested in the second one at the moment. Tina would have worked for a family with children. Do you know this Mrs Roselli personally? Is there any way we can visit her," Giò looked at her watch, "in the next 20 minutes?"

"Let me make a phone call," Vanda said. "But didn't you mention we have at least two leads? What's the second one?"

"The family in Naples."

"But what's Naples got to do with Trecchina?"

"We need to find out. Maybe nothing, but so far that's the closest we can get to connecting Tina with Trecchina."

"It will be difficult to persuade the family to speak to us. Naples is not Trecchina."

"You make your phone call, I'll make mine." Giò couldn't ignore Vanda's quizzical look. "It's to my secret information service. How about a trip to Naples tomorrow?"

"Are you kidding, Giò?"

"Nope. In fact, I'm counting on having an appointment with the Caracciolo family shortly."

"But there will be plenty of families with the name Caracciolo in Naples, how are you going to know which is the right one?"

Giò just winked and scrolled down to a number on her phone, leaving Vanda wondering whether her friend was pulling her leg.

"Hello, Gran," said Giò, speaking into her phone. "No, I'm still in Trecchina, and I'm staying here for dinner too. But I need your help. I need to make contact with an Elda Caracciolo Sciarramanna – a wealthy woman in Naples. We're looking for information about her former housekeeper, Tina Melly. Her name at the time was Tina Mica – you know, the woman who was murdered in Trecchina. If she'll speak to us, it may avoid the embarrassment of the carabinieri calling on her, asking for information. Yes, I'll leave it with you. I'll see you later."

"Your granny Rosa? How would she know somebody in Naples?"

"My gran works in mysterious ways, but having been a primary school teacher has given her a certain power over people, rich and poor, including some who now live in Naples."

"I'd better make my call too, then," Vanda said as she picked up her phone to call her boss. "Hello, Pompeo, it's Vanda here. If I remember correctly, you were the best man at the Rosellis' wedding? I'd love to speak to your friend's mother, Rachele... it's about the woman who passed away last week. I was wondering if maybe she worked as a nanny here in Trecchina. And of course, if Rachele does agree to see me – possibly in the next 15 minutes – I've got plenty of exclusive gossip I can share with her."

She stopped speaking, presumably while her boss was telling her something.

"Very good, I'll wait for a message from you, then. By the way, I almost forgot – you remember that fancy I had to take a sabbatical after Christmas?"

Vanda pulled the phone away from her ear and Giò could hear the man going through a whole range of communication methods, from heart-rending pleas to dire threats. Vanda let him rant for a while, then stepped in.

"Well, I wanted to tell you that I've thought it over, and instead, I'd prefer to take a couple of days off this week. I'm not completely recovered and I need to have some check-ups."

There were murmurings of assent on the other end of the phone, clearly audible to Giò.

Vanda concluded, "I knew you would understand. I'll just wait for you to call Mrs Roselli, then." Putting her phone down, she confirmed, "Fine for tomorrow, we're going to Naples, if you can get us an appointment."

"Consider it done."

Five minutes later, Vanda's boss called her back to let her know that Mrs Rachele Roselli was waiting for them.

They entered through a beautiful wooden gate framed by a creamy stone arch and columns that opened onto the main road.

Once inside, they found themselves in an uncovered courtyard with a view over the mountains behind Trecchina. In front of them was a garden of fruit trees with patches of colourful leaves at their feet, and an explosion of yolk-yellow Jerusalem artichoke flowers covered the fence. On the right, steps invited them to climb up to the house.

A woman in her sixties opened the door. She was as short as she was wide, and had quite a masculine face due to her square jaw, hair that had been cut too short and the heavy shadow of a moustache. But it was the hideous smell of stewed cauliflower that took the visitors' breath away.

"Who are you?" she asked fiercely.

Vanda hesitated. The dark inside the house, the woman's appearance, and the overpowering odour made her feel sick, and her head felt heavy, as if she had not yet recovered from her concussion. She called up all her willpower and was finally able to speak.

"Hello, Assuntina, I think we met when Mrs Roselli helped us with the school fundraising. I'm Vanda Riccardi and we have an appointment with Mrs Roselli."

Assuntina may have recognised Vanda, but she didn't give in. There was something bulldoggish in her stubbornness as she stood on the threshold defending her territory, almost growling.

"Assuntina, did someone ring the doorbell? Who's there?" A powerful voice rang through the darkness inside.

"Just Jehovah's Witnesses, I'm afraid."

"Mrs Roselli," cried Vanda, "it's me, Vanda Riccardi. Mr Limongi called you to arrange my visit."

Assuntina smiled malevolently. "She's almost completely deaf. It's dinner time, what do you want?"

"It's not even six," Vanda said in surprise. In southern Italy, it was rare for anyone to have their dinner before 8pm.

"We're *preparing* our dinner," the other woman growled, determined not to give them a centimetre's advantage.

Then from the shadows there materialised a shape even shorter and rounder than Assuntina.

"Oh, Vanda, is that you? Pompeo told me you were coming." Then, with reproach in her voice, she added, "Assuntina, why didn't you let them in?"

"I thought they were Jehovah's Witnesses as this is not a Christian time for visits."

Mrs Roselli didn't even bother to respond to this comment. Instead, she let the two guests in, finally switching on a light in the corridor that was so feeble, it hardly made any difference. Giò and Vanda had to feel their way towards the living room, which was no better lit than the rest of the house.

When Vanda and Giò's eyes had got used to the ill-lit environment, they distinguished a couple of dark sofas, an impressive library of books and a table in the middle of what was a large room, but was so suffocated with furniture that it felt claustrophobic. Mrs Roselli sat on an ample chair, specially made to accommodate her plus-sized bottom. Evidently, it would have been too risky for her to venture onto the sofas.

She indicated towards the chairs. "Please take a seat." Her roundish face was slightly gentler than Assuntina's, but her sagging cheeks gave her a certain similarity to her housekeeper. She had the commanding voice of someone who was more used to issuing orders than obeying them and the loud tones of someone with hearing problems.

"Who's this skinny thing with you, Vanda?" she asked.

Giò introduced herself.

"Brando, I see. You're from Maratea, aren't you?"

Giò nodded.

An avalanche of questions followed: who were her parents? Her grandparents? Did she have sisters and brothers? Where did they live and what did they do for a living? Only when she'd stored all of this information in the complex filing system of her brain, which already held a lifetime's worth of gossip, did Mrs Roselli ask if they wanted a cup of coffee.

Both friends refused, thinking that anything they were offered would be contaminated by the cauliflower smell, but Mrs Roselli was merciless.

"Assuntina, prepare some coffee for our guests, and cut the Christmas pandoro."

Assuntina had been about to protest, but when she heard that the pandoro would be on offer, she almost looked happy.

Giò and Vanda just had time to exchange a concerned look before Mrs Roselli asked them the reason for their visit.

"Maybe you've heard, but on Monday, a woman was found dead," Vanda said.

"The Swiss lady, you mean?"

"Exactly," Vanda answered. Mrs Roselli clearly knew all the details already.

"Her family has been here today," Giò explained. "They've been to see the carabinieri and confirmed she was Tina Melly, formerly Tina Mica, a nanny who worked in Southern Italy in the past. But 20 years ago, she met her now-deceased husband and left for Switzerland."

"I see, so she's Italian by birth?"

"Yes, she originally came from a small village between Lazio and Campania."

"Why did she come here?"

"Not even her stepdaughter knows. We suspect she might have had an appointment with her killer. After she'd left the bar by the bus stop to go to the town hall, no one admits to having seen her again. That is, until Vanda found her in the forest."

There followed more questions for Vanda than even the carabinieri had asked her. Mrs Roselli wanted to know everything about her finding the body in the forest, and the way she'd been hit. Why had she carried on searching for the body, and why in the adventure park? Only when she was completely satisfied did Mrs Roselli allow the two friends to ask their own questions.

Giò took out her phone. "We have a few photos of Tina Melly.

You can see what she looked like when she died, and also what she looked like when she was young. We wondered if you had ever seen her. She had to have had a reason to come here all the way from Switzerland, so maybe she worked for a Trecchina family in the past."

At that moment, Assuntina wobbled in with a tray, two cups of coffee, a dish of pandoro slices and a few paper towels. Not daring to refuse, but concerned about the dried up condition of the cake, Giò thought on her feet.

"We had such a late lunch, Vanda, I'm not really hungry. Shall we share a slice?"

"Oh no," insisted Mrs Roselli, "you should have a proper taste. It comes from Acerenza, where they make an excellent pandoro."

Unexpectedly, Assuntina came to their rescue. "As your son says, you shouldn't feed your guests to death. Let them take what they want." From her greedy gaze at the cake, it was obvious why she was on their side.

The pandoro was worse than Giò had expected, stale to the point of rottenness. Mrs Roselli must have kept it from the previous Christmas, and during its stay in the house it had functioned as a sponge, capturing all the foul smells from the kitchen. The two friends' only chance of survival was to distract the older women for a couple of seconds under the pretext of asking about an ugly picture on the wall and slip the prehistoric cake into Vanda's new bag. There was no time to wrap it in a paper towel first, but at least they were safe.

"So, do you want to show me the picture of this Tina woman?" Mrs Roselli's hand was searching for her glasses next to a hideous centrepiece on the table featuring the Ten Little Indians of the nursery rhyme.

Giò searched for the pictures on her phone. "We wondered if she had worked for you in the past."

"No, I never forget a name." Mrs Roselli grabbed Giò's mobile phone and skilfully enlarged the picture with greasy fingers. Assuntina, gnawing on her slice of pandoro, moved her head forward to see the picture.

"I saw her."

"Don't lie!" Mrs Roselli admonished sharply.

"I saw her on Saturday in the bookshop. She was nosing through the cook books."

"You always want to be the centre of the attention," said Mrs Roselli, shaking her head and rotating a finger on her temple.

"Do you mean Friday?" asked Giò hopefully.

"No, if I say it was Saturday, I mean it was Saturday. The bookshop owner had opened at a funny time, as usual. I went in, and then she arrived."

"I'm afraid she was already dead by then," Giò murmured.

"And she told me she liked my new coat." The bulldog preened, for the first time displaying an almost feminine side to her character.

At that, the two friends decided to concentrate on Mrs Roselli, who was still scrutinising the pictures.

"You're going to hell if you keep telling lies, Assuntina," she said, making the sign of the cross.

Assuntina, quick as a vulture, snatched the last slice of pandoro and retired in silence, leaving Mrs Roselli grasping at not-so-fresh air. She too had been going for that slice. She shot her housekeeper a dirty look, but carried on talking to her guests as though nothing was amiss.

"No, I'm sure I've never seen this woman in my life, but why don't you send me those pictures on WhatsApp? I'm the administrator of the Trecchina Kind at Heart group and I can ask all the ladies if they recognise her."

Giò did as she was asked, astonished at the old woman's familiarity with modern technology. *She's not so unlike my granny after all*, she thought.

It didn't take more than five minutes before the first beeps came from Mrs Roselli's mobile phone, revealing that the Trecchina population (the female half, anyway) regularly checked their WhatsApp accounts. Giò wasn't sure that even the carabinieri had access to such a powerful network.

But the results were discouraging. Apparently, nobody was familiar with the victim, either as a young woman or in her most recent portraits.

"Trecchina has become such an unsafe place to live," Mrs Roselli grumbled. "Until a few years ago, we never had so much as a robbery, never mind a murder. And now we've had two in a year."

"Two?" asked Giò.

"Hasn't Vanda told you?"

"No," said Giò, looking at Vanda. Her friend nodded as if to say, 'Keep listening'.

"It was back in January when a young woman was found dead. She was the daughter of the miller, a sensible girl, and was properly dressed, not one of those going around half naked…"

Giò had to bite her tongue hard. She couldn't accept that in the twenty-first century, some people still regarded the way women dressed as reason for them to be attacked. But Mrs Roselli wasn't the woman she wanted to have that conversation with, if for no other reason than she was longing for some fresh, clean air.

"So there's a precedent – this could be important," said Giò, as exhilarated as a hound that's picked up a scent.

"Not really," said Vanda. "Her ex-boyfriend is in prison, he'd been threatening her ever since they broke up. He was the possessive type who could accept their relationship had ended."

"How old is he?"

"Mid-twenties, I believe," said Vanda, and Mrs Roselli nodded. "He was born and bred in Trecchina."

"Then he can't have had anything to do with Tina," Giò said.

Mrs Roselli nodded again, then added, "I wonder what the carabinieri plan to do. I don't think they're very competent. With that poor girl, we'd worked out who the killer was before they did."

"Well, they have to gather evidence. It doesn't matter what they feel and think, so in a way it's much easier for us." Giò surprised herself by sticking up for the carabinieri. She was thinking of Paolo. Certainly there were stupid, vainglorious officers like Maresciallo Mangiaboschi, but the carabinieri were no different from anyone else: you get the good ones, the less efficient and the stupid.

The conversation had slowed down, Mrs Roselli and her bulldog experiencing a post-pandoro lethargy. Giò and Vanda exchanged a glance, disheartened by the wild goose chase and desperate for fresh air. It was pure terror that showed on their faces when Mrs Roselli extended an invitation.

"Do you want to stay for dinner?"

A feral glimpse livened up Assuntina's sleepy eyes. It was survival instinct, as if their mere presence threatened her share of whatever food was on offer. The two friends declined as politely and firmly as they could.

"It's just vegetables," Mrs Roselli continued. "My son says at my age, I should eat healthily. Apparently, onions, garlic, cauliflowers are good for you. I should also lose a couple of kilogrammes."

"But the stew is made with lamb, goat and beef as well," Assuntina revealed.

"That's just to give it a little flavour." Mrs Roselli tried to slap her housekeeper's hand. "You can't live on vegetables alone, they make your intestines go runny."

"And we've added a few beaten eggs too." Assuntina, knowing the guests weren't going to stay, felt she could safely describe the details of their 'delicious' meal.

"That's very nice of you," Vanda said politely, "but I'm afraid we need to go. We've been out since this morning, and I've still not entirely recovered from my accident."

"And ham cubes…"

With the help of Assuntina – and it was quite a job – Mrs

Roselli stood up from her chair and accompanied her guests to the door.

"And grated cheese…"

"Let me know if you need more information," Mrs Roselli said, attempting to sound sweet and inviting while trying and failing to silence her housekeeper. "And come to visit more often, Vanda."

"I will," Vanda lied. "And should you discover anything new, please give us a call."

Before they shut the door, Giò caught the wild, ravenous look on the two women's faces. The smells in the kitchen were about to get a whole lot worse.

12

A TRAVELLING BOOKSHOP

By tacit agreement, Vanda and Giò rushed in silence as far as they could from the house, breathing deeply to purify their lungs. Only when they were close to the main square did they exchange their first comments.

"Back to the drawing board," grumbled Giò. "Not one single clue as to why that woman came all the way from Switzerland to Trecchina."

"Do you think she lied to Martine and Gaspard when she said she was going to visit Naples?"

"I'd say so. It would have been different if she had stopped in Naples for a few days, then come here. Also, she booked her agriturismo from Switzerland. No, whatever her reason was, it was a decision she made back home."

They had stopped just in front of Edoardo's bookshop, and the man, impeccably dressed in a light blue jacket and navy chinos, a pastel scarf around his neck, came forward to greet them. He was wearing a nice, fresh cologne and his eyes were disarmingly blue, the clear irises outlined in black.

"I hope I'm not intruding on you charming ladies?"

"Of course not, Edoardo. Giò hasn't been into your bookshop yet, and she's definitely a bookworm."

"Please come in."

On this occasion, Giò was particularly grateful that the bookshop wasn't the stuffy kind. It had white walls, and islands in the middle of the room held a collection of globes. On the wall space above the bookshelves, a few display maps showed the names of writers and books from each continent. For a travel enthusiast like Giò, that was the doorway to heaven. She plunged into the travel section that, to her delight, included not only travel guides but prose and poetry from authors from every country, travel memoirs, and cookery and lifestyle books.

When Giò 'came back' to the real world of Trecchina, she saw Vanda and Edoardo talking earnestly and she recognised the rather concerned expression on his face.

"I don't think you should take this affair so lightly," Edoardo was saying as Giò joined them, his blue eyes seeming to see straight through the two women. "Either of you. Someone has been killed, and if the murderer is still here, he won't appreciate you nosing around."

"How could he know we're doing anything of the sort?" The moment anyone told Giò she shouldn't do something, the stronger her determination became to do it all the same, and even something that may have seemed insignificant to her would suddenly take on immense importance.

"Vanda found the body, and today the whole village has been bursting with the news that you two took Mr and Mrs Savioz on a murder tour."

Giò looked guilty. Having lived in London for so many years, she still tended to forget how people in small villages scrutinised you and noticed everything you did. Edoardo was right to be concerned for Vanda; she had already been hit by the murderer once, and she could easily become his next victim if he felt she was going to stir up trouble for him.

How stupid of me not to have given my friend's safety a single thought.

Giò's phone rang: it was Granny. She replied, trying to sound as casual as possible, but she felt Edoardo's piercing eyes on her. But when the good news came, she could no longer hide her enthusiasm.

"So, it *was* her... That sounds great... Is she expecting us tomorrow?... Well done, you're a marvel of a granny."

Edoardo looked suspiciously at Giò, instinctively knowing the news she'd just received was connected to their discussion, but he had no proof to back up an accusation.

"Don't you worry," said Vanda lightly, her red curls dancing as she tossed her head, "tomorrow we're heading for a change of scenery."

"What are you up to, you bad girls?"

"I guess we're heading to Naples?" Vanda looked at Giò for confirmation.

"Yes," she admitted proudly. "The name Martine remembered is correct: Tina Mica worked for Mrs Elda Caracciolo for a few years. And more importantly, she's agreed to see us tomorrow. Finally we're going to discover something about Tina's past in southern Italy."

"Naples?" Edoardo asked. "What's Naples got to do with the murder?"

"It is the closest place to Trecchina where we know Tina once worked. But we hope to find out more, perhaps a link to here. There *has* to be a reason why Tina made a long journey to an unknown village like Trecchina."

"Well you're certainly taking a broad view of the case. But I'm concerned about you two." Edoardo looked at his watch. "It's closing time, so shall we have dinner and you can tell me more?"

Giò flushed. She didn't want to play gooseberry if Edoardo would prefer a romantic dinner for two with Vanda, and after suffering the smells emanating from Mrs Roselli's kitchen, she wasn't sure she was ready to eat anything anyway. But Vanda, as if reading her mind, looked at her with almost imploring eyes.

Giò figured it out: her friend – the woman who had brought up two kids alone; the woman who basically ran the company she worked for – had not had a date with a man for such a long time, and was nervous of being left alone with one. But at the same time, she wanted to get to know him better. And of course, this was a time when a good friend would know exactly what to do.

"Where do you suggest we have dinner?" Giò asked.

"At my home. I bought some fresh tuna this morning from Pietro. He didn't have much choice, but what he did have was only caught last night and is wonderfully fresh and tasty."

"Tuna sounds perfect. I'm happy with something light after what we had to suffer at Mrs Roselli's," said Vanda, flashing a grateful smile at Giò.

EDOARDO'S HOUSE WAS MINIMALIST AND ELEGANT. THERE WEREN'T many books around – he had his store for that – but he did have a few pieces of artwork, including a series of prints of Titian's famous women.

It's obvious the guy is continuously on the move and prefers to own as little as possible. How fascinating. Giò was always ready to admire those who combined work and travel.

Roasted tuna and a colourful salad accompanied by an Aglianico – a full-bodied red wine from Basilicata – were the ingredients for the simple meal they were all longing for. While they ate, the two women shared with Edoardo all the evidence they had collected, which when they came to think about it amounted to very little. But what was clear was the affection Edoardo felt for Vanda. And it was obvious that Vanda wasn't immune to his attentions either.

Once they had finished discussing the murder, Giò asked Edoardo about himself.

"You're not from Trecchina, are you?"

"No, I was born in Pavia and I've spent my whole life wandering from one Italian town to another. My father was a bank manager, and at that time, you had to move every one to two years if you wanted to make a career in banking. And my father was rather ambitious."

"But what brought you to Trecchina? Why here?"

"We had a couple of holidays in Maratea when I was a child. I loved the place, although during the summer it's a little too busy for my tastes. Trecchina represented the perfect solution."

Giò laughed. "You make it sound so normal, but come on! To open up a bookshop in the middle of nowhere is an odd choice. When did you arrive in Trecchina?"

"It will be one year in December, and no, I didn't say it was an obvious decision. But you see, a childhood like mine has imprinted the nomadic gene in my DNA."

"But if you're a nomad at heart, why would you open a shop? Unless you can employ plenty of staff, that's the end of your travelling career," said Giò, thinking about her sister's shop.

"It depends on your definition of travelling. I don't mean taking long weekends away or holidays for a week or two. I travel with my job."

Giò already knew from her sister how Edoardo travelled around, giving struggling bookshops a new lease of life, but she wanted to hear his story from him.

"You mean, although it doesn't look much like it, your bookshop is your camper van?" Vanda teased, impatient for him to tell Giò.

"Well, that's almost true. You see, I look for small villages. There's almost always at least one old bookshop on the verge of shutting down wherever I go. I take over the business, and usually within six months – it depends on how bad the situation is – I manage to break even, and after a while turn a profit. I stick in a place for a year or two, then sell the business on and search for a new venture."

"That's fascinating," cried Giò in admiration. Then she caught Vanda's disconcerted expression and asked him, "So you're planning to leave here too?"

"Not immediately, no. There comes a time when I feel I don't have any more to give or get from a place, and then I know it's time to move on."

A shadow fell over Vanda's face.

It's not easy to fall in love with someone who's going to leave, Giò thought, feeling her friend's pain, *unless you're ready to follow him. But it's possibly too early. They need to get to know each other better.*

"And how many places have you lived in so far, making a success of their bookshops?"

"Until I was thirty, I wanted to follow in my father's footsteps, working for the same bank. Then I realised I wasn't happy with my life, and the bookshop project followed when a friend of mine mentioned she'd have to close her shop in Panzano-in Chianti. That was my first bookshop and I stayed there for a couple of years. Then, during a meeting of independent bookstore owners, I got to know of a little bookshop on the Elba Island that was closing down. I sold the Panzano store and started a new venture. Once I turned a profit on Elba Island, I realised the business model was replicable."

"And what happens to the bookshops you leave?"

"By the time I sell them, they are making a profit and they attract some booklover who's passionate about running a shop. You know, in bookshops you don't make huge money, but you make enough if you love the job."

Giò was in the position to ask the question that mattered the most to Vanda more easily than her friend could.

"How about relationships? Do you fall in love in each place and leave a broken heart behind along with the bookshop?"

Vanda flushed. Edoardo looked Giò in the face, his blue eyes emanating the strange innocence that she was starting to associate with him. It was as if he had the power to say what he meant without inhibitions.

"I've had a few relationships with women, but not that many, in truth. At times I have lingered longer that I wanted to in a place to see how things developed; at other times the woman was willing to follow me. But none of those relationships lasted, if that's what you want to know, and no, I don't have the solution for everything. I can't ignore the possibility that I might stop somewhere for good. I'm like a book that's being written: I don't have a clue what the future will bring. So far, so good." He looked at Vanda without embarrassment.

After dinner, Edoardo and Vanda accompanied Giò to her car. Beneath the windscreen wipers lay a sheet of paper. Giò snatched it away, thinking it was just an advertising leaflet, but when she turned it around, the yellow street lamp illuminated five words written in capital letters.

'YOU'D BETTER STOP NOSING AROUND'.

A flat tyre accompanied the message.

Without comment, Edoardo helped Giò remove the flat tyre and replace it with the spare, which wasn't easy in the darkness of the night, although the yellow street lamp and their mobile phone torches made it a little less daunting.

"It's been ripped with some sort of knife," Edoardo said as he rolled the damaged wheel into the boot of the car so that Giò could have it repaired the next day.

While driving home to Maratea, Giò called Paolo.

"You weren't sleeping, were you?"

"No, I was just watching *Midsomer Murders* on the telly and wishing I were there."

"Are Maratea crimes no longer enough for you?"

"Hardly! We only get a murder once every 20 years."

"Well Trecchina is scoring better: two in one year."

"Yeah, that's upping the average. But what have you been up to? I was expecting at least a dozen calls from you to find out what the Saviozes said to the carabinieri in Trecchina."

"I spent the afternoon with them and I'm calling you now to see if *you* want some info."

As ever, speaking to Giò left Paolo flabbergasted. She updated him on everything that had happened that day, deliberately omitting the part concerning the ripped tyre and the threatening message. If she'd shared that, surely he would have told her to stay away from the investigation.

"I'm worried for Vanda, can't you call and ask the Trecchina carabinieri to send a car to her place? I'm sure if the murderer knows she's being watched by the carabinieri, he will think twice before doing something awful."

"I'll call them up, certainly. But has anything happened that's worried you?"

"No, not really," Giò lied with ease. "But when we were with the Saviozes, I just had a feeling we were being observed."

Paolo sighed. "Do you have to go digging all the time? Can't you leave us to do our work without having to spend time guarding you two?"

"Now you're beginning to sound like Maresciallo Mangiaboschi," snapped Giò, knowing Paolo would not like the comparison. "In any case, we'll be out of your way soon enough. We're heading to Naples tomorrow." And she told him about the Caracciolo Sciarramanna family.

"That's good. Hopefully if the killer doesn't see you around, they will think you've turned your attention to something else and are no longer sticking your nose into the murder investigations. Of course, that's as long as you don't start meddling again as soon as you get back. The carabinieri in Trecchina have released the photos the Saviozes left with them to the media, but so far nobody has come forward to say he or she knew Mrs Tina Melly. But maybe it's just too early – somebody must know her."

"That's weird. Mrs Roselli hasn't heard of her either, nor have her friends." And she told Paolo about the photo the old woman had shared via WhatsApp. "But I think I've updated you on everything now. I'll speak to you again if we find anything useful in Naples."

"That would be much appreciated. Please share anything you think may be of interest with me, anything at all."

Giò grinned. "Same goes for you."

13

NAPLES AND SFOGLIATELLE

Giò and Vanda arrived in Posillipo, the sea quarter of Naples where 18th and 19th century villas stood overlooking the bay, their terraces and gardens hidden by stone walls. Only the tall maritime pine trees emerging from behind the walls gave a clue as to how much greenery you could find beyond. Every once in a while, the view would open up onto the Bay of Naples, the blue double-conic shape of Vesuvius seeming to emerge directly from the water.

They stopped at an imposing wrought iron gate adorned with intricate ornaments, to buzz on the intercom. When an expressionless young woman in white gloves came to let them in, they found themselves in the middle of a little grove. At the bottom of the garden stood a strangely shaped Art Deco building with a thin round turret and quite a few gables.

On the left of the main door, a beautiful set of steps led up to a side door which opened into a small hall, where they were invited to leave their coats. Finally, the woman led them into a large living room where Giò and Vanda's glances were drawn to the balconies and the panoramic terrace giving out onto the sea. The glimpses of the gulf they had been teased by so far became a full cinemascope.

"It's gorgeous!" Giò couldn't help but exclaim.

"It is. It's at this time of year that I generally go back to my apartment in Vomero, but it's always a pity to leave this summer residence, especially during a pleasant autumn like the one we're having now."

The two friends turned to find themselves facing a tall, angular woman. She had dyed black hair which didn't complement her deeply wrinkled face at all and her voice was as sharp as her features.

"I'm Elda Caracciolo Sciarramanna." She was standing erect, her elbow on the top of a white marble mantelpiece as if she was posing for a photograph for *AD Homes*. Indeed, the whole house was worthy of an appearance in a glossy magazine. Colourful Vietri tiles, elegant white curtains held at the sides by silken cords with fringe trims, Bohemian chandeliers, delicate tapestried sofas, fine paintings on the walls were all enhanced by the stunning view beyond the white arched balconies.

"I take it," the woman said, following their eyes, "you wouldn't mind sitting outside on the terrace?"

The two friends nodded.

"Would you prefer coffee, fresh lemonade, a glass of wine?"

"I'd love a lemonade," Vanda said.

"The same for me," Giò added.

"Pasqualina, please."

"Shall I bring one for you too, madam?"

"Yes, and a tray of sfogliatelle."

As the housemaid left, Mrs Caracciolo Sciarramanna guided her guests outside. The terrace with its wrought iron balustrade hung directly above the blue waters of the Bay of Naples. Immediately beneath them was a short dock, a stony wall creating a natural swimming pool on its right-hand side.

"It opens up to the sea," Mrs Caracciolo Sciarramanna said, indicating a gate in the side of the pool. "Nowadays there are too many boats, but when I was young we used to swim for hours in the open sea."

They sat on a sofa that shared the same pattern as the balustrade and was covered with blue and white pillows. A cascade of red geraniums hung from terracotta vases and, as in Maratea, these plants were still in full bloom. To their left, a walkway suspended above the sea led to the rest of the garden: a triumph of green-blue agaves, palm and olive trees and dark green cycads.

"Your grandmother told me you wanted to speak to me about a woman who worked for my family decades ago."

"Yes, it is about Tina Mica. The poor woman was found murdered in Trecchina."

Mrs Caracciolo Sciarramanna didn't show any surprise or emotion at the news.

"She worked for us almost 40 years ago when my children were young. What I don't understand is what right you have to meddle in the investigation into her death, if you pardon my bluntness."

Giò's face became serious. She knew the success of the interview rested on the tone of her answer.

"After Tina had been identified, Martine Savioz, her stepdaughter, came over to Trecchina. She wasn't satisfied with the carabinieri's work and decided to hire me and my partner for the case."

"Are you private detectives then? I thought you were a travel writer and Mrs Riccardi here worked for a biscuit company."

"That's what we call cover work. We find it's better not to stand out as detectives. Most people assume we're no better than the paparazzi, only there to uncover a cheating spouse and provide a reason for divorce and a substantial alimony pay-out. But that's not our line of business at all."

"And what is your line of business?" Again the woman seemed unmoved by Giò's words, her large, dark eyes piercing Giò's as if they were staring into her soul.

Giò held her gaze firmly and replied, "More sensitive cases. For the rest, there are common private detectives."

Vanda, aligning her attitude to her friend's words, put on her sunglasses to show how cool she was and tilted her chin upwards. Elda Caracciolo Sciarramanna smiled.

"I see."

"How long did she work for you?" Giò asked.

"For about five years, then the children went to boarding school and we no longer needed her services. But I don't understand why you're asking for information from me in relation to a person who's been murdered recently when I haven't seen the woman for 35 years."

"I'm not saying you're in any way connected to what's happened, we just want to reconstruct Tina Mica's life and find out if her work ever brought her to Trecchina."

"I don't even know where Trecchina is."

"A village in Basilicata, in the mountains that descend to Maratea."

"Of course I know Maratea. I don't think Tina worked there, though. After working for a family like ours, she would have wanted to be employed by a certain class of people. I'd assumed she'd have kept on working in cities rather than villages."

"That's the problem. Even her stepdaughter in Switzerland didn't know why Tina ended up in Trecchina. She remembers some of the stories Tina told about the families she'd worked for, but she never mentioned Trecchina or Maratea, or any small town in Basilicata."

"Maybe it's something related to her present and not her past."

"Maybe, but we're examining both. You don't remember who she went to work for after she left your family, do you? Did she leave Naples altogether?"

"Yes, if I remember correctly, she did leave. We gave her good references because she deserved them. She went to work for a Tuscan family in Fiesole. Mrs Aldobrandini is dead and buried now and her sons live in America, but you could visit them there if it would help your investigations."

That was an open challenge to their financial means, but Giò did not fall into the trap.

"Do you remember who she was working for before she came to you?"

"You're lucky, I do remember. She worked as a companion to an old woman, an aristocratic German lady who decided to live the rest of her life in Naples. Her name was Charlotte von Grumbach, and when she passed away, Tina Mica came to work for me."

That sounded very much like another dead end. Mrs Caracciolo Sciarramanna looked almost victorious as Giò and Vanda realised they seemed to be chasing after another wild goose.

But Giò wouldn't give up so easily. "Do you remember anything else about Tina? Maybe you spoke to other families she'd worked for when you were looking for a nanny, or maybe Tina herself asked you for another reference when she left the Tuscan family?"

"Once she'd left our home, I don't remember ever hearing from her again. I don't keep a record of all the places my employees go after they leave me. But unless I'm mistaken, Tina Mica also worked for a family in Ferrara, and their name must have been a good one if they could afford her services."

"And your children didn't keep in touch with her? After all, she looked after them for years…"

Mrs Caracciolo Sciarramanna raised her brows all the way up her forehead in disapproval. "Of course not."

A beep alerted Giò to a new message on WhatsApp – Granny.

"I thought I'd better remind you that the best gossips you can find are the workers themselves. I'm sure you know that, but just in case…"

The message ended with a winking smiley emoji. It was hard to accept, but Granny was right – again. After all, they hadn't got much out of Mrs Caracciolo Sciarramanna.

"A final question before we go," said Vanda to buy time, "where do your children live?"

"Umberto is currently in Boston, Adelaide in Paris. Do you need to catch a flight and go to speak to them too?" Again that sarcastic voice, as if jumping on a plane would be way out of their reach financially.

"Not at the moment, but should we need to, we will know how to track them. Thank you, you have been most helpful." Giò shook the older woman's hand with a big, satisfied smile that stretched from one ear to the other. Vanda glanced at her friend and settled her features into the same satisfied expression.

As they left Mrs Caracciolo Sciarramanna in the living room, the housemaid accompanying them towards the exit, Giò said casually, "And your sfogliatelle were delicious, *almost* as good as the ones in Scaturchio."

For the first time, an amused smile appeared on Pasqualina's face.

As they walked through the garden, Giò asked her, "Did you know Tina Mica?"

"Of course I did, and I was going to tell you that. It was a long time ago. I'm going out to run some errands in half an hour, so I'll meet you at the fish shop down the road. Make it look as though we're meeting by chance."

As Vanda and Giò turned towards the house to give the beautiful building a last look before the gate shut behind them, they spotted the silhouette of Mrs Caracciolo Sciarramanna at the top of the steps to the main entrance.

"See you soon, then," said Giò quietly.

"Oh, Giò," said Vanda as the gate snapped shut, "did you see? She was watching to make sure we didn't speak to the housekeeper."

"I wonder what Pasqualina wants to tell us. She looks too young to have been working here 40 years ago."

14

A FRAGRANCE BRIMMING WITH ANGER

A gnese was decorating the front window of her shop, placing ornamental pumpkins among the perfume bottles, cosmetics and trinkets. Such a pity Halloween wasn't celebrated in Maratea. Don Anastasio, the local priest, had banned all shops, schools and families from displaying bats, witches and ghosts or celebrating anything Halloween related. But at least he couldn't say anything about the colourful pumpkins and autumn leaves she was using to liven up her window display.

She went outside to take a better look at the results of her efforts. Satisfied, she was allowing herself a congratulatory grin when a voice came from behind her.

"Well done, Agnese, your shop windows look simply gorgeous."

She turned to see Amanda Triunfo.

"Amanda, such a pleasure to see you! How are you?"

"Fighting hard to find my place in the world. It's tougher than I'd expected."

Amanda had been dumped by her husband after dedicating her adult life to bringing up their two children. He had found a much younger woman, fallen for her, and asked Amanda for a divorce. Instead of fighting for alimony, she had bravely decided to sign up for a Master's degree while demanding that her husband allow her to work in his estate agency for a year to brush up her working skills.

"Spending the day with those two loved-up fools calls for a thick skin. And computers have changed the world of work completely. But at least the college in Salerno is very supportive..."

"A few ups and downs, then."

"Ups and downs? Call it a mad rollercoaster. No amusement park has anything to compare, not even in Orlando." Amanda chuckled. "Be a love and get me a waterproof mascara, would you?"

Agnese looked at her. "Is the reason you need that what I fear?"

"Oh yes," Amanda admitted frankly. "I'm reduced to tears of rage in the office every now and then, and I get so frustrated with the computers never doing what I want them to do. And then those fools poke fun at me..."

"What a shame!"

"No, I never let them see my tears, I won't give them *that* satisfaction. But I do sometimes have to run to the toilet for a good cry. And I need a waterproof mascara to back me up."

Agnese smiled. "Amanda, I think you're doing great."

"And I need one of those comforting scents of yours, something to take me to a fairy tale world and keep me from emptying the fridge when I get back home."

"I've got the right cure for you."

"I had no doubt that you would, which is why I came straight here rather than the chocolate factory."

Agnese picked up a *touche* and sprayed it with Serge Lutens's Un Bois Vanille.

"Imagine a huge green forest made up of vanilla plants, their vines and lianas hanging over your head and the pods releasing their scents..."

"That's deee-licious!" cried Amanda, smelling the *touche*. "I will plunge into the perfume rather than the fridge. Please give me a family-sized bottle."

Agnese chuckled. "I'm afraid you'll have to content yourself with the regular-sized bottle, but you'll only need a couple of squirts."

"Okey dokey," said Amanda, giving Agnese a hug before leaving.

I wonder if she's aware of what a transformation she's going through. She's getting stronger and more self-confident each day, despite a few crises here and there. Agnese felt proud of her small role in the woman's transformation. *I love empowered women,* she thought, and fell to her knees and raised her right fist, her left hand thumping the opposite arm, her face contorting into a triumphant grin that shocked the next customer entering her shop.

"I'm sorry, I was just practising a Maori haka." Agnese blushed, and the young Indian girl gave her a quizzical smile and moved her eyes around the shop. Only then did Agnese recognise her.

"You prepared those wonderful desserts in Trecchina?"

"Yes, that's me," she said, and her eyes fell to the floor in shyness and embarrassment.

"I'm Agnese."

"Ramya."

"Welcome! Please have a look around, touch, sniff, smell at your leisure, and if you need me, I'm only a step away and glad to help."

The girl lost herself among the patterned Danish wool slippers from the Island of Ærø, then moved on to the collection of Swedish lanterns, and finally crossed to the lines of perfumes displayed in colourful cabinets, their doors open to invite customers to test the wonderful scents housed within. Agnese peered in her direction. Ramya was closing her eyes every time she smelled a new *touche.*

She wants to tune into the fragrance as it is, without distractions. Good girl.

After a few minutes, seeing the girl glancing in her direction, obviously too shy to call her over, Agnese joined her and asked which fragrances she had liked the most so far. They were all light and colourful; Ramya had chosen the right perfumes for herself. In fact, she mentioned a few of the essences she recognised in each fragrance.

"It must be your love of cooking that's given you the ability to identify so many different scents."

"I never thought there was much in common between food and perfumes," Ramya said, a pretty smile lightening her serious face and dark eyes.

"We don't use our nose or sense of smell enough nowadays, but if you have a love for cooking or perfumes, then things are slightly different."

Ramya thought about it, then said, "Well, in fact, I feel pure joy when I peel a lemon or slice fresh ginger. I love the intimacy of cumin, or the velvety fragrance of turmeric. In my culture, each dish has its own smell."

"Yet the other day you were cooking an Italian dessert."

"I love all kinds of cuisine and enjoy the smell of Italian herbs too: mischievous green parsley, overpowering sage, but my favourite is rosemary. There's something mysterious about it; it may seem commonplace to you, but each time I use it, I discover something new."

"Your excellent nose would do well in a perfumery."

Ramya flushed slightly.

"How about next weekend at the fair? Are you planning to cook something as delicious as last time?"

Ramya's face turned crimson, her eyes dropping again. "Erica thinks she should give her menu one more try."

"Lasagne and parmigiana again? But they're so complicated to prepare on a small stall!"

Ramya seemed to want the floor to swallow her up.

"Maybe you should tell her?" From Ramya's lack of reaction, Agnese realised she'd said the wrong thing. *This girl is going to run away any second if you don't stop embarrassing her. You're preaching, not helping.* "How about a perfume session?" she suggested cheerfully.

"What's that?"

"A sort of game. I bet that there's the right perfume for the right person at the right time. And the game helps me to find out what that is."

Again Ramya didn't reply, but this time her eyes shone.

"You sit there," and Agnese indicated towards the usual alcove where the ebony table and two chairs waited for them. She then crossed to the entrance door which she locked, displaying the 'Back Soon' sign.

She took her seat and said, "You can distinguish individual essences, but now you've got to forget your logical thoughts and just ask yourself the question 'Which one do I like the most?'" Saying this, Agnese pulled out eight candles one by one from the drawer, selecting each carefully.

Ramya closed her eyes as she smelled them. "These are very different from the others," she said of the first two, and Agnese agreed. The iris one and the berry and musk were both well suited to her. Then Ramya made her final choice and handed Agnese a third candle, making it clear she preferred this to the previous two.

"Clove!" Agnese exclaimed. *You need to keep your wits about you today,* she thought, but she kept smiling at the girl. She would never judge a customer's choice until the game was over in case she influenced the next choice.

Agnese pulled out the bottles representing the different accords, carefully dipped a *touche* in each and placed them on a special holder just in front of each bottle.

"Again, let go of any rational thought and tell me which one you prefer."

This time, Ramya's choice was quick. "This one," and she

pointed to a fresh spicy oriental with the intriguing cool notes of cayenne pepper.

Agnese chose some more bottles of essences for the second round. She hesitated in front of the carnation bottle, lifting it then putting it back before finally selecting it and adding it to the line. Without a second thought, Ramya chose that very essence.

Am I influencing the game with my thoughts and predictions? Agnese wondered, puzzled by the direction Ramya was going in. *I should stop overthinking things and remain neutral.*

She pulled out the cardboard table representing the oriental family, picking up a nice purple and blue spinning top.

Chance is chance, I certainly can't influence this last part of the game.

She smiled encouragingly at Ramya and said out loud, "Each choice we make in life is the result of rational evaluations and chance. Whether we're aware of it or not, there's always an element of chance in what we choose to do." And she handed the spinning top to Ramya, inviting her to launch it across the perfume table.

The girl twirled it with her thin fingers, and when it stopped Agnese marked the spot with a pin. Turning the table, she slammed it back down in shock a second later.

Outrageous Carnation. Again.

Ramya jumped at the slam. Agnese flashed her a shaky smile, trying to keep her cool as her hand frantically smoothed the table.

There's something wrong, very wrong. The same perfume, three times in a row? And a perfume which is totally unsuitable for Ramya. Oh my goodness, what's happening? Agnese, keep your cool. Yes, keep your cool and try again.

"I'm sorry, there was a bump in the cardboard table. Maybe you want to give it another go?"

"It looked perfectly smooth to me."

"Well, it wasn't!"

Ramya's brows rose in alarm. Was she dealing with a lunatic?

Agnese had seemed like such a gentle and encouraging lady at the fair. Then she remembered the haka she had surprised Agnese doing. Maybe the woman had showed signs of madness from the beginning.

Agnese handed her a new spinning top, throwing the blue and purple one back in the basket.

"You don't mind if we give it another try, do you?"

"Certainly not," Ramya whispered, but her wary expression said otherwise.

Agnese used her forearm to flatten the table some more, then she turned her face away from it and asked Ramya to launch the spinning top again.

Agnese still had her head turned to the side when Ramya called her.

"It's stopped."

Agnese breathed deeply, marked the position with a pin, and slowly turned the table. Before she knew what she was doing, she found herself shaking the cardboard violently as if it was a stubborn machine that she could mend with a few good smacks.

"What the heck? What's wrong with you?" she repeated over and over again, until she realised Ramya was staring at her in horror as if she was madness personified. The poor girl then glanced helplessly towards the door, knowing it was locked.

Agnese rushed to open it and gave a nervous laugh. "I'm sorry, dear, there appears to be something wrong with my table. It has given me the same result for three very different people, which has never happened to me in the past twenty years. It's obviously broken and needs fixing."

"Maybe we actually do all need the same fragrance."

"That can't be." Agnese shook her head violently.

"And what's the fragrance?"

"That doesn't matter since the table needs fixing. I'm very sorry to have wasted your time."

Ramya, typically of a teenager, was more curious than ever to know what it was this adult in front of her wanted to hide.

Agnese was normally a master in dealing with stubbornness after years of practice with her sister Giò and more recently with her almost teenage son Luca, but she was too shocked to resist the determined girl in her shop.

Engaging in a tug of war, Ramya managed grab the table from Agnese and turn it over.

"Outrageous Carnation," she read triumphantly. "What's that?"

"A perfume, just like many others."

"Please, I'd love to try it."

"I can't see why since the whole game is a mistake."

"*Please*," the girl said, and there was, all of a sudden, something so firm and grown-up in Ramya's attitude that Agnese found herself doing as she'd been asked. She turned towards the cupboard, sprayed a touche and handed it to the girl.

Ramya smelled it and her brows rose in dismay. She had never experienced a scent so overpowering, but something enticing screamed from that fragrance. Something she wanted.

"May I have a bottle, please?"

Agnese handed her the bottle like an automaton. Her mouth opened to say something, but the words didn't come out.

"How much do I owe you?"

"Nothing, that's a tester. I've ran out of retail bottles, but you can keep that. I don't think I'm ever going to stock that perfume again."

Ramya's family had repeatedly told her never to accept gifts from strangers, but a whiff of the perfume reached her nostrils. She couldn't let it go. Grasping her treasure, she thanked Agnese.

On the threshold, she turned and said, "I'm going to cook something special for you as a thank you for the bottle."

As soon as Ramya had left the shop, Agnese approached the cabinet behind the main counter, pulled out the *London Dandy Perfumes Handbook* and read out loud, her voice trembling,

"Outrageous Carnation, a disturbingly dualistic fragrance. Velvety and honeyed in appearance with a dark streak of oud. Beguiling but dangerously sharp. Between light and darkness – where do you stand?"

She crashed into an armchair, her hands covering her face.

What have I done? What have I given this girl?

15

THE WICKED CHILD

Thirty minutes went by, then forty-five, then a whole hour passed and still there was no sign of Pasqualina.

Vanda and Giò looked at each other. It was time to return to the train station in Piazza Garibaldi, which was quite a long way from Posillipo.

"Do you think Mrs Caracciolo has kept her in?"

"I'm sure of it."

"We'll have to find another way to speak to her. But I'm afraid it won't be today."

At that moment, a figure approached them at a run. When she drew closer, Pasqualina went down on her knees as if picking something up from the ground.

"Madam, you dropped this," she said, and put a piece of paper in Vanda's hands.

"Oh no, it's not mine," Vanda replied instinctively. Giò kicked her leg.

"Oh, how stupid of me, it *is* mine. It must have fallen from my pocket, that's so kind of you."

The woman nodded and turned away.

The piece of paper just said, "*Follow me at a distance.*" They lingered where they were, pretending to be talking but making sure not to lose sight of the housemaid, then they made their way back to Via Posillipo. Looking around as if they were ordinary tourists, they followed the woman who was well ahead of them.

An imposing ancient palace came into view. It had huge glassless windows and was built on a foundation of solid rocks, seeming to rise directly from the sea.

"Palazzo Donn'Anna!" cried Giò ecstatically. She had heard of the palace but never seen it before. "The sea waters have melded the building into the rock itself. I've heard it's full of ghosts."

"Fascinating," murmured Vanda in awe. "But where's our lady going?"

"There must be access to the beach," Giò answered, seeing the woman turning into a side street.

In truth it was more of a terrace. Beside a low wall, a crowd of people were sitting and chatting or taking pictures, enjoying the sight of the Palazzo. There, hidden among the flocks of tourists, Pasqualina approached them and they could finally speak freely without being noticed.

The woman got straight to the point. "Mrs Caracciolo Sciarramanna told you only what she wanted to tell you."

Giò didn't ask her if she'd overheard the conversation. Instead she nodded and let Pasqualina speak.

"After Charlotte von Grumbach, the German lady, passed away, Tina went to work for another family. I can't remember their name, but they had a weird kid. He looked like an angel, innocence personified, but there was something wicked about him, as if he couldn't distinguish good from bad. First, the family had to give away all their pets for their own safety, then one day they just managed to save a little girl before he hurt her badly. The family paid her parents good money not to report the episode to the police, but they had to leave Naples nonetheless, and Tina decided not to follow them. She was too scared of the child and disgusted with the family for doing nothing to help him. They didn't want to acknowledge that he was sick; they just used to say he was too lively and couldn't understand the consequences of his actions."

"How long ago was this?"

"The accident happened just before Tina joined the Caracciolo Sciarramanna family, I believe around 40 years ago."

"Aren't you too young to remember 40 years ago?"

"My mum worked with the Caracciolo Sciarramanna family before me. She and Tina weren't exactly friends, but they worked together for a few years. It was Tina who told my mother, and my mum told me."

A wicked child from the past – could this be the secret behind Tina Melly's death? Frankly, it sounded too far-fetched, but while Pasqualina was with them, they may as well ask her some questions.

"And have you heard anything of that family since they left Naples?"

"No, not really. In fact, I had almost forgotten the whole story until I heard you questioning Mrs Caracciolo Sciarramanna when…" she flushed "…when I served you the lemonade."

"Of course, of course," Giò was quick to reassure her. She didn't want their only 'witness' to feel embarrassed about eavesdropping on a conversation. "You said you can't remember the family's name, but is your mum still alive?"

"She is, but I'm afraid she's too sick to be questioned. Sick in the mind, I mean. She still has some spells of lucidity, but they are rare. She lives in a hospital run by nuns."

"We really need the name of that family."

"I'll do my best, but apart from my mother, I can't imagine whom to ask…"

"This is my card. If you remember or find out anything, just let me know."

The woman put the card in her pocket, nodding and giving her own phone number to Giò.

"Do you think the boy might have killed her?" she asked.

"Honestly, I don't know. Unless we find some other links to Tina, he's our best lead so far. How old was the kid then?"

"Maybe eight, maybe ten, I'm not really sure."

"I can't imagine why he'd want to kill a woman 40 years later, it makes no sense. But we'll keep looking into it."

"You really are private detectives, aren't you?"

"As a matter of fact, we are," whispered Giò in conspiratorially, "but we're in disguise, so don't give us away."

"Of course not, my lips are sealed."

"You've been very helpful," said Giò, tipping her.

"And now I'd better go. If I'm away for too long, the wild cat will get suspicious."

BACK ON THE TRAIN, GIÒ AND VANDA WONDERED IF THE TRIP HAD turned up anything useful at all.

"Do you think Tina found out that the child – now a middle-aged man – was in Trecchina and decided to stop him?"

"Stop him from doing what? And would you come from Switzerland to Trecchina because a wicked child you hadn't seen or heard of for 40 years was there?"

"No, I wouldn't, even if I were sure it was the same person. Years have passed and he has probably grown out of whatever ailed him in his childhood. That's what I hope anyway."

"No matter how you look at it, it seems we're getting nowhere. I just can't wait to have a good bath and a long, long sleep."

"I wish I could have an early night too, but I'm supposed to be going out for dinner tonight."

"Ah, that fascinating bookshop owner …"

Vanda went scarlet. "Actually, it's not him."

"Not him? Who is it then?"

"You've met him. Enrico, the man who was at my place…"

"That rude and unpleasant man?" cried Giò.

"Yes. I don't like him much – actually, at times I almost loathe him…"

Giò couldn't hide her disappointment. "If that's the case, why date him?"

"It's not a date at all!" Vanda shrilled.

"What is it then? Don't tell me it's business?"

"He's also a sponsor at the school, and it's thanks to his donation that we've been able to get new stands for the Chestnut Fair. He's paying to upgrade the football pitch outside the school, too. It's in such bad shape, we've almost given up taking the children there. But kids nowadays spend so much time on the internet or on their mobiles, it's a real pity to deny them some outdoor sport space."

"Are you the sacrificial lamb then, going to dinner with the wicked ogre for the collective good?"

"That's exactly the case."

"He can't be that bad, though, if he's so generous to the community."

"I know it sounds very ungrateful of me, but he's hard to like. I've tried to take to him as a benefactor, but he's beyond hope."

Giò grinned. "Did he ask you out?"

"Yes, and I couldn't really say no, though I made sure he realised it's only for the sake of the school and it's nothing more than a business dinner to arrange a few things. You could come along, if you like, to keep me company."

"I did my fair share of playing gooseberry yesterday."

Vanda waved her hand as if to dismiss Giò's insinuations.

"Come on, Edoardo is a charming fellow," said Giò.

"Maybe, Giò, maybe…"

And Giò backed off, not wanting to ruin Edoardo's chances with her friend. Better the two of them sort things out in their own good time without any pressure from her.

At the train station, Enrico was waiting on the platform. As he walked towards them, his eyebrows were going up and down with strange quirky movements, and he was holding a bunch of pretty flowers. His huge sunglasses were missing today, but Giò recognised the flat tweed cap and finally placed him.

"You were at my sister's perfumery," she cried in dismay.

The man recognised her too, but didn't look embarrassed at all.

"So you're the sister of the tarot reader."

"Tarot?"

"Yes. She goes through a long prediction process only to end up giving me a fragrance which is miles away from the one I asked her for. Though I must say, it's not too bad." He leaned his neck towards Vanda, tilting his head to one side. Vanda instinctively backed off.

"I only wanted you to smell my cologne. It doesn't matter. I guess her shop's so expensive, she has to put on that show to convince people they're getting their money's worth." He grinned and looked at them for approval.

"That's Giò's sister you're talking about!" cried Vanda, horrified. "You could show a little respect."

"I'm only saying what happened. I went in for an aftershave costing 20 euros and ended up paying five times that much."

"But she didn't force you to buy anything."

"If I'd left empty handed, I would have wasted 30 minutes of my life."

Vanda banged her forehead with her hand. "Oh my goodness, are you sure you want to take me out for dinner? Agnese is one of my best friends."

"I didn't say I dislike her, nor her shop," he said seriously. "We could have dinner at Maratea harbour and your friend here can come along too."

"No, thanks," said Giò, uncertain whether to be angry and defend her sister, or just have a good laugh. "I'm rather tired and I'd prefer to head back home."

"Tell your sister I might visit her again."

"Watch she doesn't make your pockets spill more money."

"As long as she doesn't fill my head with all that mumbo jumbo about fate and chance." He smiled amiably as if he had just said Agnese was the most charming woman in the world. This time, Giò had to bite her tongue to stop herself from replying. She watched Vanda walk away with Enrico, trying to ignore the gloomy feeling that she had let her friend down by leaving her alone with this man.

As she was getting into her sister's car, Giò heard a powerful roar and the couple flashed away in a white sports car. Apparently, Mr Nasty didn't lack money.

16

MESSAGE IN A BOTTLE

When she woke up first thing, Giò reached for her mobile phone to see if Kate had replied to the numerous messages, both text and voicemail, she had left in the past few days. Silence from Kate, but she did find a message from Vanda.

"*I'm fine. Dinner was better than I'd feared, but Edoardo walked past the restaurant and saw me with Enrico – flowers, lit candles and all. I hope that hasn't scuppered my chances with him.*"

Giò thought it over. "*All the better, the guy won't take you for granted then.*" But she regretted what she had written as soon as she'd sent the text. It seemed her former fiancé had led her to become cynical, as if love was a game to be won by whoever managed to appear less involved in a relationship. The thought put her in a bad mood.

"You ruined my life once, Mr Dorian Gravy, you won't keep ruining it."

She banged the Moka pot on the table as she filled it with water and coffee. When the familiar gurgle told her the coffee was ready, Giò headed for her small terrace, a woollen shawl around her shoulders, to enjoy her breakfast in the sun. The view over the glittering sea and the whole gulf in the distance, the clear air, the panorama of mountains – the ghost of Dorian Gravy disintegrated like a vampire at dawn.

She was reading the notes she had taken a year ago while walking the West Highland Way in Scotland. The time had come to write a chapter on the best hikes in Scotland, and she couldn't help but start with the most legendary one: 150 miles from Milngavie north of Glasgow all the way to Fort William. It was a pity, as she had found out to her dismay that the charming Mamore Lodge where she'd stayed the first time she'd walked the Way had shut its doors…

Her phone ringing brought her back from the northern lochs to the Mediterranean. It was a foreign phone number.

"Hello, Martine, this is Giò speaking."

"Hello, Giò, we're just heading to speak to the *police cantonale.*"

"Has something happened?"

"Yes, we arrived at our family cottage in Chandolin to find a letter from Tina."

"A letter from Tina?"

"Yes, I think she sent it here so that if she got back safely, she could retrieve it."

"I'm not sure I understand."

"Oh, I'm sorry, I'm so agitated. You see, we normally come to Chandolin every other weekend and Tina collects the mail for us so the letterbox doesn't get clogged up. Before leaving for Italy, Tina sent me a letter. If she had come back safe and sound, she would have recognised her own letter and destroyed it, so I would never have known about it."

"But since she never came back, you received the letter."

"Exactly."

"My goodness, and what does it say?"

"Just *'Dear Martine, take this to the police. They will know what to do with it'.*"

"What does it mean? Is the rest of the letter written in invisible ink, maybe?"

"No, but there's an article, a page torn from a magazine. It's in Italian, but from what I can understand, it's about a young woman who was murdered in Trecchina. There's a picture of her and the killer."

"Oh my goodness!"

"We're at the police station, so I'll just send you a photo of the article via WhatsApp. I need to go now."

"Thanks, Martine, for informing me. I'll speak to you later."

As soon as she had ended her phone call with Martine, Giò was scrolling down to Paolo's number.

"There's a link! There's a link between the two murders!"

"*Two* murders? Who else has been murdered?"

"Who else? No, I mean the old murder in Trecchina, the young lady who was killed early this year."

"And that's connected to Tina Melly?"

"Exactly."

"But the killer is in jail…"

"Why don't you come over? I've loads to tell you about the trip to Naples and the threat…"

"The threat?"

Of course, of all her news, he had to pick up on the part he would reproach her about. Too late to backtrack now – she had to tell him about the slashed wheel and the threatening message left beneath her car windscreen wipers.

"And you didn't go to the carabinieri to report it?"

Giò decided that the best form of defence was attack. "I'm telling you now. You know what it's like: if I had gone to the station, they would have kept me in for a couple of hours to write a silly report, and then they would have done nothing anyway." The attack worked: Paolo did not protest. "Do you want to come over or shall we just stay on the phone and see who can ask the most questions?" she snapped.

"I can't," he explained. "I can't leave the station except for emergencies. Why don't you come over here? I'm alone in my room this morning."

Giò wasn't at all keen on the idea of visiting Fiumicello carabinieri station, but she was too impatient to have someone to discuss Martine's phone call with to refuse.

"Give me 15 minutes."

~

GIÒ RUSHED THROUGH THE ENTRANCE OF THE STATION AND BANGED headlong into something as large and solid as a wardrobe. When she looked up, she found herself face to belly with Maresciallo Mangiaboschi who was just leaving. He gave her a fierce look.

"Was someone murdered in Maratea last night?"

"How should I know?"

"You're always nosing around. And what are you here for?"

"I've lost my wallet."

"Go to see Brigadiere Rossi on the first floor. He can deal with that kind of trivia."

As Giò rushed past him, he roared after her, "I hope that's not just another of your fibs."

She didn't even bother to reply and the maresciallo shrugged his huge shoulders – like Nando, he was a former rugby player. He hadn't liked the Brando woman from the start, his cop's hunch telling him she was a menace. A pity he was in a hurry.

"Strazio, is my car ready?" he shouted to the small, trembling carabiniere at his side.

"It is, Maresciallo."

"Let's go then." Mangiaboschi was happy to see fear and respect in his subordinate's face. He was a firm believer that it was only thanks to rank and order that things got done, and a loose cannon like Giò Brando seemed to ignore both. He'd have to keep his eyes open for any signs of her stirring up trouble.

~

"Oh, Giò, I was trying to call to tell you that if you waited five more minutes, the maresciallo would be out of the way."

"I've just rammed my head into his stomach. Accidentally. He's already asked me what I'm up to."

"Actually, that's a good question. What *are* you up to this time?"

"Hello, Paolo, how are you doing?" she said sarcastically.

"Come on, Giò, you didn't want to indulge in polite conversation when you called me."

"True."

She showed him her phone with the magazine article and the news of the January murder. She also told him all she and Vanda had discovered in Naples. Paolo printed out the magazine article and looked at it, shaking his head.

"I wonder how Tina Melly got it."

"I don't."

Paolo looked at her quizzically.

"When I was in London," Giò explained, complacently, "loads of people in the Italian community subscribed to magazines or newspapers from their hometowns."

"But Tina isn't from this area…"

"Maybe she was visiting an Italian friend or browsing through the magazine in a dentist's waiting room or at the hairdresser's."

"Right. But what caught her attention? The face of the murderer?"

"Maybe it's him – the wicked child…"

"But Orrico committed the murder in January and he is in prison. And he's too young to be the wicked child. So who killed Tina Melly? Why would this article make her come all the way down here?" Paolo shook his head again, unconvinced.

He opened the window, and as he sat back at his desk, he saw Giò's eyes fixed on him. She wasn't buying it, not until she had more information.

"Let me call Massimo, my carabiniere friend in Trecchina. He can give us more details on this old murder. You go through the article and see if there's any loophole, anything that might have caught Tina's attention or made her think she knew the victim or the murderer."

When Paolo put the phone down after his conversation with Massimo, Giò asked him to repeat everything to her as she had only heard his half of the conversation.

"Nothing new, I'm afraid. Orrico was an extremely jealous guy, he couldn't bear the fact that Liliana had left him. After threatening her and playing nasty tricks on her, he finally snapped and killed her."

"Did he confess to the murder?"

"No, but that's pretty common. If it's your first offence, it's better not to confess if there are no extenuating circumstances. And there weren't any for him."

"Is there a possibility his family knew Tina Melly?"

"I asked Massimo, but he said the Orricos aren't the kind of family who would have employed a nanny or a housekeeper. And as Ettore Orrico is 26, he can't be the wicked child Mrs Caracciolo Sciarramanna's housekeeper told you about. And you know what else?"

"What?" she asked wearily, stretching her legs out over the only empty space on his desk.

"We shouldn't rely on her story. Maybe the housekeeper in Naples just wanted the attention and the tip, so she served you up a red herring."

"How about the girl? Liliana? Maybe Tina Melly knew her?"

"It seems improbable. Liliana and her family have always lived in Trecchina – until her death, I mean. They moved away in the spring. Having said that, the carabinieri will look into that as soon as they receive the communication from the *police cantonale*. But again, Liliana was 22 when she died, and Tina left for Switzerland 20 years ago. We have a few pieces of the puzzle, but they all seem unrelated; we need to undertake a process of elimination."

"Let's start from the beginning." Giò pulled her legs down from the desk and grabbed a sheet of paper, regretting leaving her whiteboard at home. She moved a few piles of paper around to make room to write, to Paolo's horror. "How can you work in these conditions? Haven't you gone digital yet?"

"Actually, we use both digital and paperwork, which means double the work," grumbled Paolo.

"Tina is living an ordinary life in Switzerland," said Giò, drawing a circle with Tina's name inside. "She tells her stepdaughter of her life in Italy, but from what Martine says, she had good memories of her 20 years in Chandolin too."

"What has this to do with our investigation?"

"You sound like Mangiaboschi when you speak like that. We want to know what our victim was like, understand her psychology. Martine painted a portrait of a happy woman. She wasn't pining for Italy; she wanted to spend the rest of her life in Chandolin. She wasn't looking for an excuse to return to the places of her early life, except for a short holiday."

"OK, I see what you mean," he said, but he didn't look completely convinced.

"One day, Tina is sitting in her hairdresser's chair, browsing a few magazines while her hair is styled when her eyes alight on this very article." And Giò waved the printout of the magazine article that Paolo had given her. "It's not from an area she's familiar with, but when she gets to the news of Liliana Ielpo's murder, something registers in her mind instantly and she tears that page out. Once home, she goes through it more carefully, and that's when she knows she has to come over to Italy and find out what's happening. Now the first question is: what caught her attention?"

"Not the photographs for sure, since she'd likely never seen the killer nor the victim in her life."

"We can't be sure she didn't know them."

Paolo thought it over. "But if she had met them, they would

have been small children, far too young to be instantly recognisable to her as adults... I think."

"So maybe it was the names combined with the location. Or what if Ettore Orrico or Liliana Ielpo had a distinguishing feature that would have made them instantly recognisable, despite them having gone from babyhood to adulthood since Tina left Italy?"

"May I remind you that the carabinieri asked the public to get in touch if they knew Tina? They circulated photos of her when she was young and more recent ones, but nobody came forward. She seems to be a total stranger to this community."

"Mrs Roselli's friends confirmed that, and that is strange. But let's go back to Switzerland." Giò draw a square and wrote 'news'. "Tina reads the article, she recognises something or someone in it, she knows she has to come to Trecchina to check in person. She also knows it might be dangerous. She doesn't mind risking her life, but she wants to make sure that she's left a clue behind her just in case, so before leaving, she puts the article in an envelope and sends it to Martine. But not in Berne. She doesn't want to alarm her stepdaughter if the danger isn't real; it's just a precaution in case something happens to her. She knows she might be going to meet a killer."

"That's a good reconstruction, Giò."

"But that's not all. She decides not to tell the full story in her letter. It would have been so simple to tell Martine everything, who she feared and why, but she deliberately made our lives tough, giving us no more than a subtle clue. Why?" Her pen drew a large question mark.

"It's like a part of her wanted to protect the killer, as if she wasn't sure whether to give him away or not..."

"Maybe she simply thought that if something else happened to her – a heart attack or an aeroplane accident, for example – she didn't want to give him away if she hadn't had the chance to speak to him."

"So she must have thought there was a chance he was

innocent." Paolo rested an elbow on a pile of paper, propping his head up. The fingers of his other hand were drumming on the only small space left among the papers on his desk.

"And you'd be most inclined to feel like that," Giò said triumphantly, "if you'd known someone as a child. I believe what we discovered in Naples might be the truth."

Her pen wrote '*the wicked child*'.

Paolo straightened up a little. "We're missing something that's right under our noses." But then he shook his head, pointing to a large white space on Giò's paper. "We're jumping to conclusions without considering what might be in the middle."

She nodded patiently, went back to Tina's circle and said, "In any case, she buys her flight ticket, doesn't mention anything to Martine, and comes to Trecchina. She's probably got an appointment with her killer since nobody else sees her in town; she doesn't even have time to stop off at her agriturismo before he finishes her off."

"I'm not sure about the two having an appointment. We checked Tina's phone calls with the help of the Swiss police – since we never found her bag nor her mobile, they sent us the phone records – and she didn't make any calls to Trecchina except to her agriturismo."

"You think she met him by pure chance?"

"If you think how small Trecchina is and how many people live there, it's quite possible."

"And that's why the killer left her in the forest. He was taken by surprise, he had to act fast. He got rid of her body, only to remember that there would be crowds of chestnut hunters tramping all over the forest over the next couple of days."

"Or maybe he just needed somewhere temporary while he decided where to hide the body permanently, but by the time he returned, Vanda had found it. Again he had to act quickly: he hit Vanda on the head and went on with his plan to hide Tina's corpse in the adventure park. After all, if the corpse were never found, it would save him from all kinds of trouble. And he almost got away with it."

"You mentioned you questioned the park owner and he doesn't seem to be involved."

"Yes, the carabinieri checked his alibi and Mr Nascimale was in Naples that day. The thing is, though, now the bulk of the work has finished, the area has reverted to being a popular walk for the locals. People know how to get in: there's a side gate which is left unlocked to allow them access and avoid anyone protesting that a private company is destroying one of the most popular hikes in the area. Any local could have taken the body there."

"How about the watchman? Did he see anything?"

"As he does every Friday, he went to visit his daughter in Marina di Camerota. He came back late evening, and he's got witnesses."

"So what do we do now? We should start with what Tina Melly gave us..."

"The article, you mean?"

"Exactly, it's like a message in a bottle. We should start with the old murder."

Paolo checked his mail. His colleague from Trecchina had sent him all the documentation on the Ielpo case, but it was a long print run. Even though he and Giò shared the pages between them so they could get through them more quickly, it took some time.

"My goodness," Giò cried.

"What?"

"I didn't know Liliana Ielpo had been strangled too!"

"Yes, it's a weird coincidence."

"Correct me if I'm wrong, but didn't you say during our last murder investigation that you don't believe in coincidences?"

"I don't believe in *too many* coincidences. But I do my best to keep an open mind. This time, it might not be a coincidence, but then again, it might be."

"Two women have been murdered in the same way in Trecchina within a year. And in the previous ten years, how many murders have there been in Trecchina? None at all?"

"I see your point, Giò, but the Ielpo case was cut and dried: a jealous jerk of an ex-boyfriend with violent tendencies." Paolo was reading from the papers in his hands. "During their two-year-long relationship, Liliana tried to hide from her parents how unhappy she was, but when she finally confided in them, with their help she managed to leave him."

"After two months of her being stalked," Giò summarised what she was reading, "Liliana's family finally filed a formal complaint with the carabinieri. Orrico was summoned before them and told to keep his distance from the girl, her home and her family. But a month later, he surprised her in the carpark and strangled her."

Paolo nodded. "No fingerprints on the victim, but also no alibi for Orrico. He had dropped a bottle of beer in the parking area, and forensics found his DNA on this bottle. The beer was a favourite of his – he had been drinking it in the local pub before leaving for his home."

"What happened when he was questioned?"

"He said after leaving the pub, he headed home by himself and nobody saw him. The guy who runs the pub said Orrico had drunk far too much – as usual – and he was glad Orrico had left as he tended to cause trouble when he was in that state."

"So would you agree that Orrico would have been the perfect guy to frame?"

"Or simply the perfect killer. Also, if we follow your train of thought, Giò, we end up with one less murderer, not one more."

"Well, a different one maybe." She waved her hands at Paolo, indicating that he should stay quiet until she'd shared her thoughts. "Imagine our wicked child has killed his first victim and framed Orrico. It's the perfect murder. Then ten months later, he's discovered in Trecchina by his former nanny. He kills her too, and now he's ready to strike again whenever he pleases."

"A fascinating hypothesis, Giò, but who is this child, and how did Tina recognise him from the picture of two young people she'd probably never met?" He showed her the article again. There was a picture of Trecchina with no people in the shot, along with the portraits of Orrico and Liliana.

Giò scrutinised the picture of Trecchina. "Maybe there's some little detail that screamed the truth to Tina."

"And what's that?"

"I don't know, yet."

"Giò, let's wait and see if someone gets in touch with the carabinieri, someone who knew Tina and can shed some light on the mystery. We need to find something that links her to Trecchina, otherwise it's going to be hard to prove anything."

How Giò hated this. The solution was right in front of her, but the more she tried to grasp it, the more it eluded her. So close and yet so far, and so frustrating.

"You plan to do nothing?" she snapped, venting her impatience.

"You know Trecchina is outside my jurisdiction, but I'll keep in contact with Massimo, suggest he go over the Ielpo case again and see if he can find any anomalies that didn't make it into the official documentation."

She looked at him scornfully.

"Giò, you know that I'm always working even when I pretend I'm not."

Then she smiled at him. After all, the guy had saved her life earlier in the year when she had acted impulsively and, as it turned out, very foolishly. If it hadn't been for his cop's hunch, she would now be sleeping for eternity in Maratea's graveyard.

"You're right, I'm too quick to act without thinking."

"You know what? When you're apologetic, you scare me more than ever."

"Truth is, you're always looking for the worst in me!"

"Come on, Giò, you'll see – we'll sort this out."

"Yes, after another couple of victims have been strangled."

"That's not fair!"

"And it's not fair when you don't take my opinion into consideration."

Paolo was shaking his head in denial when a familiar voice roared from downstairs.

"What's happening up there? Is that mad woman still here?" The maresciallo was back, and to make matters worse, he was climbing the stairs. "What's this chaos?" He made his way into the room and looked at the notes his brigadiere was sharing with Giò. "What are the two of you up to this time?"

Giò evaluated the situation. With a man like Maresciallo Mangiaboschi there were only two possible courses of action. She could be submissive and apologise, but she decided to opt for the other one.

"I'm glad you asked because I've wasted an hour in this station reporting the loss of my wallet thanks to your silly questions and tons of paperwork," she snapped as she lifted a pile of papers and slammed it down on Paolo's desk, "and we're still not done yet."

The maresciallo started at the noise, looking at her in surprise. "Where's this report anyway?"

"I tore it up. While your brigadiere was making me fill in form after form, I had a phone call from Maratea town hall: a street sweeper found my wallet next to the rubbish bins."

Maresciallo Mangiaboschi looked at her with suspicion and dislike, but Giò wasn't finished.

"I'm going to thank the mayor and suggest Maratea should employ more road sweepers than carabinieri!" And she slammed the door noisily as she left the room, leaving the two men looking dumbfounded.

17
___

NOT ALL GAMBLING IS BAD

Despite the satisfaction of having got the better of Maresciallo Mangiaboschi, Giò felt rage and a sense of powerlessness growing in her. She and Paolo were just a whisker away from solving the case, but something was obscuring their view.

From a previous case, she had learned that a small change in perspective could alter her outlook on a murder completely. If she could only find out how to view the mystery differently, she would uncover the elusive truth.

I'll go for a kayak ride; I'll go insane if I think any more about the case.

At the communal doorway leading into the building she shared with her family, she met Granny going out.

"Giò, what's happened?"

"Nothing much."

"You might have a talent for telling fibs to the rest of the world, but not to your granny."

Giò chuckled, "I'd forgotten I was facing the most shrewd detective since Sherlock Holmes," and she told Granny about the magazine and everything she had discussed with Paolo.

"I don't like this case. The more you dig into it, the more

complicated it looks. Be careful, Giò, don't launch yourself into it headlong. There's something wicked about it; I don't believe for one moment it was a robbery that ended badly."

"I plan to get my stuff and go for a kayak ride, enjoy this beautiful day."

As Giò went upstairs to get ready, Granny looked at her watch and decided she'd better change her plans for the morning. She returned to her flat, got something from a drawer in the living room, and then out she went.

It was one o'clock by the time Granny had finished her errands and entered the Asso di Picche, a dingy bar trattoria in a dark alley off Maratea's town centre.

"Good morning, Mrs Brando." A young woman with muscular tattooed arms looked up from behind the bar, evidently surprised to see her there.

"Hello, dear, aren't you Ildegarda's daughter?" Granny enquired.

"I am," the other replied, getting ready for the avalanche of questions about her family that would inevitably follow.

When Gran was done, she ordered her usual cup of barley coffee and went to sit at a grimy little table, facing a man who was finishing his lunch. Granny asked him if she could borrow the set of cards sitting on the table in front of him.

"Might need them later," he mumbled, his lips red with tomato sauce.

"I'll return them."

Gran set her drink on the table and started to play Solitaire, making sure to shuffle and handle the cards with the refined skill of a Monte Carlo croupier. The man turned his angular face and penetrating eyes in her direction. Clearly fascinated, he wiped his thin moustache with a napkin and spoke.

"You know how to handle cards, don't you?"

Granny stayed silent, as if too absorbed in her game to answer. It was an unusually frenzied version of Solitaire. The man's eyes rested on her quick hand movements as if hypnotised.

When she had completed the game, she finally looked up at him.

"There's no fun in playing cards alone. Oh, for a decent fellow to challenge to scopa."

The man would never generally have considered playing cards with an old lady, but he recognised excellence when he saw it.

"I've finished my lunch, so if you want, we can play a couple of games. But I play hard."

"So do I," Gran replied, making space on her table and cutting the deck to see who should deal first. It was she. She shuffled, she distributed, she played: scopa, settebello, scopa, settanta, scopa. Pearls of sweat formed on the man's forehead.

After she'd won the first three matches, Gran looked deeply into the man's eyes and said, "The warm-up is over. Shall we play for real now?" while her hands performed a sequence of overhand shuffling, riffling, weave shuffling.

"You mean… for money?" babbled the man, his small eyes glued to the cards flying from one hand to the other.

"Don Anastasio wouldn't approve of that," Granny said. "But I will stake my preserves of stuffed peppers, aubergines and chillies, mushrooms, and my limoncello of course."

The man instinctively passed his tongue over his greedy lips. Rosa Brando's cookery skills were legendary in the town.

"I don't cook," he replied drily, picking up his cards and starting a new game.

"I wouldn't expect jars of preserve from you. Scopa!" Granny said. "But I want information."

The man looked at her, his eyes full of suspicion. Gran continued as if nothing was amiss, doing even better than she had in the previous games.

"What kind of information?"

"Nothing much, really. I just want to ask a few questions about an old client of yours – Ettore Orrico. Settebello and scopa!"

The man didn't reply and Granny continued to win mercilessly. Then she stopped.

"No point continuing. Either you're not concentrating enough or you're not worthy of a place at my table," she said, gathering up the cards and dealing them out to play Solitaire again.

"Of course I'm worthy, but we weren't really playing, were we? Stop that silly game for nannies and let's start over again."

Granny lost a few matches, then looked at her watch. *Gosh, it's getting late,* she thought, and from that point onwards, she took all the points in all the games, to the great chagrin of the man who couldn't believe he had done so poorly against an 80-year-old.

"Now the questions," said Granny victoriously. The man nodded. "You were the lawyer defending Orrico, weren't you?" The man nodded again. "I'm not the police, so it'd be my word against yours if I were to share any of the information you give me. Nobody would believe me if I were to say that I won it in a scopa game."

The man nodded a third time, understanding dawning on his face. He could honour his stake without fear of anyone discovering he had betrayed a client's confidentiality.

"Also the information could do more good than harm since he's already in prison."

The lawyer nodded once again.

"Do you think he was the real killer?"

The man faltered, his head almost falling from his shoulders onto the table, but Granny kept looking at him steadily. He thought for a while, then spoke slowly.

"Honestly? He's the violent good-for-nothing type. He had threatened the girl, he had some previous for fights..."

"But?"

"Well, it's hard to explain. Most of our clients either talk to us as if they're in the confessional, telling us the truth and relying on us to unravel their mess, or they pretend to the whole world, their lawyers and families included, that they are innocent of the crime."

"And which party did Orrico belong to?"

"Neither. Yes, he declared himself innocent, but he worded it strangely: 'I don't think I killed her'. It was as if he himself couldn't be sure whether he'd committed the crime or not."

"Did he admit that he was drunk?"

"Yes, he was drunk, but he said he wasn't *that* drunk, and he had enough experience to distinguish between the different stages of drunkenness. I believed him because he admitted that if he had met her, he would have killed her, because even if he wasn't that drunk, he *was* that furious."

Granny paused, then spoke. "But you haven't answered my question. Do you believe he killed her?"

He thought over the question as if considering it for the first time. His job didn't involve finding out the truth, but giving his clients the best defence possible, whether they were innocent or guilty. The rest, the moral judgement, was up to the court.

"Had he told me blatantly that he was innocent, I would have said he was guilty. But because of the way he expressed himself, I'd say I'm only 90 per cent certain."

Granny nodded.

"Any elements of the investigation you weren't happy with?"

"Just the fact forensics found no traces of his DNA on the victim's body, as if the crime had been premeditated, which didn't fit with my client's violent but empty head."

"Nothing else?"

"Nothing else."

"May I give you a piece of advice?" said Granny, standing up and clutching her bag, ready to go. He lifted his hands in a scornful 'why not?' "You'd better develop the habit of checking the cards you play with."

The man looked at the cards on the table, shrugging his shoulders. "I know those cards as well as I know my pockets."

Granny searched her bag, pulled out a deck of cards, and told him, "I meant these cards. We played with my cards all along. But to make up for that, I'll leave a couple of jars of preserves and a bottle of limoncello for you at my daughter's perfumery. You can collect them tomorrow." She moved closer to him and waved her finger under his nose. "Just don't mention anything to her about card games."

The man nodded for a final time, his open mouth and eyes popping out of their sockets giving him the same expression as a boiled cod.

18

IT NEVER RAINS...

Agnese was on her way to open her perfumery that afternoon. She had left home a few minutes earlier than usual to give herself time to visit Nennella's newsstand. Since yesterday, she had been feeling low. For once not trusting her perfumes to offer her comfort, she'd decided she'd choose a good book instead to bring a little joy back into her life.

When Agnese reached the newsstand, which doubled up as Maratea's bookshop, Nennella was busy serving a customer. She greeted Agnese briefly from the top of her library ladder, blowing dust from a book on the upper shelf that she hadn't touched in years. The dust flew down onto the customer, a tall, sturdy man wearing thick round glasses. He was looking up at Nennella, waving away the dust with his hand but not moving from the spot.

"Thailand?" asked Nennella once she had removed enough dust to read the title.

"Nope!"

"OK, there's more." The woman moved on to the next book. "Malaysia?"

"No."

"Sri Lanka?"

"No."

"East Asia?"

"Maybe." The man stretched out his hand, wiped away the dust with the corner of his raincoat sleeve and searched for the index. Nennella waited impatiently on top of the ladder. "No, East Asia apparently does not include the damn country."

"Japan?"

"That's even further away!"

"I've got more further along." Nennella came down the ladder, moved it to the right and went up it again. "China? Maybe there's a chapter on Nepal. After all, it's nearby."

Again, he removed the dust, opened the book and checked the index.

"Nothing. The author wrote 700 pages on this stupid country and not a word on Nepal. I wonder who writes these guides."

Agnese felt like saying that you wouldn't expect to find a chapter on Switzerland or France in a guide to Italy, but she held back when Nennella gave her a warning look, her eyebrows almost touching her hairline.

"I've brought a couple of biscuits for Annina," Agnese said instead. "May I?"

"Sure, we're almost finished."

Agnese bent down to Annina, a cute Jack Russell who a few weeks earlier had saved Giò from a grisly death, the dear little dog.

"Asia!" Nennella cried triumphantly, but she stretched too far, losing her balance. The man was quick to grab her as she fell and they hit the floor. Luckily when the two of them stood up, helping each other to their feet, there wasn't a single scratch on either of them.

Annina barked repeatedly in the direction of the man, who smiled at the dog, for the first time showing a certain gentleness.

"You're right," he said, "it's my fault."

"Are you OK?" asked Agnese.

"It's all fine, dear, and we found the right book." Nennella handed the book to the man, who again went straight to the index.

"Maybe we got somewhere in the end."

"You're searching for a book on Nepal, I hear. I've got a friend there... ouch!" Agnese cried in pain as Nennella kicked her leg.

The man raised his eyes to Agnese and looked at her with interest. Then he shook his head.

"No, you look like a sensible woman. You can't be the witch."

"The witch?"

The man's face turned red in anger. "One of these modern witches, influencing young people with their honeyed words. Speaking rubbish and ruining them."

"My goodness!" exclaimed Agnese, thinking of her two kids. "What happened?"

"I have a daughter who's been doing brilliantly. She got a first class engineering degree, she enrolled for a Master's degree in Milan and was awarded the only place left. Only 30 students were taken on. Oh, the privilege of being among young, challenging minds, damn good teachers, and a great job waiting for her at the end of it. She had done it all by herself. She needed no help, my Cabiria."

Agnese jumped. Cabiria was the 'friend' she'd been referring to: a sweet young woman who had entered her perfumery a few weeks ago, burdened with sadness. And Agnese had helped her as well as she could with her perfumes, although the whole thing had taken a rather unexpected turn when Cabiria decided all of a sudden to quit her Master's and take a year out volunteering in Nepal.

"Nepal, you see, is where she is right now," he muttered, waving the book angrily under Agnese's nose. "And all because of a madwoman who manipulates young minds."

Agnese gasped, her mouth wide open as if she couldn't take in enough air to breathe. Nennella came to her rescue.

"Maybe it wasn't this woman's fault at all. Maybe your

daughter just needed a break. After all, she's clearly worked hard all her young life."

"Maybe," Agnese found a few words, "she will learn things she could never have learned in Milan."

"Life has taught me there are no second chances. All these New Age beliefs about letting things happen as and when they're ready to happen are nothing but rubbish." He held up a copy of *Eat, Pray, Love* – the very book Cabiria had found in Agnese's shop – and slammed it against the counter as if it were responsible for all the wrongs in the world. "If you want your kids to succeed in life, you have to teach them to work hard, make plans and stick to them, because life will do its best to blow them away. Do you have any kids?" he asked Agnese.

"I do," she murmured.

"Then keep them away from this woman, whoever she is. Cabiria wouldn't tell me her name – I've no doubt the witch asked her not to. But we need to stop her."

He opened the book about Asia at a picture of a Nepalese town. Cables suspended in the air went from one shattered building to the next. An unpaved street was full of people dressed in the local clothes.

"Here, look, my Cabiria is in this hole."

"Maybe her generosity and skills will help those people, and in turn she might learn from them…"

The man raised his eyes to hers. In them she read the despair of a parent who believes his child has lost her way. Agnese knew his pain; she was a parent too, and despite having two wonderful, happy kids, she had felt the same doubts. Was she too strict? Was she too sweet? Had she given them the skills and mindset necessary to cope if life turned nasty?

The storm of questions sealed her lips.

The man turned to Nennella. "How many copies of this have you got?" He pointed to *Eat, Pray, Love*.

"I've got six," Nennella said, staring in dismay at the half torn copy the man still held in his hand.

"I'm taking them all, and this book on Asia."

He left with his bundle, stopping in front of the newsstand to drop six of the seven books in the first available bin. He kept only one: the guide to Asia. That was clearly his contribution to keeping Maratea safe for young people.

Agnese looked guiltily at Nennella. "I didn't tell him I'm the witch." She dropped the book she had picked up. "Forgive me, I'll be back when I feel better." As she left, her head sank down onto her chest. Not only was it her fault that Cabiria had left for Nepal, but she had recently sold a weird perfume to another young woman. Her thoughts ran to Ramya – what harm would come from that? And what about Edoardo and Mr Nasty?

Granny always said there are two certainties in life: the sun will rise again, no matter what, and it never rains, but it pours. As poor Agnese reached her shop, a tall, thin, elegant figure spoke angrily.

"As usual, you're late." Mrs Lavecchia, one of the most difficult clients Agnese had, was waiting for her. Agnese didn't even have time to think. Her legs ran, taking her away from the shop as fast as they could and only stopping when she was hidden in a narrow alley.

Opening her bag, she took out her phone with shaky hands and called Giò. The call went straight to voicemail. Frantically she phoned Nando instead. To her relief, he answered.

"Please, I can't go into the shop. Mrs Lavecchia is waiting for me. I can't cope with her just now, I had to run away."

Nando had no idea what had happened. "So you're launching your adoring hubby into the lions' cage," he teased, trying to break his wife out of the fear and despair she seemed to have fallen into. "I'm going, sweetheart, don't you worry, I'll take care of it all. You go back home, and tomorrow you can enjoy a day off and take the kids to the fair. You need a break."

"Oh, Nando, thanks so much…"

"Shh," he silenced her. "You take things too much to heart, but then that's why I love you. Go home, now."

19

NIGHT-TIME HUNTERS

G iò didn't get home until the evening. After a soothing outing on her kayak, she had gone to the local library to do some research, reading and note-taking. As she opened the main door of the building to go up to her attic, she found Granny waiting for her on the threshold of her ground-floor flat. She asked Giò to come in, a strange expression on her face.

"You weren't nosing out of the window, were you?"

"I was waiting for you," Granny corrected.

"That's what mobile phones are for: arranging to meet people."

"But they don't stimulate your observational skills as much as…"

"…spying from the window!"

Granny shook her head in denial. Looking out of her window was a favourite hobby of hers. She hadn't exactly been spying, as Giò had intimated; she had simply been waiting to exchange a few words… OK, gossip with any passer-by worthy of her attention.

"I think your sister has had a bad day."

"Why? What's happened to her?" Giò was instantly worried.

"Nothing much really, it's just that perfume game she loves

so much. It hasn't worked out as she thought it would a couple of times, and I think that's been the last straw for everything that's been building up inside her."

"What's that?"

"You know what she's like: she wants to be the perfect mum, wife, sister and granddaughter. In her shop, customers come to her with problems of all kinds, and she wants to help everyone who confides in her…"

"Oh the poor love," Giò said, thinking how many times she had complained at her sister for being too maternal with her.

"Come on in and I'll tell you more."

They sat in the large white living room and Granny told her what had happened. Giò laughed, imagining Mrs Lavecchia's face, but she was still concerned for her sister.

"I saw a missed call from her, but as she didn't leave a message and I was in the library, I forgot to call her back. I'll go to see her now."

"Oh no you don't, I haven't finished with you yet. Sit down. Your sister will be fine; she's got broad shoulders, she just needs a little break. Nando is going to stand in for her in the shop over the weekend so she can go to the fair in Trecchina, but he's also planning to fly her away somewhere for a week, just the two of them. I said we'd take care of the perfumery and the kids."

"Oh my goodness, if Mrs Lavecchia comes in then, it will be fun," said Giò, rubbing her hands together mischievously.

"I hope you won't put your sister out of business."

"Come on, I was only kidding."

"Now to the serious stuff," and Granny told Giò what had passed between her and the lawyer, leaving out any mention of anything related to cards and gambling.

"How did you manage to get anything out of that man? He's renowned for being as chatty as a brick wall."

"He couldn't resist a frail old lady."

"I'm not buying this," said Giò, looking suspiciously at Granny. "But well done, it's another piece of our puzzle. So the killer's lawyer suspects his client may have been innocent, and this coming from a man who's defended the worst criminals in Southern Italy. That's a piece of evidence not to be taken lightly."

"Do you want to stay with me for dinner?"

"No thanks, I'm really into writing at the moment, and as long as the inspiration lasts, I want to get down as much as I can."

"I see. How about your writing conference?"

"The results should be out tomorrow. I still have hope, though it's impossible to get hold of Kate."

"Hmmm."

"My suspicious Granny! I'd better go, but just remember: thanks to Kate, your granddaughter will finally be able to publish a real book rather than boring travel guides."

"Hmmm."

"You'll see."

Giò kissed Granny goodnight and retired to her attic. After writing for a while, she texted Paolo to update him, simply getting an irritating *"OK"* in response. She followed that with a better dinner than she'd anticipated as her fridge housed a spinach and ricotta pie from Granny, accompanied by a salad and a piece of paper saying, 'It's already been washed.' Granny couldn't cope with the thought of her granddaughter using bagged salad from the supermarket, which was never as fresh and tasty as a hand-picked version, but had the benefit – according to Giò – of being readily scoop-able out into a dish.

She sat on her balcony and ate her dinner, looking out over the sea into the distance. The fishermen's lamps shone here and there on the dark surface. When she'd finished, she tried once more to call Kate, and this time the woman picked up.

"Hello."

"Hello, Kate, this is Giò."

"Giò?"

"Yes, Maratea's Giò." She paused, waiting for a reaction that didn't come. "Giò Brando, the travel writer in Maratea."

"Joe Brando? Are you a man? Where's Maratea?"

"No, I'm Giovanna Brando. You and Mike met me in Maratea, you stayed at the Buon Giove Hotel…"

"Oh, that gorgeous place. Do you want us to come back?"

"Ahem, no, not really. I mean, I just called you for a quick update. I'm working hard to finish my Scottish travel guide so that I can make a start on my travel memoir…"

"*Another* travel memoir? Libraries and bookshops are bursting at the seams with travel memoirs. Everyone who's ever visited a nice resort or done a world cruise thinks they should write a memoir, and even worse, publish it."

"But you and Mike said my writing style was good enough…"

"Sure, sure, dear, you may be different. Why not write your memoir, and when you're done, we might come over to discuss it and review it. We want to make sure it won't sit on the shelves, only selling about twenty copies a year to family and friends. You will need an expert's advice. I must go now, but it was a real pleasure to hear from you. Let us know when you're done. Bye, dear."

"Bye, Kate, and thanks."

How strange was that? Why hadn't Kate recognised Giò from the outset? But then again, she must meet hundreds of people each week. But what about once she had realised who Giò really was? Surely she had only wanted to open Giò's eyes to the realities of the publishing industry, but Giò already knew it wasn't going to be a walk in the park. And having Kate on her side, available to review her work… wasn't it great?

Giò went to bed early to make the most of the following morning, her most productive time for writing, but she found herself tossing and turning, her thoughts on the murder, the wicked child, Tina Melly. The more she tried to soothe herself to sleep, the more her frenzied thoughts tormented her.

"Sleep and dreams, fiddlesticks!" she grumbled, finally switching on her bedside lamp and throwing off her duvet. The only remedy for her sporadic attacks of insomnia was walking. She threw her jeans on over her pyjamas, put on her jacket and shoes, and out she went.

As she walked down to Piazza Buraglia, a few bars and restaurants were still open. After all, it wasn't that late, and it was a Friday night. But she didn't fancy socialising, so she crossed the piazza with fast steps to take a little alley leading to the upper part of the village.

She loved Maratea by night: the shadowy paved streets; the yellow lamps projecting a warm light onto the white houses; an old building to let, its windows only half closed as if someone like Granny was peeping out from behind them. There was something mysterious and fascinating in each backstreet.

Giò climbed up to a small square – so small you could hardly call it a square – that could only be reached via a series of steps. In the middle of it stood a large, old wooden door, surrounded by an imposing wall. The funny thing was that behind the door, there was no building, but the view opened out over the mountains embracing Maratea. Tonight, even in the dark, she could still recognise their profiles thanks to a slice of moon shedding a feeble light.

Giò collected doors – or rather, photos or memories of them – that led nowhere. At times, they opened onto gardens, or directly onto the sea, or onto a wild landscape. She made an inventory of them and regarded them as magical, there to remind her that a surprise might lie behind the most mundane of things.

When she heard a strange noise coming from behind her, she turned abruptly but couldn't see anything unusual. She continued her walk, quick to immerse herself in her imagination. Reaching Maratea's main church, she stood by the small fountain to take everything in: the little square, the church standing off to its side; the 20-metre-high illuminated statue of Christ the Redeemer on top of the mountains, seemingly suspended in the black sky.

What was that? That noise again – were they footsteps? And again, the disturbing feeling of being watched. A black cat ran across the square and looked at her with shining green eyes. Was it he who had made the noise? Or was he running away from something, or someone?

Giò looked back in the direction she had come from. She had walked Maratea's streets countless times in the past, at a much later hour than today, but now – for the first time – she was feeling uneasy in her small town. Was that the shadow of a person hiding behind that low wall? Or was it her imagination?

She had no intention of finding out. Better head for home, taking the alley opposite. She moved quickly, trying to make as little noise as possible and relying on the labyrinth of alleys and streets to lose anyone who might be following.

As she started to descend a flight of steps, she heard the unmistakeable sound of someone walking behind her. She hurried on, holding her breath, but the footsteps continued, following her closely. Heading for a junction from which a tiny flight of steps stemmed, known only to a few people, she decided to hide and let the follower go ahead of her.

Running down the stairs in search of the spot, she turned abruptly to her right, squatting down and keeping her ears wide open.

Her blood froze in her veins as she felt a hand on her shoulder. She looked up slowly in horror, opening her mouth, but no sound came out of it.

Mr Nasty was facing her, his face distorted in a hideous grin, his hand shaking her shoulders.

"Why were you running away?"

Giò, still unable to speak, gulped a few times.

They were in the oldest part of the town. Not a single light shone from any of the windows; in fact, most of the houses were in a rundown state and were up for sale, and even the habitable ones were mainly empty, being second homes of holidaymakers.

Nobody lived in this area in autumn. She'd have to be ready to fight her way out.

Mr Nasty was breathing loudly. He was clearly not used to exercise, which she could turn to her advantage if she could free herself from his grasping hand.

"Why were you running away?" he repeated after a few deep breaths.

"Why were *you* chasing me?" she finally managed.

"I wasn't chasing, just following…"

"I could argue that point, but then again, it's not important. Why were you *following* me?"

"Because I need to speak to you."

"Why?"

"Well to start with, can't we find a more comfortable place to talk?"

This was good news. Giò could hardly imagine a better place for someone to strangle her than where she was squatting right now. Anywhere else would be a safer place.

She simply nodded her assent. He handed her his claw of a hand to help her stand up and surprised her with his next question.

"Where's the main square?"

"Down that way," she murmured.

In silence, they descended to Piazza Buraglia and Leo's bar.

"Hello, Giò, not writing tomorrow morning then?" Leo said, looking at his watch. He could be a writing coach, he knew the habits of authors and creatives so well.

"Taking a break for the weekend," lied Giò.

"Well done. You look pale, you're definitely working too hard. What can I get for you? A lager?"

"A double whisky."

Leo's brows almost reached his bald patch in surprise.

"And for you, sir?"

"A beer and no more chat, if that's possible."

As Leo left the table, Giò looked at him in anger.

"How dare you address Leo so rudely! Especially after what you've just done to me."

The man looked flabbergasted, as if he believed he had merely invited her for a drink.

"What have I done to you? You make me run like a madman all over town, and now I'm tired and thirsty and the guy wants to waste 15 minutes talking to you before taking my order. If he does the same with every table he serves, I'll get my beer in two days' time."

Giò banged her forehead with her hand. "My goodness, you're totally deranged, but maybe you really don't realise what you did. But let's leave it at that. What do you want from me?"

A waitress put down their drinks. The man took a few large gulps. Giò took a sip from her glass, coughing hard.

"Not used to whisky, are you?"

"Of course I am," she lied as soon as she'd recovered from the fire burning her throat and stomach. The man smirked at her, and Giò shrugged as dignified a response as she could manage. Then imitating the man, she addressed him bluntly.

"Well, I don't have the whole night. What do you want?"

For the first time, he seemed to have difficulty coming up with a suitable reply, grimacing more than ever as if his mouth was made of dough. Giò drummed her fingers on the table.

"I'm waiting, but not for long," she snapped, even though her glass was almost as full as when the waitress had brought it to the table.

"Well, you know that woman. The one with the red curls."

"Vanda?"

"That's her. You're friends with her?"

The answer was so obvious, Giò didn't even nod.

"Well, I've seen her around. I mean, around that stupid man. The one from the bookshop who's always dressed up as if he's going to dance the night away at an old-fashioned ball."

"That's none of your business."

"I thought you cared for your friend."

"Of course I do, but I can't see how Edoardo is a problem."

"I don't like the stupid fop. I don't think he's good for her."

"My goodness, is that it? Are you jealous? Do you fancy Vanda?"

"Fancy who? The red-haired woman? Never! She's as stubborn as a herd of mules."

"Then why are you bothering me?"

"I thought you were her friend and you'd care. I think that fop is after something."

"What makes you say that?"

"Just the way he behaves around her."

"Quite frankly, I can't see the point of this conversation at all, Mister…" Realising she didn't know his real surname, she carried on regardless. "I think you should mind your own business, and if you've got feelings for Vanda, speak to her directly. But I wouldn't badmouth an honest man, that won't help you to get what you want!"

She stood up.

"You ain't finished your whisky."

"You need good company to drink whisky."

"You're just as stubborn as the red-haired woman. I can see I've wasted my time."

Enough was enough. Giò turned around and left the man to protest to fresh air.

20

MYSTERIOUS WAYS

It was the phone ringing that woke Giò the following morning, at nine o'clock. Damn! She had probably switched the alarm off earlier on and gone back to sleep. And where was the wretched thing?

When her hand landed on her phone, she looked at the screen: Annika, a fellow travel writer from Sweden. Giò said a couple of sentences out loud before answering, not wanting to sound as though she'd been fast asleep at nine o'clock in the morning.

"Hello!"

"Hello, Giò, how are you doing?"

"Fine, thanks."

"You weren't sleeping, were you?"

"Course not, just got a bit of a cold."

"Imagine catching a cold when you live in such a sunny climate."

"Quite!"

"Anyway, have you seen the results? They're having the Travel Writers' Con in Italy this year."

"Yesss!" Giò shouted. She was already picturing herself in front of the audience, thanking them for coming over to her hometown and sharing with them the secrets and hard work of finding a publisher and a solid project for her new book. She would tell them of the strain and the pain, and that by the time next year's conference came around, she'd have a book out.

"And not too far from you," Annika was saying.

"Maratea?"

Annika laughed. "Don't take me so literally! It's to be in Rome, which is… what? Only three hours' drive from your home?"

"Rome?" Giò gasped. Kate and Mike had never mentioned Rome. "How do you know?"

"It's on the Travel Writers' Conference website. But why are you so surprised? The organisers have been taking an interest in Rome since last year, when an important publisher first suggested it."

"It can't be Rome, it has to be Maratea!"

"Come on, Giò, you know how far you are from an airport."

"But it's supposed to be a travellers' conference, attended by people who have visited the remotest places on earth!"

"But it's still a conference. You weren't really expecting it to be in as small a place as Maratea, were you?"

"I thought you loved the place."

"Of course I do. In fact, as soon as I saw the conference was to be in Rome, I thought how nice it'd be to come on a writer's retreat there, either before or after the conference. I'd love to spend some time in Maratea, maybe even live there for a while."

No reply.

"Giò, are you still there?"

"I am, but I don't understand. If Rome was already a done deal, why did Kate and Mike come here at all?"

"Kate? You don't mean Kate Advantage, do you?"

"Yes, her. She's on the committee to decide the location for the conference each year."

"More like the committee to scrounge free nights in fabulous locations. She and her sidekick."

"Mike Profit?"

"Him. Don't tell me they came to Maratea?"

"They did, a week ago."

"I hope you didn't pay for their accommodation."

"In fact, that's exactly what I did."

"Oh, Giò, by that time the committee would have already decided to host it in Rome. How did you think they'd decide in such a short time?"

Giò was finally realising what in truth had been staring her in the face. Then an even worse thought flashed across her mind.

"My book!" she whispered frantically.

"Giò, they didn't say that you're a fabulous writer and they're going to introduce you to a top publisher or an agent, did they?"

"How did you know?"

"And that was before you paid their hotel bill?"

"How stupid! How stupid of me! But they said I was special, that they had read my guides and found something unique in my writing style…"

"They're scammers, especially as they know how much endeavour we put into our work and how welcome compliments and appreciation are. I'm so sorry, Giò, that it had to be me who shattered your dream."

"Deep down, I think I knew it was too good to be true. But if you don't mind… I'll call you back. It's a bitter pill to swallow."

"Sure, but I just wanted to tell you about plans to organise a retreat for independent authors, maybe in springtime. Olga Thross is creating something beautiful where we can help each other. Giò, are you there?"

"Annika, I need to go now, but I promise I'll call you back soon."

Giò put down the phone, but she didn't have time to lie on the sofa and cry all her misery away. There was a knock on her door.

"Auntieee, are you at home?" Lilia, her niece, wanted her to accompany the family to the fair.

Sorry, Lilia, not today. I'll be no company to you, or to Agnese.

And to exacerbate how miserable she felt, she ignored her niece, pretending not to be in.

∽

Agnese, Luca and Lilia participated in the treasure hunt in Trecchina Forest. The carabinieri had patrolled the area early that morning, fearing the killer might have dropped another corpse there, but they'd found nothing and had allowed the game to go ahead. When Nando joined them at lunchtime, he found that his family had come sixth, winning ten kilogrammes of chestnuts and a tray of *marrons glacés* from the local pastry shop. Agnese's cheeks were rosy and red from the exercise and the fresh air. She was smiling and hugged her husband in gratitude.

"Mum, I'm starving," Luca said, proud of having led his family to victory. "It must be the mountain air, I'm always hungry when we're in Trecchina."

"The school street food stalls should be ready to serve food by now. Shall we go check them out?"

"Maybe that girl will be serving the same dessert she cooked last time." Lilia was especially fond of dessert.

As they made their way through Piazza del Popolo, Vanda joined them. She had been working hard, organising her teams as she wanted to make up for her absence the previous weekend.

"You've done an excellent job of fundraising," said Agnese. "The arts and crafts stalls are literally swamped with customers."

Vanda smiled. "And the food stalls too, from what I've seen."

"That's exactly where we're heading, the menus last time were unbelievable," Luca said, patting his tummy.

"I've just come from there and the smells are delicious… except for team three, I'm afraid."

"The lasagne team?"

"Yes, they're doing the same menu again."

"We're still going to have a look at their stall," Agnese said. "Last time, they managed to serve an excellent dessert."

As Vanda left, Agnese and Lilia sat on the long benches among the trees, while Nando and Luca headed for the stalls. When they came back, they had trays full of all sorts of delicious food that the people sitting next to them were already eating with satisfaction.

"Just a pity about the lasagne. I don't think there's any chance we'll get anything from that stall."

"Lilia and I will go over later to see if Ramya is cooking her dessert."

Despite the laughter and chatter around them, despite the loud music, Agnese and her family could still hear Erica shouting at her team. A line of boys and girls, all crimson with embarrassment and mostly looking down at their feet, they weren't daring to acknowledge the few encouraging remarks from clients queuing in front of them.

"You're so stupid! Yet again, we're not getting anywhere. Giuseppe, you're a total idiot, and you, Mariangela, are so slow. And, Ramya, don't even think about making that dessert of yours. You won't get all the glory this time." And with that, Erica threw a glass of vinegar in the dough Ramya had been trying to hide from her as a last resort.

Ramya raised her gaze from the ruined dough to look straight into Erica's face, her black eyes burning with anger. Erica backed off a couple of steps.

"Yes, you'd better walk away as quickly as you can," Ramya growled in a low voice, all the more menacing for being so quiet.

There was a long pause as the two looked fiercely at each other. Then in the same low voice, Ramya continued.

"You stubborn, stupid, spoiled brat, you'd better disappear."

Erica clearly wanted to regain her authority, but before she could utter a single word, Ramya roared, "NOW!"

Again the two girls stared at each other for a long moment,

like two gunslingers in the Wild West, then unexpectedly, Erica removed her apron and threw it in Ramya's face.

"I should have left earlier and had nothing to do with such a bunch of losers."

Ramya turned to the rest of the team, who were staring at her with incredulous expressions on their faces.

"Now, let's get back to what we were doing." Her voice was firmer than they'd ever heard it before. Ramya showed Giuseppe exactly how she wanted him to cut the onions, then she moved on to Mariangela to help her prepare the lasagne layers.

"The sauce first, not too much, not too little, then plenty of parmesan, some cubes of mozzarella and fresh basil leaves. Come on, you can do it."

One by one, Ramya encouraged each of her teammates, giving commands, shouting praise, correcting when necessary and controlling her little army. How she could find the time to do her own work as well was a mystery to Agnese, who had stopped eating to watch the girl.

"Hurry up, Simone, you're almost there. But be quick."

"Mariangela, that works perfectly. It's beautiful, they will love it. Now, you've just got to repeat the process all over again, a bit faster."

"Come on, Giuseppe, you've got the right idea, but you need to be much faster. I'll show you."

No one on the team had time to look at their feet; they were all concentrating hard on what they were doing and learning from Ramya. Thirty minutes later, the queue in front of the stall had grown huge. The delicious aroma of the lasagne had spread all over the square, and despite people already having full stomachs, they didn't want to miss out.

"Antonella, you need to cut equal slices. Take your time… but hurry up. And don't forget to tell the customers to come back for dessert."

"Simone, have you changed the oil in the frying pan?"

"Mariangela, this is too big, let's start all over again together.

I'll show you how to do it."

One hour later, not a single crumb was left on the third stall. Every now and then, a hopeful customer would approach, just to make sure there wasn't a delicious morsel left. Agnese was excited and proud to see the transformation in Ramya; she and Lilia left the menfolk happy and contented at the table and went over to compliment her.

The girl had just finished coordinating her team in cleaning up, but now a lost expression was crossing her face. She exchanged glances with Agnese, then looked at her team, who were still staring at her, amazed at the radical transformation that had occurred. Only then did Agnese recognise it was pure horror on Ramya's face. She unlaced her apron and let it fall to the floor as she ran away, sobbing.

"Lilia, you're faster than I am. Please follow her and find out what's the matter."

Lilia hurtled along Trecchina's main street ahead of her mother. When Agnese finally caught her up, she and Ramya were in front of the little Forraina Chapel at the end of the village. Ramya was sitting on a bench below the chestnut trees, crying her heart out. Lilia had an arm around her shoulders, but neither she nor her mother could make sense of what Ramya was saying.

"My dear girl, what's the matter? You did a great job," said Agnese, sitting beside Ramya and catching her breath. Between gulps and sobs that were almost choking her, Ramya finally uttered a few coherent words.

"I was shouting. I was hollering at them, bullying them. I don't know what happened to me."

"No, you were wonderful, Ramya. What are you saying?"

"I was acting like a monster. I think it was the perfume. I felt a dark shadow coming over me."

Agnese shook her head in disbelief.

"Ramya, I don't know what you felt, but you were the best leader I've ever seen. You weren't bullying them; you were fighting beside them, helping and supporting them, showing them exactly what they had to do, and working hard yourself."

"I swear it wasn't me, I could never be that rude."

"But nobody thought you were rude!" Agnese continued, caressing Ramya's shiny black hair. "You were energising. There are moments when we can't be all kindness and tenderness."

"You were a perfect role model," Lilia said. "When I grow up, I want to be just like you."

Ramya finally smiled at Lilia, accepting a tissue from Agnese.

"I think we should go back to the fair. Your team is missing you."

"I don't know if I can ever face them again," Ramya said, hiding her face in her cupped hands, her voice the soft and gentle one Agnese remembered. Nonetheless, they left the little chapel, the forest on their left and a patchwork of red-tiled roofs below them on their right.

In the main square, Ramya's team was waiting for her.

"We won!" they screamed at her in delight. "We won the competition for the best dessert *and* first course."

Ramya again covered her face with her hands, saying, "I can't believe it." Her team surrounded her, and before she knew what was happening, they were launching her slight body into the air as she laughed and screamed at the same time.

"For our captain, the best captain ever, hip-hip hooray!" And up into the air Ramya went as the headmistress officially proclaimed Team 3 the competition winners, inviting the whole team to join her on stage. The crowd clapped enthusiastically, grateful for the best lasagne they had eaten in ages. Only one stubborn, stupid, spoiled girl and her mother didn't join in, instead glaring at the stage with livid faces.

We can't be goody-goodies all the time, Agnese thought, still marvelling at what had happened. *There's a time for laughing and for gentleness, but there's also a time for fighting. Perhaps Outrageous Carnation wasn't such a bad choice for Ramya after all. I shouldn't have doubted my perfumes – they work in mysterious ways.*

21

TIME TO TURN THE PAGE

After a hideous lunch consisting of a microwave meal she had in the fridge, Giò made an attempt to do some more research and take notes on her laptop, slamming books down whenever she couldn't find what she was looking for.

"To be fooled by two old scammers like them. How stupid of me. Paying all that money for the stupid hotel, and dinner, and going to the airport to pick them up. Damn!" And she let a heavy dictionary fall onto the floor. Agnese and her family weren't in anyway. But the truth was that she was so hurt, it'd take a lot more than a bit of slamming and banging to make her feel better. "Telling me how good a writer I was when they'd never read a single line written by me." Here a little tear of self-pity made its way from her right eye and rolled down her cheek. She was quick to wipe it away angrily with the back of her hand.

"Agnese isn't well, but instead of supporting her, here I am thinking about myself. But no, I can't go to the fair in this state. I'd hurt her rather than help." She started to read another paragraph about the Scottish Grampians, but stopped short.

"I'm going mad!" she howled, springing up. "I need to get out or I'm likely to destroy this home of mine."

Kayaking had become her cure-all medicine. Was she feeling

stuck in her work? Was she mad at her sister? Was she thinking about her called-off wedding? Was she having doubts about ever making it as a writer? Once on the water, once she had the paddle in her hands and had found her rhythm, it would ease her mind. Maybe she wouldn't find all the answers to her questions, but her brooding thoughts would give her a break.

Giò packed her rucksack, changed into something comfortable and, without even brushing her teeth, opened her door. A second later, she was screaming and backing off – someone was standing in front of her.

"It's only me," said Granny.

"Is everyone in Maratea determined to be the death of me?" Giò cried, thinking of Mr Nasty the night before. "What are you doing hiding behind my door?"

Giò was sure that Granny blushed, a rare phenomenon.

"I was going to slip this article under your door. It's about Scotland and I thought you might find it useful for your guide."

Giò grabbed the page from Granny's hands, but kept glaring at her. "And you weren't eavesdropping, were you?"

"There was no need for me to do that, you were shouting so loud."

"I was shouting because Agnese is not at home, and you're on the ground floor so you shouldn't have been able to hear me."

"You weren't saying anything I didn't already know. It was obvious that those two were con artists from the moment they refused to go to the Conference Hotel. As for Agnese, as I said, she's made of tough stuff, and Nando will help her through, so no need for you to drown in a sense of guilt."

"I can't believe it, you heard it all! You could at least pretend you hadn't."

"If you want, I can do that…"

"Never mind, what's this?" And Giò flattened the sheet of paper Granny had handed to her on the table. "But this is about Icelandic literature, nothing I'm working on at the moment."

"Turn it over."

And on the other side was a beautiful article about Glencoe and a few Scottish legends – just the kind of thing Giò adored. But she didn't even think about thanking Granny. She held the page in her hand and kept turning it.

"Turn it over! Have we been that stupid? Wait here, and please try not to speak for the next five minutes."

Giò frantically recovered her phone from her rucksack and made a call.

"Hello, Giò, so good to hear from you."

"Hello, Martine, I'm afraid I don't have any news. But I do have a question. You remember the article you found in your stepmother's letter?"

"Of course I do."

"Was it a photocopy or a real page torn from a magazine?"

"It was a page torn from a magazine."

"But you only sent me a photograph of one side of the page."

"I didn't think there was anything relevant on the other side."

"What was it?"

"I can't remember, really. But why?"

"Explanations later. Do the police have the page now?"

"Correct."

"Can you ask them to let you see what's on the other side?"

"I'm not sure they will return it to me while the investigations are ongoing. Also we're in Chandolin for the weekend. I could go to the *police cantonale* in Berne on Monday and let you know. Do you think it's that important?"

"It's just an idea at the moment. I'll check with the local carabinieri, maybe they have both pages."

Giò phoned Paolo, who phoned Massimo, but the answer was that the Swiss police had only sent a copy of the page that seemed to be more relevant.

"Oh my goodness, am I really supposed to wait till Monday?" Giò growled, putting down the phone.

"That depends on you," Granny interrupted her train of thought. "Do you want that magazine page now?"

"Of course I do, oh wise one."

"Then I'd suggest you go to the library. They should have a subscription to all the area's magazines. Maybe you can make out the name of the magazine from your picture."

"The library! Why didn't I think of that?" Giò patted Granny's cheek and left with her rucksack and all she needed for a kayak ride, forgetting she was no longer going kayaking at all. Left behind, Granny looked in horror at the remains of Giò's lunch.

"Microwaved food? This girl really needs a husband to take good care of her!"

PAOLO WAS ALREADY IN FRONT OF THE LIBRARY, WAITING FOR GIÒ IN response to the voicemail message she had left. On the photocopied page he held, the name of the magazine wasn't visible, but the librarian was easily able to identify it from its format and style.

"We don't have many magazines from the area," she explained. "This one comes out weekly, so I'd start with the January and February issues from this year, when the murder occurred." And she handed them the journals.

"There it is!" Giò cried after a few minutes. With trembling hands, she turned the page. "The monthly readers' club, presenting the book it has chosen for January, and an article on Mr Enrico Nascimale, a successful local entrepreneur!"

"I know that man," said Paolo.

"I know him too," said Giò, looking at the magazine photograph that was unmistakeably of Mr Nasty. "Do you think this was the photograph that Tina Melly wanted us to look at?"

"Well, I don't know what you know about him, Giò, but he's the adventure park owner."

Giò gasped. "You mean where Tina Melly's body was found?"

"Exactly."

"And the carabinieri didn't interview him at the time?"

"Of course they did, but he had a cast-iron alibi. But now we should investigate in more depth."

"Does this mean we might have solved the case?"

"Possibly. Tina Melly pointed us in the direction of this man, but didn't accuse him just in case her suspicions were wrong. Now we need to find out if there's a link between Nascimale and Tina."

"I can find that out easily." She searched for the phone number of Pasqualina, the housekeeper in Naples, and after some small talk, Giò asked her if she had ever heard of Mr Enrico Nascimale, putting her mobile on speakerphone mode.

"Oh yes, that's the name I was looking for. He was the awful child, always doing bad things to little girls. Particularly those with red hair, if I remember rightly. Tina told Mum he'd make them cry by locking them up and cutting their hair, and then he'd try to strangle them. Luckily, he was too small to really harm them. Tina said to my mum that he needed serious help, but his family did nothing and just said he was a lively kid."

When they finished the call, Giò looked triumphantly at Paolo. "I think we've found the killer, haven't we?"

"Yes, Giò, we finally have our suspect, and maybe we can piece together the chain of events. Tina recognised the child in the photo of the grown man."

"Look at this birthmark on his forehead," Giò said, thinking of how she had only ever seen him wearing a hat. "It makes him instantly recognisable even as a grownup, and when Tina read his name, she would have had no doubt it was him."

"Then she turns the page and reads about a murder that has been committed where he now lives. And the victim was a young woman with red hair, and she was strangled."

"She reads that another man has been charged with the murder, but she is suspicious – too many coincidences. She decides to come and have a look in person, to speak to

Nascimale and make sure that an innocent man hasn't been falsely accused."

"She knew it might be risky, so she drops the magazine article in an envelope and writes a letter to Martine, hoping that if she doesn't return, the police will do all necessary checks and uncover the relationship between her and Nascimale. But none of us made the connection because we were looking at the wrong page, until now!"

"Are you going to arrest him?"

"Arrest him? Come on, Giò, there's no proof. We will certainly check his alibi thoroughly, though, and his past."

"I bet he was the one who threatened me, slashing my tyre. And he was following me last night."

"Following you?"

Again my big mouth has given me away, Giò thought gloomily, and she had to tell Paolo all about the previous night.

"Didn't I tell you to be careful?" was Paolo's angry reply. "And the first thing you do is go walking by yourself late at night."

"I would never have done that in Trecchina, but I thought in Maratea I would be safe."

"Giò, he could have hurt you, badly."

"I'm surprised he didn't. I wonder why."

"I believe he thinks he's safe. Tina knew his story and had to die, but despite you and Vanda looking around, so far no evidence has pointed in his direction."

"Until today."

"Exactly."

"Could it be that he's killed other women before?"

"If he's really the wicked child, that's likely. Not in Trecchina, but maybe he found his victims in large cities where it's far easier to remain anonymous. We will check unsolved cases of murder by strangulation, especially where the victim was a red-haired woman."

"Vanda!"

"Vanda what?"

"She went for dinner with the man on the day we went to Naples. He's got some sort of interest in her – he spoke to me about her last night. And she has red hair."

"Tell her to stay away from him. I'm sure the carabinieri in Trecchina will put him under strict surveillance, don't worry."

Giò stood up and walked up and down the library, brooding. She finally stopped in front of Paolo.

"We can't take that route, Paolo."

"What route?"

"The do-nothing-and-see-what-happens route. It's too risky – he's killed twice and he's attracted to Vanda. And we know how these things work. There aren't enough carabinieri; they will do their best, but as soon they lower their guard, he will strike. Or maybe he doesn't intend his next victim to be Vanda at all…"

"You've already got a plan running through your head, haven't you?"

She grinned.

"You surely don't want to use Vanda as bait?"

"Nope, there's no need to expose her to further danger. Let's use the same strategy we used for Mr Rivello a few weeks ago…"

"That was very risky, Giò. We only saved you by chance."

"This time you will be there all the time. I will tell Nascimale that I have incriminating evidence against him and provoke him into confessing all."

"I don't like it."

"But, Paolo, it's the only way we can stop him. He'll either confess or attempt to murder me. It seems he doesn't use any weapon but his hands, so you will have plenty of time to stop him. He knows I've been investigating the case, he knows I'm Vanda's friend – it's our chance to stop him before he hurts someone else."

"How are you going to convince him to speak to you?"

"That will be the easy part. As I told you last night, he was chasing me because he wanted to know things about Vanda, and maybe if I had stayed longer, he would have asked me about the investigations too."

Finally Paolo gave in.

22

GREAT EXPECTATIONS

Giò didn't sleep a wink. Mindful of what Paolo had told her, she kept her word to him and didn't venture out on any more night-time meanderings. Maybe it was safe and secure for her to stay at home, but it did nothing for her impatience.

When the first ray of light finally lit up the sea beyond her terrace, she sighed with relief: the long night was finally over.

At 8am, she couldn't resist any longer and called Vanda.

"You're up early on a Sunday," Vanda said.

"I hope I didn't wake you up."

"Of course you didn't. I'm meeting Edoardo for a picnic in the forest and…" she laughed nervously, "I have butterflies in my stomach. I'm like a teenager on a first date."

"Oh my goodness, you've finally dropped your guard?"

"You're right, Giò, I've been putting barriers up for far too long. But it seems this guy has worked his magic on me."

"Aren't you busy with the fair anymore?"

"Not really. Yesterday we had the grand final of the cookery competition, which was so good – it's a pity you weren't there. Today, Edoardo and I will drop in at some point in the afternoon, but I will be relaxing as a guest. Then there's the official opening of the adventure park this evening."

"Busy schedule."

"And you called because you smelled romance in the air?"

"Not really, I didn't think the first kiss moment had arrived."

"Giò!"

"Come on, it's the natural course of things. But you're right, I did call you for a reason. You've got Mr Nasty's phone number, haven't you?"

"Yes. I'm not particularly proud of it, but I have it. What do you need it for?"

Giò had been expecting that question. "I know someone in the UK interested in his line of business and they asked me for a contact."

"Well, I'm happy to hear that. Did I tell you that the dinner I had with him wasn't as bad as I thought it'd be?"

"Yes, but I prefer to know that you're having your picnic with Edoardo. And by the way, it's not nice to date two men at the same time," Giò teased.

"Giovanna Brando, how dare you imply anything like that! I just said that he isn't as bad as he seems, not that I have any interest in him."

"Of course, I was just pulling your leg."

"I'll send you his contact details via WhatsApp."

"Thanks a lot, and enjoy your picnic. I'll possibly see you two at the fair this afternoon, hand in hand …"

"Shhh! I already feel sick with nerves." Vanda laughed, ending the call.

Now the hard part, thought Giò, *the call to Mr Nasty*. She had agreed with Paolo not to give herself away from the outset. They didn't want Enrico Nascimale to suspect anything until he and Giò met; she would catch him by surprise then.

"Hello?"

"Hello, it's Giò Brando here. Vanda's friend. Do you remember?"

"Course I do, the whisky drinker. But what time do you call this?"

"Almost 8.30."

"On a Sunday?"

His voice sounded even more grumpy than usual. Had she made her first mistake? Had she called him too early to be believable? She couldn't allow herself the luxury of doubt, not now.

"I'm sorry if I dragged you out of bed, but I've been thinking over what you told me about Vanda and the bookshop owner. In fact, I'm quite concerned myself."

He muttered something undistinguishable, but he sounded more satisfied. Encouraged, she continued.

"I need to speak to you, and it would be better in person than on the phone."

"Do you want me to come to Maratea?"

"No, I'll come to Trecchina. I've been working so hard recently, I wouldn't mind a walk in the forest, and we can talk privately along the way."

"At least there won't be one of those silly treasure hunts today," he replied, back to sounding grumpy.

"Shall we meet in the main square?"

"Oh no, there will be tons of people there – that stupid fair is still on. How about leaving our cars by the Forraina Chapel? There's a nice path into the forest from there."

"That's perfect," she said, in her mind adding, *and that's not far from where you took Tina Melly's body and hit Vanda on the head. Killers always return to the crime scene.*

A shiver went down her spine.

"Ten o'clock at the chapel," he said. She would have preferred to get it over and done with as soon as possible, but if she were to insist on urgency, she'd arouse his suspicions.

"Absolutely fine," she said, wondering if the man needed the extra time to organise things. Things involving her…

∽

VANDA PUT ON HER FAVOURITE WHITE DRESS PRINTED WITH POPPIES. She'd heard some say that red-haired people shouldn't wear red lipstick or clothing, but she felt a little red on the white background was just perfect. Her children would hardly have recognised their mother, so often in severely tailored trousers, now looking girlish, and frankly, dating wasn't how she'd imagined passing her time once her children had both flown the nest.

She looked at her face: she looked exhilarated, but maybe also a little scared. Giò had mentioned a kiss. How long since she'd last kissed a man? After the divorce she'd had a couple of love affairs, but they'd done nothing to help her regain her trust in men. On the contrary.

She sighed, but it was more as a matter of habit than with real conviction. In fact, when she looked up at the mirror, she found a smile printed on her face and a certain twinkle in her eyes she hadn't seen for a while. The past was the past; it was the present that now mattered.

FINALLY, THOUGHT PAOLO, ANSWERING HIS PHONE. IT WAS GIÒ, telling him where and when she had arranged to meet Nascimale. Paolo reassured her he'd follow in his own car at a distance and park somewhere out of sight, coming after them along the path from the Forraina Chapel.

"Have you already planned what you're going to say?" he asked.

"Not really, but had you met the guy, you'd know it doesn't take much to make him furious. He's of the foul-tempered kind, so I know how to handle him."

"I just hope this isn't the most foolish plan we could have come up with."

"Oh please! This isn't the time for doubt."

At 9.30 they met on Town Hall Square, chatted, and cracked a couple of stupid jokes to try to diffuse the tension. Ten minutes later, they got into their separate cars and drove towards Trecchina. Paolo stayed close behind Giò's car as they headed up to Passo Colla, then he dropped behind as they approached Trecchina. She passed the village and took a small road on the right that led to the chapel. Paolo stopped before the last curve, 300 metres before the chapel, and waited a couple of minutes, then got out of his car. Heading slowly towards the chapel, he made sure he'd spot Giò and Nascimale before they could see him, using the large horse chestnut trees along the road as camouflage.

When he reached Giò's car, there was a white car parked beside it. The two drivers had already gone.

"I hope I haven't given them too much of a head start," he murmured, leaving the chapel behind and heading for the path into the forest.

ENRICO NASCIMALE WAS ALREADY WAITING IN FRONT OF THE chapel, standing beside his car when Giò arrived. He showed her where she should park, and as she got out of her car, he opened the door to his.

"Let's go up to the Madonna del Soccorso Sanctuary. It's much more beautiful up there; here there are still too many chestnut pickers."

"But it's so nice in the forest here."

"From there, we will be able to enjoy the view all the way down to Calabria and the Isola di Pino."

Giò had no choice but to get into his car. *Paolo will follow us.* But as they left, a white car passed them, coming down from the direction of the Sanctuary, and parked right beside Giò's car.

I hope that won't mislead Paolo, she thought. *I wonder if he saw it or whether he's still too far down the road. I'd better send him a text, just in case.* Also, she needed to get some sort of conversation going with the man in the driving seat so as not to arouse his suspicion. But how do you chat with a man who would rather bark than speak?

"It's another sunny day," she threw out dejectedly. Was that the best she could come up with?

He didn't reply.

"Yesterday was such a lovely day too – it's weird to think we're in the middle of autumn."

He gave her one of his weird contorted smiles as if he was responsible for the wonderful weather, then turned his attention back to the winding road. Only then did Giò notice the brown leather gloves he was wearing. Were they the reason why no fingerprints had been found on any of his victims? Why was he wearing them now? Had he already made a plan to get rid of her?

With as casual an air as she could manage, she completed her text and sent it to Paolo. Looking again at the gloves, she felt grateful, knowing the brigadiere would be behind them in a matter of minutes.

Nascimale stretched out his gloved right hand. Giò gulped with fear, but he only switched on a CD. The lovely voice of Ella Fitzgerald filled the car.

"This is real music, not the crows who pretend to be singers nowadays."

Giò nodded in approval – the same approval she'd give to a lunatic asserting that the sun was green.

"So where are we heading?" asked Vanda.

Edoardo had dressed with his usual effortless elegance: sporty blue jacket over jeans, a scarf around his neck. His cheeks were pale, almost translucent above his trimmed beard, but he had no distinctive features apart from his blue irises outlined in black. There was something innocent about his appearance that surprised Vanda each time they met.

He smiled his warm smile, displaying white teeth between pink lips.

"Are you ready for our picnic?"

"Of course, I can't wait for it. But I promised the headmistress I'd visit the fair after lunch. There will be prizes to award to the students."

"We'll stay close to the town, don't worry."

He closed her passenger door and they left.

"So where are we heading?" she asked again, full of curiosity.

"As we don't have all day, I thought we could have a look at the attraction park before it fills up with people for the grand opening this afternoon."

That's where we found Tina Melly, but Vanda nodded to Edoardo. *It's such a popular destination, I'd better get used to the idea of it being just an ordinary place like any other.*

"And there's a beautiful view from there," he added.

"The tourists will love it too," Vanda replied. "I have to hand it to Mr Nasty, he had a great idea to build a park here."

"Mr Nasty?"

"Oops, I meant Mr Nascimale, Enrico Nascimale. Giò calls him Mr Nasty for fun, and I'm afraid it's stuck."

"Is he that strange man with the lopsided face? And quite a number of nervous tics? Always grumbling and giving people a hard time?"

Vanda laughed. "That's him!"

"He doesn't like me at all. He's always giving me dirty looks and muttering things – rather too loudly – when I pass."

"I don't think it's anything personal, he behaves like that with everybody."

"Well he didn't seem that nasty the other night when you were having dinner together." Edoardo's blue eyes lingered on her for a couple of seconds before returning to the winding road.

Vanda blushed, but she couldn't help feeling contented that

Edoardo had shown a hint of jealousy. She laughed to dispel her embarrassment.

"That was only a business dinner – he's an important sponsor for our school. I was dreading it, to be honest, but I must admit, he behaved much better than I'd expected."

He looked at her again, and before she knew what she was doing, she'd slipped her hand over his.

"Really, you've no need to worry. At least not about him."

His right hand left the gear lever and gripped hers strongly – maybe a bit too strongly.

"Ouch!" she whispered, pulling her hand from his grip.

"I'm sorry, it's this stupid winding road," he said, and the hand returned to the gear lever as he smiled sheepishly.

When they arrived at the adventure park, Edoardo parked his car a few hundred metres from the main entrance.

"We can park closer…"

"Only closer to the main gate." He walked around the car to open her door. "We'll get in through the other gate that's open at all times." As she got out of the car, his eyes moved from her slender figure to her curly red hair, and his hand gently invited her to spin around as if they were dancing. She laughed as he gave her an appreciative look.

"Did I tell you, you look so very pretty?"

"You didn't," she said, her finger wagging in front of her eyes as if she were admonishing him.

He laughed. "Then I apologise. You look gorgeous." He put an arm around her shoulders as they walked towards the gate, giving her goose bumps. She looked around her, wondering if a cloud had covered the sun.

You stupid woman, have you forgotten everything? It's got nothing to do with the temperature.

PAOLO ENTERED THE FOREST APPREHENSIVELY, CAREFUL NOT TO

make any noise. He'd rather have Giò in his radar, as he suddenly realised he couldn't remember whether there were any forks in this path.

He hurried forward. *I wonder where they are, I can't hear a single noise.* Well, except for the rustling of the fallen leaves under his shoes and a few birds singing in the distance, probably to raise the alarm that another two-legged animal was making its way into the forest.

Could they have walked this far already? Has Giò realised yet that I'm not within earshot?

Then came the moment that Paolo had been dreading: he was facing a fork. The main path split into two, one track heading upwards, the other downwards. He stopped and studied the leafy carpet, trying to find tracks to follow. Standing still, silent, he was ready to capture any whisper, any words spoken in the distance. But to his frustration, no sound reached him and he couldn't see any signs of the leaves having been disturbed.

It was pointless to linger. He took the path heading upwards, running as fast as the hidden rocks and stones would let him. The path climbed rather steeply, and within minutes he was sweating profusely.

It was then that the wind carried the sound of voices to him, but it seemed they were coming from beneath him. He couldn't hear any cries, so maybe Giò was still safe, but he launched himself downwards at full pelt nonetheless. It didn't matter if he ruined their plans and burst into the open before Giò had the chance to accuse the murderer. He wanted her to be safe and hated himself for having consented to this dangerous plan.

His thoughts gave him extra momentum, but before he had a chance to think of the consequences, he felt a cracking pain in his ankle. He lost control and his body tumbled down the slope, beating painfully against rocks and stones. He finally came to a stop against a tree trunk, his breath cut short by the impact.

When he managed to sit himself up against the trunk, he felt dizzy as if he was still spinning down the escarpment. Both his ribcage and his right shoulder hurt, but the worst of the pain was coming from his ankle. It was sprained at the very least, maybe broken – he didn't know. He just knew it was far too painful to walk on. And Giò – Giò was alone with a killer, while he lay battered and bruised in the gut of the forest.

He pulled himself upright – he had to conquer his agony and help her. But as soon as his foot touched the ground, a spasm of pain made him cry out loud and he fell helplessly down to the ground again.

GIÒ PRETENDED TO STUDY HER REFLECTION IN THE PASSENGER SIDE mirror. As they went around one of the bends in the road, she spotted the shadow of a blue car behind: Paolo was following them. A wave of relief washed over her as Nascimale parked by the path that led to the chapel.

"Wait," he said, rushing around the car to open her door. It was a gesture that was meant to be elegant, but he just made it look gawky. She thanked him nonetheless and his contorted grin spread onto his right cheek, causing his right eyebrow to rise in a weird curve on his forehead.

"This way." He pointed to the gravel path that led among rocks and vegetation to the Sanctuary of the Madonna del Soccorso. In summer, it was a popular destination for tourists searching for a little fresh air, or worshippers hiking up the mountain to pray to the Madonna. But in late October, there was nobody around.

In they went, through the little gate any visitor could open, the chapel in full view. Giò stopped for a second, pretending to tie her shoelaces – long enough to see a car parking next to theirs. She resumed their walk, fearing Nascimale would spot what she'd just seen too – Paolo had arrived, and now was the right time to take the bull by the horns.

"You know when Vanda and I went to Naples a few days

back? We met some people there who were familiar with Tina Melly and one of the children she took care of."

He shrugged as if he had no interest at all in their findings. Giò, irritated by his indifference, continued.

"The point is, he wasn't a normal child; he was a cruel monster."

DON GEPPINO PARKED HIS BLUE VEHICLE BESIDE A SPORTY WHITE CAR in front of the path leading to the Sanctuary. He came every Sunday for a quick inspection to make sure no one had vandalised the premises during the week. Looking at the car, he walked the path to the chapel and spotted the two visitors in the distance along the path. They had walked on to the belvedere where they could enjoy the view from the top of the mountains over the sea.

It was a pity he was in a hurry today; he normally loved to chat to people, especially when visitors appreciated the charm of the sacred place. Not all were religious, not in the traditional way at least, but this spot tended to bring all hearts together despite their differences.

The chapel was locked. Don Geppino did a quick check, but everything was fine – he didn't even find any beer bottles or empty pizza boxes along the path this week. With the fair going on in Trecchina, he decided he'd better get back as soon as possible. Enjoying a last look at the scenery, he glanced towards where he'd last seen the couple. They were out of sight, probably enjoying the view.

With a shrug, he made his way back to his car.

NASCIMALE LOOKED AT GIÒ WITH AN EXPRESSIONLESS FACE AS SHE continued.

"Years passed and we don't know what happened to the child. But I fear his wickedness grew. I suspect that once he became an adult, no longer under the control of parents and nannies, he committed quite a number of heinous crimes. But he was smart and always made sure to choose his victims in different places."

Nascimale didn't say anything, but his head was now tilted to the left as he listened intently. Giò paused again to make sure she had given Paolo enough time to reach them, pretending to consult notes on her mobile phone before continuing.

"Just making sure my sister Agnese hasn't called."

"I don't think any of the phone company networks can cover this area," he replied dryly.

Of course, he was right: no mobile coverage, not one bar. And only then did she notice that the text for Paolo had never left her mobile. Luckily, he had followed her anyway. So far, so good.

"Don't you want to continue my story?" Giò asked.

"Me?"

"Yes, you. Don't you want to tell me how back in January, the wicked man killed someone close to this place, someone in Trecchina, because he knew he could frame his victim's former fiancé?"

His head tilted further. "Am I supposed to know this murderer?" he asked.

"I think you've heard of Liliana Ielpo, killed by Ettore Orrico."

He nodded.

"Only it wasn't he who killed her."

"Goodness!" was his sarcastic reply.

"Fate had it that the news of the murder reached Tina Mica. By now, she had got married and was living in Switzerland, but by chance she came across a copy of the *Gazzetta del Lagonegrese*. She wasn't familiar with the victim, nor with the presumed killer, but when she turned the page, she found an article about a successful entrepreneur in Trecchina. And guess what?"

"What?" He finally seemed curious.

"The entrepreneur's name was the same as that of the wicked child she'd cared for 40 years earlier in Naples. She recognised his picture too thanks to a rather peculiar birthmark on his forehead."

Nascimale's hand reached instinctively for his forehead. Their gazes, that had been wandering all over the place, finally met. Surprise and something elusive were painted on his face. Instinctively, Giò glanced over towards the car park, looking for Paolo's car, but she couldn't see it. Then, along the serpentine road, she saw a glimpse of blue heading round one of the bends. What was happening? Why had Paolo left her alone with this lunatic at such a critical moment?

Then realisation flashed in her brain. The SMS had never left her mobile, so what if the blue car hadn't been Paolo's at all? What if he had never followed her up to the Sanctuary?

23

_____

THE PENDULUM SWINGS

P aolo breathed deeply; he had to regain his cool. Panic wouldn't help anyone. He couldn't help Giò – not physically, anyway; he had to raise the alarm.

He reached for his mobile phone, only to find his pockets empty. It must have dropped out during his fall. Had it broken as well?

Shouting out the frustration of the powerless, he crawled across the leafy ground, his hands touching and searching all around. To be methodical about his task, he had to clear his mind of both anger and pain, and search from where he had landed upwards. Even crawling wasn't a painless exercise, but at least it was a pain he could manage, sometimes by biting his lip, at other times by swearing or taking deep breaths.

His search didn't turn up anything. He had to get back up the escarpment, his hands dipping among the leaves and grasping whatever solid surface they touched. Then a couple of metres ahead of him, he saw something shiny. Crawling and sliding along the loose terrain where he couldn't find a single thing to hang on to, the pain in his ankle flaring as his body slipped downwards, he tried again where the carpet of leaves was less thick and the earth not so wet and slippery. His eyes locked on to the shiny object and, grinding his teeth, he reached for it.

Feverishly, he turned his mobile phone over, fearing that he would find a broken and useless display. It was cracked, but still working. The only coverage in the area was for emergency calls, and that was enough for him.

He dialled 112 and in a few words told his colleagues to come up to Trecchina Forest with an ambulance and plenty of men, advising them to search where he was and the road to the sanctuary. The more he thought about it, the more convinced he was that Giò had never entered the forest. Maybe Nascimale had meant the other chapel, which was much more isolated than the Forraina.

Damn! How stupid of me, and he crashed a fist against a chestnut tree trunk. He didn't feel any pain in his fist; all his torment was coming from his ankle and the fear of having left Giò in the hands of a killer.

EDOARDO STOPPED NEXT TO A LITTLE GATE, HALF HIDDEN BY THE vegetation.

"The main gate will be closed, we'll get in from here."

Vanda smiled at him. "You seem to know the place well."

"I love to walk around here," he replied, unlatching the gate.

In they went, the oak and chestnut trees embracing them. It felt suddenly cold now that the sun could no longer reach them.

"You were telling me you've known Giò since childhood?"

"Yes, I was best friends with her sister Agnese as we're about the same age, but I always admired Giò. And once we'd all grown up, even though she travelled a lot and lived in the UK for years, we still kept in touch. Mind you, we'd sometimes go for ages without speaking or writing to each other, but you know how it is with people you're close to. When you meet again after being apart, it's like you only spoke to them the previous day."

"And she's serious about this sleuthing thing?"

Vanda shook her head. "I don't know whether it's serious or not, but Giò definitely has a talent for sleuthing," and she told him about the couple of times that Giò had been involved in solving murders.

"Who does she suspect this time?"

"There isn't a suspect, but we found a connection to Tina Melly in Naples."

"Oh yes, your trip to Naples. Did it help?" he asked, but then he carried on without waiting for an answer. "Wait a second, there's the goat's pen. It's inside, so we'd better close it – the stupid animal can get quite wild." As he spoke, he fastened the gate. The sturdy goat gave him a dirty look and kicked at the air with his leg.

"But that's Guglielmo," cried Vanda. "He's not that bad, he just guards the place."

"I prefer to know it's safely locked away," Edoardo replied, grinning. Vanda tried to call Guglielmo over to the gate, but the goat kept looking fiercely at Edoardo.

"He doesn't like you," Vanda laughed.

"The feeling's mutual. Let's go – I don't even want to look at those yellow eyes."

As they turned their back on Guglielmo, Edoardo returned to their previous conversation.

"Weren't you telling me about Naples?"

"Yes, of course. We were looking for a link between Tina Melly and Trecchina."

"And you found it in Naples?"

"Maybe," she said, and told him about their visit to the Caracciolo Sciarramanna family.

"Caracciolo is quite a common surname among the aristocratic families in Naples," he commented as the path opened onto the tubing track.

"Children and their families are going to have great fun on

that," said Vanda. From the upper part she'd visited with Giò, she hadn't appreciated how long and winding the track was.

"It will be fun, but let's make our way towards the restaurant beyond the great slides."

The sun was high in the sky and the slight climb looked pleasant after the coolness of the forest.

"Of course there are lots of people called Caracciolo, but Caracciolo Sciarramanna is much rarer as a surname, and Giò's gran has put us in touch with the right family," Vanda continued. "It was their housekeeper who told us that Tina Melly had previously worked for a family with a problem child."

"What sort of problem child?" he said in surprise.

"It seems this child was a little peculiar. He enjoyed torturing insects and small animals, then he progressed to hurting other children. Giò and I believe there might be a connection between him and what happened in Trecchina."

"Isn't that a little far-fetched?"

"I'd say no because we haven't been able to find a better explanation as to why Tina decided to come from Switzerland to Trecchina, of all places."

He smiled incredulously. "You believe she came here to catch up with her deranged little boy?"

They had reached the closed restaurant. Beyond it was a terrace on the crest of the mountain from which you could view the distant coastline. There stood the four massive metal pillars Vanda had seen with Giò, only this time they were holding something in the centre that had been covered up and not showing on their last visit.

"There's the pendulum!" she cried.

"Tonight the first brave visitors will enjoy a 360° view of the valley, the sea and the sky."

"Wow!"

As they got closer to the ride, Edoardo took her hand. "You were telling me about the deranged child. What else have my two sleuths discovered?"

"It seems Tina found a magazine article about the murder in Trecchina in January. Do you remember the case of young Liliana Ielpo?"

"Of course I do, but I believe the killer was caught."

"Maybe things are not what they seem. Maybe the deranged child found a way to frame Ettore Orrico."

Still holding Vanda's hand tenderly, Edoardo led her to sit on the pendulum. The safety bars were in the open position, allowing them to sit comfortably. They looked at each other, then at the landscape at their feet.

"It's beautiful!" Vanda said, not knowing whether she meant the view or having Edoardo beside her, starting a new chapter in her life. Then their eyes met and he kissed her.

"Why don't you finish your story?" Nascimale said, his hands, in their leather gloves, clenching and unclenching.

Giò rapidly assessed the situation. Paolo wasn't there, but she knew from their night-time chase in Maratea that the monster in front of her wasn't that fit. She only had to run faster than him, which didn't seem too difficult – as long as he had no weapons on him, of course. By now, Paolo should have realised his mistake and come searching for her.

"Tina read that Ettore Orrico had declared himself innocent." Giò marched on determinedly. "She read that the young woman had been strangled, which was what the wicked child used to like doing to children in Naples, and that she'd had long red hair, just like those little girls. Suspecting what may have really happened, she decided to travel all the way to Trecchina to see for herself. When she arrived, by chance she met him soon after the bus from Lauria dropped her in the main square. She recognised him immediately and talked to him, leaving her in no doubt who the real killer was. Unfortunately, he also had no doubts; he killed her there and then, and hid her temporarily in the forest. He needed the cover of darkness to get rid of the corpse permanently, but when he went to fetch the body, he found Vanda bending over it. He hit her hard over the head, knocking her out, and took Tina's corpse back to his car."

"My goodness, then what?" Nascimale was looking at her with his usual smirk.

"As owner of the new adventure park, he knew there was a concrete platform yet to be finished. He threw Tina's body into the works and laid the concrete on top, and there it would have stayed forever were it not for Guglielmo the goat."

She looked at him, hoping he'd confess before she had to finish the story. But he remained silent, rocking from one foot to the other.

Then he stopped abruptly and looked back at her. "But you said he owned the land," he snapped. "That can't be!"

"Why not?"

"Because I own the land."

"That's it, then! The game is over," Giò cried, ready to run for her dear life.

The man gulped, as if only now recognising the game Giò had been playing. He banged his forehead with his gloved hand and burst into raucous laughter.

"I told Vanda to stay away from you, and that madwoman in the perfumery. I knew you were a few sandwiches short of a picnic. You really believe I did the nanny in?"

Of all the things Giò had imagined happening, amusement was not on the list.

"All pieces combine perfectly, you'll have a hard time to prove otherwise."

"Hard time, rubbish. To start with, on the Friday in question, I was in Naples, lecturing to young entrepreneurs. There are dozens of people who can verify my story, unless you think they are all accomplices."

So saying, he put a hand in his pocket. Giò jumped back, sure he was going to draw a gun.

"It's only my mobile," he sneered, holding up his phone as he opened his photo gallery, pointing at the dates. There were pictures from the Friday when Tina had met her killer, showing Nascimale in a classroom full of people and the programme for the whole day. Apparently, he had been lecturing from 9am to 5pm.

"How is that possible?" cried Giò, for the first time doubting her theory. "It all coincides: the magazine article, the story the housekeeper in Naples told us. Have you ever lived there?"

"Yes, as a kid. My family spent a few years there during my childhood, but I was never considered a problem child."

That Giò could hardly believe – he was definitely a problem adult with his bad manners. How had he ever been a nice child, or even just an ordinary one? But something in his reaction told her more than a million words: she had made a bad mistake. She didn't know where exactly, but something had misled her.

"So you didn't want to speak to me about that poseur who's romancing Vanda at all; you laid a trap for me. And you came all by yourself?"

Giò nodded. What was the point in telling him that a carabiniere had also been misled by her theories?

"I imagine you have a weapon on you if you wanted to trap me."

Giò shrugged without replying, her mind filled with all the coincidences that had led her to this point. Through her confusion, she realised they had retraced their steps back to Nascimale's car.

"Before we do anything else, I'd like to stop the fop from leading Vanda astray."

"Why are you so concerned about him?"

"I don't like him. Nascimbene looks like butter wouldn't melt in his mouth, but there's something about him I don't trust."

"Nascimbene? Is that his second name?"

The man nodded.

"And yours is Nascimale."

"Correct. Things are never as they seem, are they?"

As they entered the car, Giò jumped as if she had received an electric shock before she had even touched her seat.

"The book club! The magazine! The names so similar! Could it be?" Panic filled her face.

"What now? A new suspect?" he teased.

"I might be wrong again, but on the magazine page that Tina sent to her stepdaughter, along with your profile was the Book of the Month, a column written by the local bookshop owner."

"That fop? Nascimbene?"

"Him."

"His picture too?"

"His picture, yes."

"And you never considered he could have been the killer?"

"Never," Giò admitted. "But it all fits! He moves every two to three years, taking over bookshops in different towns, and he was already in Trecchina at the time of the first murder. And he said his family travelled a lot. And maybe, when I phoned her for confirmation, the housemaid in Naples got confused as your names – Edoardo Nascimbene and Enrico Nascimale – sound so similar. And then… my goodness! All the portraits in his house."

"Portraits?"

"Yes, Vanda and I went to his home for dinner and he had a collection of prints of famous paintings, but only ones depicting red-haired women… Liliana had red hair."

"And Vanda has too. Where is she?"

"She's gone for a picnic, with him!"

"Where, though?"

"In the forest. I think I spotted his car just before the adventure park entrance."

"Yes, I saw a car next to the second entrance. But with the Chestnut Fair on, there's virtually no one around this afternoon. It must be them."

As Nascimale's car took off in a cloud of dust and raced

along the road at full speed, Giò frantically tried to call Vanda. But once more she was reminded of the terrifying truth: there was no phone coverage in the area.

Vanda was on her own with a ruthless killer.

EDOARDO SLID SOFTLY FROM HIS SEAT.

"What do you say to a little ride?" He silenced Vanda before she could protest. "I mean a gentle swing, not the real ride. It could be our loveseat."

Vanda eyes shone. "Is that possible?"

"You should never doubt me!"

"Come on! The owners won't leave the controls open for just anyone."

"I'm not anyone; I'm a friend of the watchman and I know where he keeps things…"

He unlocked the cabin and turned on the control panel. The pendulum started to move gently. Edoardo stood in front of Vanda as she swung slowly to and fro, her eyes closed, enjoying the rhythm and the soft breeze on her face.

When she opened her eyes, she found him following her movements with his disarmingly innocent gaze.

"This is picking up speed."

"I know. What a pity."

"Edoardo, this isn't a nice joke. Please stop this thing."

Her hands held on to the iron safety bar, which was still sticking up above her head instead of closing down over her body to protect her. Edoardo was looking at her, his face showing no emotion whatsoever. Vanda was reminded of the stare children give when they don't know how to distinguish right from wrong. But children learn to make the distinction, whereas he…

Then the truth hit Vanda and her blood froze.

"The carabinieri will know it was you," she cried. "Don't be so stupid."

The pendulum was rising higher, and when it came back down at full speed, she could no longer speak. A cry of fear burst out of her as her hands tightened on the bar, her legs swinging freely in the air, her stomach jumping at the emptiness in front of her.

Edoardo was still looking up at her impassively.

"Such a pity it should end like this. It's all your friend's fault, she's so nosey. If only she'd left everything to the carabinieri, they would never have found me out."

As the swing approached 90°, slowing before plunging down again, Vanda found the strength to speak.

"Please, stop this. They already know it was you, and they will be on your tail soon."

"No they won't, I've always managed to avoid trouble everywhere I've been. But we've talked enough, it's time for you to enjoy the full ride."

As he said this, the pendulum rose to a new height. Vanda knew that the next peak would throw her out of her seat, and even if her hands managed to hold on to the bar, her body would crash back down against the seat as the pendulum fell. Would she be able to hold on then?

She closed her eyes, fighting with all her will to keep her hands tight on the bar above her head, but her arms were tiring rapidly. Her muscles spasmed in pain that overrode the adrenaline pumping through her.

When the pendulum started to rise again, she found the courage to open her eyes just in time to catch a brownish mass launching itself at full speed against Edoardo. The impact threw the man a few metres from his position. He fell onto the rocky ground and could only manage to raise himself a little way on his elbows, uncertain what had happened, just feeling the pain of the impact. Then he recognised Guglielmo, his head low, ready to charge again.

"That stupid animal will end its days as goat ribs on the barbecue," Edoardo said, a flick knife in his hand shining in the sun. Guglielmo charged again, unaware of the danger…

But just then from the depth of the forest, Enrico Nascimale jumped on Edoardo, who swung the flick knife at this new assailant. The knife cut into Nascimale's left shoulder at the same time as a powerful punch landed on Edoardo's right cheek. Then Guglielmo charged once more and Edoardo fell to the ground, knocked down for good.

Vanda cried out in terror as her body was launched into the air before falling back heavily onto her seat. The sight of Edoardo being overpowered by a man and a goat gave her an extra dose of courage, but she knew her hands wouldn't maintain their hold on the bar much longer.

GIÒ WAS STANDING IN FRONT OF THE CONTROL PANEL, UNCERTAIN what to do. When her gaze finally landed on the red emergency button, she pushed it with all her strength. Instantly the height of the pendulum decreased, and with a few soft swings, it came to a halt.

When the carabinieri arrived a few minutes later, they found Enrico Nascimale, the adventure park owner, holding Edoardo Nascimbene, the Trecchina bookshop keeper, down, apparently oblivious to the blood pumping from his shoulder. A fierce goat was looking around in case there was anyone else who needed knocking down, and Giò Brando was holding Vanda Riccardi as the red-haired woman leant against a rock.

"Perfect timing!" said Giò sarcastically. "Shouldn't Brigadiere Rossi be with you?"

"He raised the alarm, but he broke his ankle down in the forest."

"Don't you want to handcuff this guy?" Nascimale cried out

as the pain in his shoulder became unbearable. "Or do you want to enjoy a ride on the pendulum first?"

Then his eyes fell on the large amount of his own blood that had pooled around him and he fainted.

24

A VISIT TO THE HOSPITAL

Giò arrived at the hospital and lingered in the reception area, wondering whom she should visit first. Vanda? Nascimale? Paolo? She decided to go to see her friend, but when a nurse guided her into Vanda's room, she was surprised to find an empty bed.

"She will be on the floor below," another woman on the same ward told Giò. "I believe she's got a friend there."

When Giò entered Enrico Nascimale's room, she saw Vanda sitting beside him, caressing his hand while speaking softly to him.

"So here you are!"

Vanda turned to face Giò and blushed slightly, taking her hand away from the man's.

Enrico protested immediately. "Here's the nosey one," he said in dismay and Vanda shot him a dirty look. "Come on, I was only joking. If it weren't for her, you'd still be swinging on that pendulum."

No matter how hard Vanda tried to keep a straight face, she ended up laughing out loud. Giò, a firm believer that laughter is a good cure for a number of ills, soon followed suit.

"So how do you feel?" she asked Vanda as soon as they'd recovered their breath.

"The doctors want to keep me in overnight because of my recent concussion, but I'm fine. Aching all over, a little dizziness every now and then, but nothing serious."

"How about you?" Giò asked Nascimale.

"It's damn painful, it hurts awfully," he said, but he had a pleasant smile on his face.

"Come on, with all those painkillers the nurse gave you, she said you should be fine."

"That nurse doesn't know what she's talking about. It's not the painkillers, it's this magic that does the trick." And he pointed to the hand Vanda had been using to caress him.

She smiled. "You're so spoiled."

The two of them clearly wanted some time alone, so Giò told them she was going to visit Paolo. As she left the room, she glanced at Nascimale. She had never noticed that there was something interesting about his square face, if not exactly handsome. And as Vanda started stroking his hand again, it seemed his quirks and tics had quietened too.

When Giò entered his room, Paolo looked as though he was sleeping, but he opened his eyes as she approached him.

"Hello, my protector." Giò smiled softly.

"Please, don't tease me, Giò." His eyes were sheepish, lank locks of brown hair falling over the tired face of someone who's not had an easy night.

"I'm not teasing you," she said, but her eyes were dancing. "In the end, the carabinieri arrived just in time."

"Indeed."

"What did the doctors say? Anything broken?"

"Some bruised ribs, one broken, a severely sprained ankle that might take four to six weeks to recover completely…"

"Head is fine?"

"Still spinning. When I was investigating the case, I never thought about the bookshop owner."

"Neither did I, I was concentrating so much on Mr Nast… ahem, Enrico Nascimale, I couldn't see past him. I guess we always tend to judge people by their appearance and manners. When I read the back of the magazine article and saw the book club thing, I never even considered for a second the culprit could be Edoardo."

"Was it Mr Nascimale who led you to the truth?"

"Once he'd proved beyond all doubt that he was somewhere else when Tina was killed, as improbable as it seemed at the time, I realised he must be innocent. Then he called Edoardo by his surname, Nascimbene. Imagine, two people with such similar names: Nascimale and Nascimbene. I immediately saw how easy it would be to confuse the two, especially for Pasqualina who had only ever heard stories about the wicked child from her mother."

"That was a weird coincidence. So we have the hero and the antihero…"

"And neither of them seemed to be what they really are. Did I tell you about Agnese's perfume game?" And she told him about the two men's sessions leading to the same perfume.

"Next time we'll start our investigations from your sister's perfumery. She was close to revealing the truth from the beginning."

Then it was Paolo's turn. He told Giò how the white sports car parked next to hers had indeed misled him into thinking she was in the forest with Nascimale as they had planned, when in fact she had already left in Nascimale's car. He told her how he had fallen, but for some reason, he omitted the despair and anguish he'd felt when he realised she was elsewhere and he was powerless to help.

"Has Edoardo confessed?" Giò asked.

"Not really, he's refusing to answer any questions, but the

whole picture is getting clearer. It's all as you said, Giò, in your early reconstruction: you did a damn good job."

She flushed.

Paolo went on, "We believe that Tina read the *Gazzetta del Lagonegrese*, not giving the report of the brutal murder in the crime news much thought until she turned the page and saw the portrait of Edoardo. It was a small picture, but he has such unusual eyes, it caught Tina's attention. Reading the article fully, she found the guy's name and knew he was her wicked little boy. Then she went back to the previous page and saw that a red-haired woman had been strangled in the very place the man lived. Was it a coincidence?"

"So it wasn't Nascimale's birthmark she recognised at all, it was Edoardo's distinctive eyes. No wonder we were confused." Giò thought things over for a moment before adding, "From the way Martine described her, Tina had a strong sense of moral duty. She'd never have just let it lie if she had any doubt at all."

"Exactly. The article went on to say that the murderer had been caught, but what if he hadn't really? And that 'if' kept troubling her, until she decided to visit Trecchina. She got off the coach, went to the bar, asked for directions to the town hall, then went to look for the bookshop. I imagine she knew it'd be closed at 3pm, she only wanted to see where it was so she could come back later. But by chance, Edoardo was passing by…"

"How stupid of me!" Giò cried. "Edoardo wasn't passing by, he was in the shop. When Martine and Gaspard came over, he was working in the bookshop with the shutter half-closed. I asked him if he had been around at that time the previous Friday and of course he said no. And I took his word for it!"

Paolo considered what she had said and nodded sadly. "It's easy to believe what people say, especially when we like them."

"Exactly!"

"I imagine Tina knocked on his shutters and in her forthright way told him what she suspected, not realising he wouldn't think twice about what to do. He killed her there and then. At

3pm, no one was around, so he drove her body to the forest so that nobody would associate her death with him. Once back home, though, he must have thought it would be even better if the body was never found."

"Vanda told me Edoardo loved to walk around the adventure park. He was friends with Nicola the watchman and knew he'd be away from the area, as he was every Friday."

"That's how he managed to get into the control cabin, then – he must have seen where Nicola left the key."

"That's right. And as Edoardo had no compassion in him, Guglielmo's animal instincts told him Edoardo wasn't to be trusted, despite the man being friends with his master."

"All the pieces fit," said Paolo. "He went to fetch the body from the forest and found Vanda staring at it. Again he acted fast, hitting her on the head and knocking her out, then he hid Tina's body in the adventure park. He had seen the concrete mixer and wanted to bury the body where no one would ever find it."

"When I asked him if he had seen Tina, he said that he had opened his bookshop at 5pm, but that was another lie – he didn't want us to find out that on Friday, he'd opened up much later than usual because he'd been hiding the body. Again I made the mistake of taking his word for it…"

"In a small place like Trecchina, people would hardly find it strange if a shop opened later than usual – unless it's the local bakery."

"It's unfortunate that Assuntina, Mrs Roselli's housekeeper, told us lies about having seen Tina on Saturday. That meant we took no notice when she said the bookshop opened at funny times."

"At that point Edoardo thought he was safe. But then he met you and Vanda, and I suspect you shared all you knew with him…"

"We did," Giò confessed miserably, looking at the floor.

"And he tried to scare you with the threatening message, but soon realised it hadn't been enough."

"But why did he decide to kill Vanda and not me?"

"She was the one with red hair. And as they were out together, he would have claimed it had been an awful accident, admitting how stupid they'd been to try the ride before the official opening. He would have taken care of you later, if you'd kept nosing around, but maybe he hoped you'd be so devastated by Vanda's death that you'd stop your investigating."

Giò shook her head. "I would never have believed that it was an accident."

"So the man underestimated who he was dealing with," Paolo said, winking at her.

Giò grinned. "How about the Ielpo case?"

"If Nascimbene doesn't confess, we'll have to dig some more, but from our liaisons with the carabinieri in other areas where he's lived, we're already uncovering some nasty incidences. I'm sure we'll bring him down with a number of charges. We believe he's a serial killer so we'll have to reconstruct his life."

"And to think I admired him so much for his travelling bookshop."

"That, I'm afraid, was a cover for all his wicked deeds. Giving himself a legitimate reason to move every couple of years has allowed him to escape time and time again." Then Paolo changed the subject to a more cheerful note. "By the way, I heard Guglielmo played an important part in saving Vanda."

"Enrico had a splendid idea. Once we realised who the murderer really was, we rushed to the adventure park and found the goat nervous and furious. Enrico realised he'd get to Edoardo quicker than we could. They're good friends – Enrico and Guglielmo, I mean."

"So he freed the goat?"

"He did, and Guglielmo had no doubt about what he had to do. He'd knocked Edoardo down once by the time we got there and was ready to charge again."

"Such a hero!"

"Indeed."

For some reason, Giò now felt slightly embarrassed, as if she didn't know exactly what else to say. She looked at the pale carabiniere, his face clearly showing the pain he was in, even though he was heroically trying to ignore it. For the first time, Giò realised it must have been pretty hard for him, lying injured in the woods, knowing she was risking her life, and she felt an unusual pang of tenderness.

"Hi there!" Five or six heads popped around the door as a mixture of carabinieri from both Trecchina and Maratea came into the room. Behind them came Maresciallo Mangiaboschi and Maresciallo Bevilacqua, congratulating Brigadiere Rossi on his successful investigation.

"It was Giovanna Brando who worked it all out," said Paolo, but the other men barely listened. The two marescialli looked at each other and Giò heard the whispered words that passed between them.

"The concussion must have been worse than we feared, he doesn't know what he's talking about."

Giò managed to catch Paolo's eye and signalled him to keep his mouth shut. She was quite happy for him to take all the credit for the investigation. After all, her dream was to be a writer, not a detective.

Quietly, she left the noisy room.

EPILOGUE

Agnese was in her bedroom that evening. Nando was watching TV and Giò, after having had dinner with them, had said she'd go back to her flat, have a good night's sleep and get up early the next day to work on her Scottish guide. She was tired of adventures; writing was such a safe, healthy job.

In the comfort of her room, Agnese picked up the turquoise notebook she used as a diary. Since she usually wrote at the end of a long day when she was tired, she had learned to make bullet points of anything significant that had happened.

Her last note was from early October, so she started a new page with an exclamation. *What a weird Chestnut Fair it was in Trecchina this year! Nothing was as it seemed:*

- Mr Nasty, now just Enrico, revealed himself to be not only the hero who risked his own life to save Vanda, but also the generous (and anonymous) benefactor behind a lot of charity work in the village. Certainly he has a long way to go to learn some manners and not be so provocative. He looks like a devil, but he acts ~~like an angel~~ *almost* like an angel. But I have a feeling that Vanda will help him improve his manners. It will take some time, but they're not in a hurry.

- Edoardo Nascimbene, the perfect gentleman with his childlike face and elegant manners, revealed himself as the man who's never learnt the difference between good and evil, and has been responsible for a number of murders wherever he's lived. The police are investigating any unsolved murders of women with red hair to see if they can connect them to him. I can't believe his parents turned a blind eye to his actions when he was a child, making feeble excuses rather than helping him to live a decent life.

- It's been a trying time for me too: I doubted what my perfumes were telling me. In the fragrance handbook it says, *"Between light and darkness – where do you stand?"* about Outrageous Carnation. And I didn't realise the importance of the question. If this was a "disturbingly dualistic" fragrance, who was Dr Jekyll and who was Mr Hyde? Edoardo, with his nice manners, or Mr Nasty? The answer wasn't the obvious one. Only Guglielmo the goat could see beyond the appearances. He knew beyond any possible doubt who the devilish murderer was.

- The big takeaway for me is that if I hadn't doubted my perfumes, maybe I'd have recognised the truth sooner. To trust in ourselves is not selfish, it may benefit the people around us.

- Since her triumph at the fair, I'm sure Ramya has gained the confidence and esteem of her schoolmates, but more importantly she can trust what she's able to achieve. And that awareness helped her teammates too: from losers, they became winners.

- As for Giò, she faced another disappointment in her dream to become a travel writer, but I don't have any doubt she will go forward now that she knows what she wants in life. She might also consider a career on the side as a private investigator. After all, she's shown she has a certain talent for it. I guess it comes from reading too many mysteries when she was a kid.

- I need to speak to Cabiria's father, no matter how angry he might be; I can't believe how I acted. I don't regret having run away from Mrs Lavecchia as I'm sure she will be back soon, but I feel so childish about not owning up to him. Let's say that I've had my afternoon of silliness...

- One last thing before I crash into my pillow. That weird man, the lawyer who defended Orrico, approached me at the fair with the most astonishing accusations about Granny gambling and cheating at cards. As if she would be seen in the squalid bars he frequents, or play any card games apart from Solitaire. I mean, my sweet Granny!

THE END

Is there any way a reader may help a newbie author? Yes! Please leave a review on your favourite store, Goodreads and/or Bookbub. It doesn't matter how long or short; even a single sentence could say it all. We might be in a digital era, but **this old world of ours still revolves around word of mouth**. A review allows a book to leave the shadow of the unknown and introduces it to other passionate readers.

Grazie :)

GLOSSARY

APERITIVO – this is a convivial social event, often in a bar with friends before heading home for the family lunch or dinner. Let's say it's a sort of appetiser before the real meal. It can be simple or lavish, merely a drink or a variety of finger food. In Italy, we also invite people home for an aperitivo, which is not as formal as a proper meal, but beware! Like Granny's panzerotti, it can be delicious, moreish and *very* filling.

BARLEY COFFEE – In Italy, this is an alternative to coffee that's not coffee at all, nor does it contain caffeine. The drink was popular during the Second World War when the price of real coffee rocketed, with barley and chicory being cheaper local ingredients available in the countryside. In the case of barley, the tradition continued after the war as a healthy alternative where caffeine might cause problems. The grains are roasted and ground, and a Moka pot or bar machine is used to brew it like a regular espresso.

BRIGADIERE – plural brigadieri: this can be loosely compared to a detective sergeant. In the carabinieri ranks, a brigadiere operates below a maresciallo.

CARABINIERE – plural carabinieri. In Italy, we don't only have the polizia (much like the police in most countries), we also have the carabinieri. Essentially, this is another police force, but it's part of the army and is governed by the Ministry of Defence, whereas the polizia depends on the Ministry of the Interior. The two are often in competition with one another (though they will never admit it), so never confuse one with the other (especially if you're talking with Maresciallo Mangiaboschi, he is rather touchy). For me, the only difference between the two is that we have a number of cracking jokes about the carabinieri and none about the polizia. Don't ask me why.

In Maratea, there's only the carabinieri and no polizia. But Paolo would have been a carabiniere and not a policeman in any case. By the way being a military corps carabinieri tend to wear their uniforms more than the police even when investigating crimes.

CORNETTO – plural cornetti. This is the equivalent of a French croissant. I have to admit it was the French who invented them, but they're very popular in Italy too.

GASSOSA – a popular non-alcoholic lemon-scented soda used mainly in Southern Italy.

MARESCIALLO – this rank is similar to detective inspector. A maresciallo is superior to a brigadiere, carabiniere semplice and appuntato.

MOUILLETTE – see 'TOUCHE' below.

NASCIMBENE and NASCIMALE – These two surnames could be translated respectively as Well Born and Badly Born. The first is a common surname in Southern Italy, while – luckily – I've never met someone with the second. But it was just the name I needed for Mr Nasty.

PANZEROTTO – plural panzerotti: small calzones made with the same dough as pizza, filled with mozzarella, tomato and fresh basil leaves, and deep fried.

SALUTE! – or CIN CIN (pronounced chin chin)! This is the equivalent of "Cheers!" When celebrating an event with a glass of wine or prosecco, we love to accompany the word by clinking our glasses together.

SCOPA (SETTANTA e SETTEBELLO) – Scopa is a popular card game in Southern Italy. It is played with the Italian 40 card deck and literally means 'broom', possibly because the goal of the game is to sweep up all the cards. As a kid, I loved to play with my grandma and granddad, and I swear we never played for money. (Some treats, maybe…)

Scopa is not only the name of the game, but along with settanta and settebello, it is an important score to win the game.

SFOGLIATELLA – This is a pastry from Campania, so named because of its many crunchy sfoglie (layers), typically with a shell shape. The inside is soft and made out of ricotta flavoured with orange blossom water. They're so complicated to make, you'd better fly over to Naples to enjoy one.

SCATURCHIO – is a bar and pastry shop in Naples renowned for its sfogliatelle. Whether or not they are the best in town is the subject of many heated disputes among the inhabitants, but the final proof is in tasting its wares for yourself.

TARANTELLA – You may already be familiar with this one. Tarantella are traditional folk dances to a fast rhythm that can get almost frenzied. If you come south, don't miss your chance to be involved in one, and yes, you'll be required to dance too. But don't worry – it's impossible to stay still.

TOUCHE – this is a French word that refers to paper strips onto which you can spray perfumes for people to smell. They're also called *mouillette*, again a French word.

VIETRI TILES – Vietri is a small village on the Amalfi Coast (two hours north of Maratea) that has specialised in the production of hand-painted ceramic tiles over the centuries. There's a renowned international ceramic school there, and the tiles are characterised by fascinating patterns and joyful colours.

If you have found other Italian words in the story and would like to know what they mean, please let me know.

Contact me on:
    Twitter: @adrianalici
    Join the Maratea Murder Club

JOIN THE MARATEA MURDER CLUB

Keep in touch and you'll get exclusive content:

- Book 0, *And Then There Were Bones* – the prequel to the *An Italian Village Mystery* series available nowhere else
- **Giò Brando's Maratea Album** – photos of her favourite places and behind-the-scenes secrets
- **A Maratea Map** – including many places featured in the series
- **Adriana Licio's News** – new releases, news from Maratea, but no spam – Giò would loathe it!
- **Cosy Mystery Passion:** a place to share favourite books, characters, tips and tropes

Join here – it's free: www.adrianalicio.com/murderclub

ALSO BY ADRIANA LICIO

And Then There Were Bones, prequel to the *An Italian Village Mystery* series, is only available by signing up to **www.adrianalicio.com/murderclub**. You can unsubscribe any time you like, but of course, I hope you will stay.

Book 1 *Murder on The Road* is available on Amazon (it is free if you are on Kindle Unlimited).

Book 3 *The Mystery Before Christmas* (a novella) will be released on 20 November 2019 (free if you are on Kindle Unlimited).

ABOUT THE AUTHOR

Adriana Licio lives in the Apennine Mountains in southern Italy, and whenever she can, she visits Maratea, the seaside setting for her first cosy series, *An Italian Village Mystery*. Adriana returns to Maratea looking for peace and quiet, but inevitably stumbles on beguiling places and intriguing stories every time. She says time for relaxing will come – sooner or later.

She loves loads of things: travelling, reading, walking, savouring good food, exploring small villages, and home swapping. A long time ago, she spent six years falling in love with Scotland, and she has never recovered. She now runs her family perfumery, and between a dark patchouli and a musky rose, she devours cosy mysteries.

She resisted writing as long as she could, fearing she might get carried away by her fertile imagination – she was already renowned for living in the clouds. But one day, she found an alluring blank page and the words flowed in the weird English she'd learned in Glasgow.

Adriana finds peace for her restless, enthusiastic soul by walking in nature with her adventurous golden retriever Frodo and her hubby Giovanni.

Do you want to know more?
Join the **Maratea Murder Club**

You can also stay in touch on:

www.adrianalicio.com

facebook.com / adrianalicio.mystery

twitter.com / adrianalici

amazon.com / author / adrianalicio

bookbub.com / profile / adriana-licio

AUTHOR'S NOTE

The idea for this book came from the tester of a certain perfume I found in an almost forgotten cabinet in my perfumery. This particular perfume – Vitriol d'œillet by Serge Lutens, with its dark notes and duality – fascinated me. And when an idea keeps tormenting you, even when you're desperate to get rid of it, you have no choice but to follow it and see what happens. Which is what I did.

In the autumn of 2018, my husband, my dog and I found ourselves in Trecchina for the annual Chestnut Fair, and I thought it would be an ideal location for *that* story – which at the time wasn't a story, merely a seed that had yet to sprout. There were schoolchildren displaying their works and selling the chestnuts they had picked that morning; there was a dance floor for traditional dances; there were stalls offering delicious food. When the evening arrived, we had a walk up to the Forraina Chapel and I found myself looking at a patchwork of red-tiled roofs under a sickle moon. I wanted that image to last.

Before joining the fair the next morning, we had a walk up on the mountains of Trecchina to the Sanctuary of Madonna del Soccorso. I had been there before, but the little church and the rough rocky mountains, where your eyes can travel from inland

Basilicata to the sea of Calabria and Basilicata combined, is a feast for the heart. On the way back, we saw a tubing track and discovered an adventure park that hadn't opened yet. Actually, I'm not sure it ever opened, but a watchman told us that if we were curious, we could have a look inside (how unfruitful a writer's life would be without such precious collaborators). And in we went, the three of us.

On a sort of belvedere, we spotted four powerful metal arms shining in the sun. The central part of it was wrapped up for protection, and not being a fan of rides, I wasn't sure what I was looking at. But it must have stayed in my memory and made its way back to dominate the final scene of this book.

Guglielmo was a Scottish sheep I met over 20 years ago during my time in Dufftown. I remember his owner telling me that he not only protected her like a guard dog, but he was also a clever chap with – according to her (and I've no reason to doubt her) – a good sense of humour. No, the sheep's name wasn't Guglielmo, but I could hardly call a goat in Southern Italy Glenn Mackinnon.

I regularly share photos of the places I use in my books on Facebook, so you might want to give them a look here: www.facebook.com/adrianalicio.mystery/